The Mystery of
the Black Jungle

The Mystery of the Black Jungle

Emilio Salgari

Translated by Nico Lorenzutti

ROH
PRESS

The Mystery of the Black Jungle
By Emilio Salgari
Original Title: *I misteri della jungla nera (bound edition 1895)*
First published in serial form in 1887 as *Gli strangolatori del Gange* in "Il Telefono di Livorno"

Translated from the Italian by Nico Lorenzutti

ROH Press
First paperback edition
Copyright © 2008 by Nico Lorenzutti

All comments and questions can be addressed to:
info@rohpress.com

Visit our website at
www.rohpress.com

Cover design: Nico Lorenzutti

Special thanks to Mario Lorenzutti, Franca Lorenzutti and Michiko Sakata.

ISBN: 978-0-9782707-1-1

Printed in the United States of America

Contents

Part I: The Stranglers

Part II: Tremal-Naik's Revenge

Part I

The Stranglers

Chapter 1
A Murder

The Ganges, the great river sacred to Hindus, rises among the snowy mountains of the Himalayas and flows through the rich provinces of Kashmir, Delhi, Agra, Benares, Patna and Bengal, giving life to some of the most populous cities in India. Three hundred miles from the sea, it divides in two, forming within its branches a vast delta unique to the world.

A multitude of streams emanate from those imposing arms; large and small canals crisscross that immense tract of land bounded by the Bay of Bengal, creating an infinite number of islands, islets and sandbanks, known to the world as the Sundarbans.

No sight is stranger, more desolate or more frightening than the Sundarbans. No cities, no villages, no huts or hovels; endless forests of thorny bamboo stretch from north to south, east to west, the tops of their tall stems swaying in the wind among the deadly miasma rising from the rotting foliage and human corpses set adrift in the Ganges.

By day, a dismal silence reigns supreme, instilling terror in even the bravest of souls, but once darkness descends, the air fills with a frightening cacophony of howls, roars, and hisses that make the blood run cold.

Ask a Bengali to set foot in the Sundarbans and he will refuse; an offer of a hundred, two hundred, five hundred rupees, will not sway him. Ask a Molango[1] and he will refuse just as adamantly, to set foot in those jungles is to ask for death.

A thousand dangers lurk beneath those forests among the mire and sallow waters. Giant crocodiles swim in search of prey; tigers lay in wait

---

[1] A member of a tribe that lives on the outskirts of the Sundarbans.

1

for passing boats, ready to pounce upon the first sailor that dares get close to shore. Rhinoceroses roam the land, ready to attack at the slightest provocation; snakes abound in infinite varieties, from tiny poisonous serpents to enormous pythons large enough to grind an ox within their coils. But perhaps the most deadly of all are the Indian Thugs, dreaded stranglers that skulk in the shadows, searching for victims to sacrifice to their bloodthirsty goddess.

And yet, despite these dangers, on the evening of May 16, 1851, a large fire blazed in the southern part of the Sundarbans, about four hundred paces from the three mouths of the Mangal, a wide muddy branch of the Ganges that empties into the Bay of Bengal.

The flames shone brightly against the dark sky, casting their light upon a large bamboo hut at the foot of which slept a man wrapped in a large dugbah[2]. He was a handsome Bengali, about thirty years of age, with muscular limbs and deep bronze skin. Three horizontal lines of ash streaked his brow, marking him as one of Shiva's devotees.

Though he slept, his dreams must have been troubling, for he frowned at times, his forehead beading with perspiration. His strong chest heaved against his dugbah, as mumbled whispers escaped his lips.

"It's almost time," he smiled. "The sun is setting, the peacocks have fallen silent, the marabous have flown off... a jackal cries... Where is she? Why isn't she here?... What have I done? Isn't this the place?... Come, sweet vision... I long to see you... I must see you... even if only for a minute...

"Ah, there she is, there she is!... Looking at me with those dark eyes, a smile on her lips... Such a beautiful smile! Divine vision, why do you stand before me in silence?... Why do you look at me so?... Don't be afraid; I'm Tremal-Naik, Hunter of the Black Jungle. Speak, let me hear your sweet voice... the sun is setting, it's growing dark... No! Don't go! Don't go! Please!"

Suddenly the Bengali let out a sharp cry, his face twisted in anguish.

Drawn by the noise, a second Indian ran out of the hut, a shorter agile man with strong powerful legs. His proud bearing, dark eyes, earrings

_____
[2] A cape made from coarse cloth

2

and the languti[3] about his thighs, indicated he was a Maratha, a warrior from a tribe in Western India.

"Poor master!" he murmured, studying Tremal-Naik. "Another nightmare!"

He stirred the fire then sat beside the hunter, taking up a fan of peacock feathers.

"What a mystery!" mumbled the sleeping man. "Is that blood!?! Are those nooses? Run, sweet vision, run… it isn't safe!"

"Blood, visions, nooses?" murmured the Maratha, surprised. "What a dream!"

Without warning, the hunter shook himself awake, opened his eyes and sat upright.

"No, no!" he exclaimed dully, "Don't…!"

The Maratha looked at him.

"Master," he said, a note of compassion in his voice, "What troubles you?"

The Indian closed his eyes, opened them once again and fixed them upon the Maratha.

"Ah, it's you, Kammamuri!" he exclaimed.

"Yes, master."

"Watching over me?"

"And keeping the flies away."

Tremal-Naik took several deep breaths and wiped his brow.

"Where are Hurti and Aghur?" he asked after a brief silence.

"In the jungle. They found some tiger tracks last night and went off in search of it this morning."

"Ah!" Tremal-Naik replied dully.

He frowned as a heavy sigh died upon his lips.

"What troubles you, master?" asked Kammamuri. "You seem ill."

"Nothing, I'm fine."

"You were talking in your sleep."

"What!?!"

"Yes, master, you spoke of a strange vision."

---

[3] Short loincloth

3

A bitter smile spread across the hunter's lips.

"I'm suffering, Kammamuri," he said angrily. "I'm suffering terribly."

"I know, master. I've been watching you for the past sixteen days. You've grown melancholy, taciturn, and yet not so long ago you were not like this."

"That's true."

"Have you grown tired of the jungle?"

"Don't even think it, Kammamuri. This is where I was born and raised; this is where I'll die."

"Well then? What's caused this sudden change?"

"A woman, a vision, a spirit!"

"A woman!" Kammamuri exclaimed in surprise. "A woman?"

Tremal-Naik nodded then pressed his brow as if to stifle a disturbing thought.

Silence fell between the two men, broken only by the murmur of the stream and the cries of the wind.

"Where did you see this woman?" asked the Maratha after a few minutes had passed.

"In the jungle," Tremal-Naik replied darkly. "I'll never forget that night, Kammamuri! I was hunting for snakes along the bank of a stream when a vision appeared just twenty paces from me, among a thicket of blood-red mussenda. She was radiant, superb.

"I never thought the gods could create such beauty. She had large black eyes, fair skin, and long dark curly hair.

"She looked at me, sighed sadly, and vanished. Stunned, I just stood there, unable to move. Once the shock had faded, I went to look for her, but it had grown dark and she was nowhere to be found. Was she an apparition? A woman or some kind of spirit? I'm still not certain."

Tremal-Naik fell silent. He was shaking visibly and Kammamuri wondered if his master had been taken with fever.

"That vision affected me deeply," Tremal-Naik added angrily. "A strange feeling took hold of me, as if I'd been bewitched. Since that day, I see her everywhere, dancing before me in the jungle, swimming before the bow of my boat when I'm on the river; my thoughts always turn to her; she appears in all my dreams. I think I'm going mad..."

"You're scaring me, master," said the Maratha, glancing about nervously. "Who was she?"

"I don't know, Kammamuri. She was beautiful though, very beautiful," Tremal-Naik exclaimed passionately.

"A spirit!?!"

"Perhaps."

"A goddess?"

"Who knows?"

"And you've never seen her again?"

"I've seen her several times. I returned to that stream at the same hour the following night. When the moon rose over the forest, that divine apparition appeared amongst the mussenda bushes once again.

"'Who are you?' I asked. 'Ada', she replied. Then she sighed sadly and disappeared, as she had the first time, as if the ground just swallowed her up without warning."

"Ada?" exclaimed Kammamuri. "What kind of name is that?"

"Not an Indian one."

"That's all she said?"

"That's all."

"Strange, I would never have returned."

"Yet, I did. A powerful force kept drawing me towards that place; I tried to resist it several times, but no matter what I did, I always went back. It was as if I'd been bewitched."

"How did you feel in her presence?"

"My heart pounded wildly."

"And you've never felt like that before?"

"Never," said Tremal-Naik.

"Do you still see her?"

"No, Kammamuri. She appeared for several nights, always at the same time, always in the same mysterious way. She would look at me in silence then disappear without a sound. Once, I waved to her, but she did not move; another time I tried to speak, but she put a finger to her lips and signalled me to be silent."

"You never followed her?"

"Never, Kammamuri, that woman frightens me. Fifteen days ago, she appeared dressed in red silk and remained longer than usual. The next night I waited for her again; I called out to her several times, but to no avail; I never saw her again."

"A strange adventure to be sure," murmured Kammamuri.

"It's terrible," Tremal-Naik continued hoarsely. "I can't eat, I can't sleep, it's like I have a fever; I have this burning desire to set eyes upon that vision once again."

"I think I understand your problem."

"Yes?"

"You're in love."

"What?"

Several sharp notes sounded from near the vast swamp south of the hut. The Maratha shot to his feet.

"A ramsinga!⁴" he exclaimed, terrified.

"What of it?" asked Tremal-Naik.

"It heralds misfortune, master."

"Nonsense, Kammamuri."

"The only other time I've ever heard a ramsinga sound in the jungle was on the night poor Tamul was murdered."

The hunter frowned at that sudden recollection.

"Don't worry," he said, forcing himself to appear calm. "Playing the ramsinga is a common skill; you know the odd hunter ventures into the jungle from time to time."

He had just finished speaking, when they heard a bark followed by a roar.

Kammamuri trembled from head to toe.

"Master!" he exclaimed. "Hear that? There's trouble nearby."

"Darma! Punthy!" yelled Tremal-Naik.

---

⁴ A long Indian trumpet made of four pipes of fine metal which can emit sound over a great distance

A superb Bengal tiger came out of the hut and fixed her eyes upon her master. She was followed by a black dog with sharp ears and a long tail wearing a large collar bristling with metal thorns.

"Darma! Punthy!" repeated Tremal-Naik.

The tiger grunted then leaped and landed at her master's feet.

"What is it, Darma?" he asked, gently stroking the animal's back. "You seem uneasy."

Instead of running to his master, the dog planted his four legs firmly on the ground, pointed his head towards the south, sniffed the air and barked three times.

"Could something have happened to Hurti and Aghur?" the hunter murmured uneasily.

"I fear so, master," said Kammamuri, glancing at the jungle nervously. "They should have returned by now."

"Did you hear any shots during the day?"

"Yes, a few in the middle of the afternoon, then nothing more."

"Where did they come from?"

"South of us, master."

"See anyone suspicious roaming about the jungle?"

"No, but Hurti told me that one night he spotted several shadows lurking about the shores of the island of Rajmangal, and then Aghur reported hearing strange sounds emanating from inside the sacred banyan tree."

"From inside the banyan tree!" exclaimed Tremal-Naik. "Have you heard or seen anything?"

"Maybe, I'm not sure. What are we going to do, master?"

"There's not much we can do. Best we wait here."

"But they could be..."

"Shh!" said Tremal-Naik, squeezing Kammamuri's arm tightly.

"What is it?" whispered the Maratha, growing uneasy.

"Look over there, the bamboo's moving."

"Someone's coming, master."

Punthy whimpered a third time as more sharp notes from the ramsinga filled the air. Tremal-Naik drew a pistol from his belt and quickly loaded it. Suddenly a tall man dressed in a dhoti[5] and armed with an axe, rushed out from among the bamboo, running towards the hut at full speed.

"Aghur!" Tremal-Naik and Kammamuri exclaimed simultaneously.

Punthy ran towards the newcomer, howling sadly.

"Master... master!"

He reached the hut in a flash. Eyes bulging, limbs trembling, he let out a soft cry and collapsed among the grass.

Tremal-Naik immediately rushed to his side and cried out in surprise.

The Indian appeared to be on the verge of death. Numerous cuts lined his blood-streaked face and his lips were covered in bloody foam; he looked about wildly, panting heavily.

"Aghur!" exclaimed Tremal-Naik. "What happened to you!?! Where's Hurti?"

At the sound of that name, Aghur's face twisted in fear. He tore at the ground, clawing up the dirt around him.

"Ma... ster... ma... ster," he stammered, deeply terrified.

"Yes, Aghur."

"I'm... suff... occ... I... ran... ma...ster!"

"Think he's been poisoned?" murmured Kammamuri.

"No," said Tremal-Naik. "The poor devil ran here at full speed, he's just winded; he'll be fine in a few minutes."

As the hunter had predicted, Aghur began to settle once he had caught his breath.

"Now tell me what happened," said Tremal-Naik, once the Indian had rested for several minutes. "Why did you come back alone? Why are you so afraid? Where's Hurti?"

"Master!" the Indian murmured with a shudder. "What a tragedy!"

"I knew that ramsinga was a bad omen," sighed Kammamuri.

"Continue, Aghur," urged the hunter.

"If only you'd seen the poor wretch... I found him lying on the ground, as stiff as a board, his eyes wrenched from their sockets..."

"Hurti's been killed!" exclaimed Tremal-Naik.

---

[5] A large rectangular piece of cloth worn about the waist

8

"Yes, they murdered him at the foot of the sacred banyan tree."

"Who murdered him? Tell me and I'll avenge him."

"I don't know, master."

"Start from the beginning; tell me everything."

"We'd set off to look for the tiger and spotted the beast in the jungle about six miles from here. It had been injured by a blast from Hurti's carbine and was heading south, trying to escape. We tracked it for four hours and came upon it once again near the shore, not far from the island of Rajmangal; however, before we could kill it, it spotted us, leaped into the water, swam to the island and hid beneath the great banyan tree."

"And then?"

"I wanted to come back to camp, but Hurti refused. He said the tiger had already been injured and was easy prey so we swam to the island then split up to go look for it."

The Indian stopped. He had turned pale with fear.

"Night had begun to fall," he continued gloomily. "All fell silent as darkness spread over the jungle. Suddenly, I heard a sharp note from a ramsinga and my eyes met those of a shadow half hidden in a bush just twenty paces from me."

"A shadow!" exclaimed Tremal-Naik. "A shadow?"

"Yes, master, a shadow."

"Who was it? Tell me, Aghur, tell me!"

"A woman."

"A woman!"

"Yes, I'm almost certain it was a woman."

"Beautiful?"

"It was too dark to tell."

Tremal-Naik put a hand to his brow.

"A shadow!" he repeated several times. "A shadow on the island! Continue, Aghur."

"It looked at me in silence, then raised an arm and gestured for me to go. Surprised and scared, I obeyed, but I had not gone more than a hundred paces when a cry of agony reached my ears. I recognized the voice immediately: it was Hurti."

"And the shadow?" Tremal-Naik asked excitedly.

"I didn't turn to see what had become of it. I headed through the forest, carbine in hand, and soon reached the great banyan tree. Poor Hurti was at the base of it, lying on his back. I called to him, but he didn't move; I touched his arm, he was warm, but he had no pulse!"

"Are you certain?"

"Positive, master."

"Where had he been hit?"

"I didn't see a single wound on his body."

"Impossible!"

"Yet, that's how it was."

"And you didn't see anyone?"

"Not a soul and I didn't hear a sound. Frightened, I dropped my carbine, jumped into the river and swam back as quickly as I could. Once ashore, I raced back towards our hut, never once looking back, never once stopping to take a breath, that's how frightened I was! Poor Hurti!"

Chapter 2
The Mysterious Island

A deep silence followed Aghur's story. Tremal-Naik, having suddenly grown sullen and restless, began to pace before the fire, head lowered, arms crossed, a frown upon his brow. Kammamuri had curled up into a tight ball, frozen with terror. Even the dog had fallen silent as he stretched out by Darma's side.

Several sharp notes from the mysterious ramsinga tore the hunter from his thoughts. He reared his head, cast an eye upon the deserted jungle then quickly made his way towards Aghur.

"Have you ever heard that ramsinga before?"

"Yes, master," replied the Indian, "Once."

"When?"

"Six months ago, the night Tamul disappeared."

"Kammamuri thinks it heralds tragedy."

"I'd agree, master."

"Ever seen anyone playing it?"

"No master, but I'd wager the musician is connected to the mysterious people on Rajmangal."

"Who do you think they are?"

"Spirits, master."

"What? Impossible!"

"Pirates then," said Aghur.

"Why would the suddenly start murdering my men?"

"Who can say? Maybe just to scare us or keep us away."

"Have you seen their huts?"

"No, but I know they gather beneath the sacred banyan tree every night."

"That's a start," said Tremal-Naik, "Kammamuri, go get the oars."

"What do you have in mind, master?" asked the Maratha.

"We're going to the banyan tree."

"No, master!" the two Indians cried simultaneously.

"Why not?"

"They'll kill you just as they did poor Hurti."

Tremal-Naik's eyes blazed darkly.

"I'm a hunter. I've never trembled before anyone in my life; we're going to that island, Kammamuri!" he exclaimed in a tone that did not allow for debate.

"But, master…"

"Are you afraid?" Tremal-Naik asked disdainfully.

"I'm a Maratha," the Indian replied proudly.

"Then let's go. I'm going to find out who these mysterious people are, why they've declared war upon us, and who that woman is."

Kammamuri picked up a pair of oars and headed towards the shore.

Tremal-Naik entered the hut, pulled a carbine from the wall, picked up a flask of gunpowder and tucked a large knife into his belt.

"Aghur, you'll remain here," he said, turning to go. "If we haven't returned in two days, take Darma and Punthy and come look for us on Rajmangal."

"But, master…"

"Have you lost your nerve?"

"No, master. I just don't think you should go to that cursed island."

"I won't let my men be murdered at will, Aghur."

"Take Darma with you. She could be of great assistance."

"She'd give us away. I want to land unseen. There's no need to fear, we'll be back soon. Goodbye, my friend."

He slung the carbine over his shoulder and headed off towards Kammamuri, who was waiting for him beside their gonga, a small canoe carved from a tree.

"Let's go," he said.

They jumped into the boat and slowly pulled away from the shore. Fog rippled over the canals, islands and sandbanks, shrouding the stars.

Vast forests of thorny bamboo stretched out on either side of them, the tall stalks tangled in vines and creepers. At times, growls and hisses emanated from among the grass and bushes lining the shore.

Rows of palms and latanie towered above the dark horizon, a few coconut and mango trees growing among them laden with exquisite fruit.

A heavy silence filled the air, broken only by the murmur of the sallow waters lapping against the mangroves and the sound of a gentle breeze rustling through the bamboo.

Tremal-Naik, stretched out on the stern, clutching his rifle, remained silent, his eyes darting from shore to shore as he scanned for hidden dangers. Kammamuri, sitting in the middle, made the small gonga fly, a long, sparkling wake stretching out behind it. From time to time, however, he would stop, hold his breath and fall silent, straining his ears to catch the slightest sound.

They had been afloat for more than thirty minutes when several notes from a ramsinga suddenly broke the silence. It had come from the right bank and sounded as if the musician were no more than a hundred paces away.

"Stop!" whispered Tremal-Naik.

He had barely uttered that word, when a second ramsinga sounded in reply. It had come from further off; a melancholy tune, contrasting oddly with the bright lively notes they had just heard.

Indian music is based on four styles, closely related to the four seasons of the year, each one having its own particular tone. It is melancholy in winter, lively in the spring, languid in the stifling summer heat, and sparkles brilliantly in the fall. Why were those two instruments playing so differently? Kammamuri feared it was a signal.

"Master," he said, "They've spotted us."

"Looks like it," replied Tremal-Naik, listening intently.

"Should we head back? They'll be expecting us."

"I never retreat. Keep rowing, they can play that ramsinga all night for all I care."

The Maratha began to row once again, driving the gonga ever forward. The river began to narrow and the air grew warmer. Several fireflies appeared in the distance, their light shining bizarrely over the black surface of the river. Suddenly, as if drawn by a mysterious force, they swirled before the gonga's bow then flew off as quickly as they had appeared.

"We've arrived at the cemetery," said Tremal-Naik. "We'll reach the banyan tree in ten minutes."

"Do you think we should cross in the gonga?" asked Kammamuri.

"All we need is a little patience."

"It's never wise to offend the dead, master."

"Brahma and Vishnu will forgive us. Start rowing, Kammamuri."

With a few strokes, the gonga entered a small basin; enormous tamarind trees towered about them, their branches arching over the water in a tangle of vegetation. Several corpses floated nearby, the tributaries of the Ganges having dragged them to the Mangal.

"Keep rowing!" said the hunter.

The Maratha was about to pull on the oars, when the dark canopy suddenly gave way to open sky and their eyes fell upon a storm of long-legged, black-winged birds with large sharp beaks diving towards the water.

"What now?" Kammamuri exclaimed, surprised.

"Just a few marabous," said Tremal-Naik, "Probably come for their next meal."

Hundreds of those sombre birds, common to the sacred river, were swarming upon the cemetery, their wings fluttering cheerfully as they alighted upon the dead.

"Keep rowing, Kammamuri," repeated Tremal-Naik.

The gonga headed ever forward. A half hour later, the two men had crossed the cemetery and arrived at the mouth of a large basin. An island divided it in two, an immense tree towering a few paces from the shore.

"The sacred banyan," said Tremal-Naik.

Kammamuri shuddered at the sound of that name.

"Master!" he whispered, gritting his teeth.

"Don't worry, my good Maratha. Take in the oars; let the gonga coast to the island. There may be someone about."

Kammamuri quickly did as instructed then lay flat against the bottom of the boat; Tremal-Naik loaded his carbine and stretched out by his side. Carried by a light current, the gonga turned about and headed towards the northern tip of the island of Rajmangal, home to the mysterious men that had murdered poor Hurti.

A profound silence reigned over that place. The breeze had ceased to blow and the bamboo had fallen quiet, even the waters appeared to have lost their voice.

Disturbed by that eerie calm, Tremal-Naik would cautiously raise his head as they drew nearer and carefully scan the shore.

With a light thud, the gonga landed a hundred paces from the banyan tree, but the two Indians did not move. Ten anxious minutes passed before Tremal-Naik peered over the side. The first thing he spotted was a black shape lying among the grass, about twenty metres from the river.

"Kammamuri," he whispered, "Load your pistol."

The Maratha did not wait to be told twice.

"What is it, master?" he whispered.

"Look over there."

"A body!" said the Maratha, his eyes growing wide.

"Shh!"

Tremal-Naik raised his carbine and aimed it at the dark silhouette stretched out before him, waited an instant then lowered it without firing.

"Let's go see who he is, Kammamuri," he said. "I don't think he's alive."

"What if he's only pretending to be dead?"

"Then he'll regret it."

The two men disembarked and silently headed towards the body, keeping close to the ground. They had arrived to within ten paces of it, when a marabou squawked noisily and flew off towards the river.

"It is a body," murmured Tremal-Naik. "If only…"

He did not finish the sentence. Upon reaching the corpse, an exclamation of rage escaped his lips.

"Hurti!" he cried.

The poor man was lying on his back, his arms and legs strewn about, frozen in the final throws of death. His face was twisted in terror, eyes bulging from their sockets, tongue jutting from his mouth. His knees and feet were broken; someone had dragged him there.

Tremal-Naik picked up the unfortunate Indian and looked for a wound, but at first glance could not find a single scratch. However, upon closer examination, he found deep marks around Hurti's neck and a large bruise on the back of his head that appeared to have been made by a rock.

"They knocked him out before they killed him. We'll avenge him. Quickly now, back to the boat."

"Poor Hurti!" murmured the Maratha. "Why would anyone want to kill him?"

"We're going to find out, Kammamuri; I won't allow this act to go unpunished, you have my word."

"What about Hurti? Are we going to leave him here?"

"We'll set him adrift in the Ganges come morning."

"The tigers will probably get to him before we return."

"I'll stand watch over the body."

"What? You're not coming back with me?"

"No, Kammamuri, I'm staying here. I'll return once I've dealt with his murderers."

"You're going to get yourself killed…"

A disdainful smile spread across the proud Bengali's lips.

"I was born and raised in the jungle! Go back to the hut, Kammamuri."

"Never, master!"

"What?"

"If something were to happen to you, who'd be here to help? Let me stay; I'll follow your every order."

"Even if I decide to set off and find my vision?"

"Yes, master."

16

"Very well then, you may stay, my good Maratha; the two of us will do the work of ten men. Come!"

Tremal-Naik went off towards the river, grabbed the gonga's starboard side, tipped it over, and forced it beneath the waters.

"What are you doing?" Kammamuri asked, surprised.

"No one must know we're here. Now, let's try to solve this mystery."

To ensure they would not miss their first shot, they replaced the powder in their carbines and pistols then headed towards the large banyan tree looming proudly in the darkness.

Chapter 3
Avenging Hurti

Banyan trees, also known as *Pagoda fig trees,* are stranger and larger than one might imagine. Their trunks are as tall and as thick as the largest oak trees. Thin root-like shoots tumble from their infinite branches and imbed themselves in the soil, infusing the tree with nutrients and thickening as they age.

As the branches continue to spread, they generate a labyrinth of bizarre columns, at times an entire forest can be comprised of a single tree.

In the province of Gujarat a banyan tree named *Cobir bor,* revered by the Indians, for it is believed to be more than three thousand years old, extends for six hundred metres and has no less than three thousand column-like roots. It covered even more ground in ancient times, but part of it was destroyed as the waters of the Nerbudda River eroded its island home.

The banyan beneath which the two Indians were about to pass the night was enormous, it having more than six hundred columns. Its immense branches were laden with small vermilion fruit, and its strong thick trunk appeared to have been severed at the top.

Having carefully scouted their surroundings to ensure they were alone, Tremal-Naik and Kammamuri sat down before the base of the tree, side by side, their loaded carbines resting upon their knees.

"And now we wait," whispered the hunter. "I wouldn't want to be the first person to come within range of my carbine."

"You think Hurti's murderers are going to come back here?" asked Kammamuri.

"I'm certain of it. We'll solve this mystery before the night is up."

"So, we'll kill the first man that dares show his face."

"It depends on the circumstances. Now keep your eyes open and try not to make any noise."

He pulled a betel leaf out of his pocket, added a bit of walnut and some lime to it and began to chew.

Two hours passed slowly. All remained quiet beneath the giant tree. It must have been close to midnight when Tremal-Naik, who had been straining his ears to catch the slightest sound, heard a strange rumble emanate from beneath the ground.

The hunter began to grow uneasy.

"Kammamuri," he whispered, "Stand ready."

"See something?" asked the Maratha.

"No, but I heard a sound."

"Where?"

"I think it came from underground."

"Impossible, master!"

"I doubt I was mistaken."

"What do you think it was?"

"I don't know yet, but we'll find out soon enough."

"Master, I don't like this place."

"Are you afraid?"

"Afraid? I'm a Maratha."

"Then let's see who's behind all this."

A second rumble emanated from beneath the ground. The two men looked at each other in surprise.

"It almost sounds as if someone's playing a hauk[6]," said Tremal-Naik.

"It couldn't be anything else," replied Kammamuri. "There must be some caves beneath this island. What are we going to do, master?"

"We'll stay right here. Someone's bound to come out from somewhere."

"Tikora!" yelled a voice.

The two men jumped to their feet. The voice had come from nearby, so close in fact, it sounded as if the speaker were standing behind them.

---

[6] A sacred ceremonial bass drum of enormous proportions

"Tikora!" murmured Tremal-Naik. "Who's calling out?"

He scanned his surroundings but could not see anyone; he looked up and saw only the tangled branches of the banyan tree stretching out in the darkness.

"Could someone be hiding among the branches?"

"I don't think so," said Kammamuri, trembling. "The voice came from behind us."

"It's strange."

"Tikora!" repeated the same mysterious voice.

The two Indians looked about once again. There was no mistaking it; someone was close by, but to their surprise and terror, that someone remained invisible.

"Master," whispered Kammamuri, "It's probably a spirit."

"I don't believe in spirits," replied Tremal-Naik. "It's a man and we'll find him soon enough."

"Oh!" exclaimed the Maratha, stumbling back three or four steps. "Look up there... master! Look!"

Tremal-Naik raised his head, fixed his eyes on the banyan tree and spotted a sliver of light rising from inside the severed trunk. Despite his courage, his blood turned cold.

"A light!" he stammered, dismayed.

"Let's get out of here, master!" begged Kammamuri.

For the third time, a mysterious rumble emanated from beneath the ground, but this time it was followed by the brassy notes of a ramsinga. The music seemed to come from inside the banyan's trunk. Instantly, a reply sounded off in the distance.

"Let's get out of here, master!" Kammamuri repeated, terrified.

"Never!" Tremal-Naik exclaimed resolutely.

He placed his dagger between his teeth and grabbed his carbine by the barrel, planning to use it as a club, but quickly changed his mind.

"Come, Kammamuri," he said. "It's best we learn who we're dealing with before we start a fight."

He led the Maratha to a spot behind four thick roots about two hundred paces from the banyan tree, from where they could spy on the large trunk without being seen.

"Not a word now," said Tremal-Naik. "We'll attack on my signal."

One last sharp note emanated from the colossal trunk and was greeted by wild cries from the Sundarbans. The sliver of light projecting through the tree's summit went out, and a head wearing a yellow turban appeared in its place.

It scanned its surroundings for a few minutes, as if to ensure that no one was lurking about beneath the giant tree, then it protruded further, and a man, an Indian judging by his appearance, came out, and grabbed onto one of the branches.

Forty Indians followed, grabbing onto the roots and sliding to the ground. They were naked to the waist, each man's chest marked by a tattoo: a series of ancient Sanskrit letters encircling a Nagi, a snake woman with a coiled serpentine body. They wore dhotis of yellow cloth about their hips and silk rumaals[7] weighted with a lead ball about their waists, their sharp daggers peering menacingly from behind those strange belts.

The band of Indians silently gathered round an old man.

"My sons," he said gravely, "Our mighty hand has struck down the wretch that dared set foot upon our sacred shores. Another victim for the altar, but our work is not yet done. Our beloved goddess demands more blood."

"Command us, great leader, and we shall obey."

"You are brave," said the old man, "but this is not the time. We face a grave danger, my sons. A man has dared to look upon the Guardian."

"Blasphemy!" exclaimed the Indians.

"Yes, my sons; a man has dared look her in the face. He will not escape the goddess' wrath!"

"Who is this man?"

"You'll know all in time. Bring me the victim."

Two Indians stood up and headed towards the spot where Hurti's body lay. Tremal-Naik had watched that strange proceeding without batting an eyelash, but as soon as those two men grabbed the body by

---

[7] A kerchief used as a strangling cloth

21

the arms and began to drag it towards the banyan tree, he shot to his feet, carbine in hand.

"Wretches!" he murmured, taking aim.

"What are you doing, master?" whispered Kammamuri, grabbing the rifle barrel and pulling it down.

"Let go, Kammamuri," said the hunter. "They killed Hurti and I'm going to avenge him."

"You'll get us both killed! There are forty of them!"

"You're right, Kammamuri. We'll wait for better odds."

He lowered his carbine and crouched back down behind the roots, biting his lip to reign in his anger.

The two Indians had dragged Hurti's body into the middle of the circle and dropped it before the old man's feet.

"Kali!" he exclaimed, raising his eyes towards the heavens.

He drew the dagger from his belt and plunged it into Hurti's chest.

"Wretch!" howled Tremal-Naik. "This is too much!"

He jumped out of his hiding place. A flash of light tore through the darkness followed by a loud discharge. The old Indian, struck in the chest by the hunter's bullet, fell forward onto Hurti's body.

Chapter 4
In the Jungle

At that sudden discharge, the men had jumped to their feet, drawing their daggers and nooses. Seeing their leader fall, covered in blood, they quickly rushed to his aid, too stunned to think of looking for the shooter. Taking advantage of the confusion, Tremal-Naik and Kammamuri quickly slipped away.

Paces from them, the jungle, teeming with thorny bushes and giant bamboo trees, offered a variety of hiding places. The two Indians dove in among the vegetation, ran desperately for five or six minutes, then dropped to the ground in a thick grove of bamboo trees no less than twelve metres high.

"If you value your life, Kammamuri," Tremal-Naik whispered quickly, "don't move."

"Why did you do that, master?" said the poor Maratha. "We're done for; they'll strangle us."

"I avenged my friend. Don't worry; they won't find us."

"They're spirits, master."

"They're men. Now keep quiet and keep your eyes open."

The terrible cries of those mysterious men still thundered off in the distance.

"Revenge! Revenge!" they yelled.

Three sharps notes, the notes of a ramsinga, echoed throughout the jungle while the dark rumbling they had heard earlier resumed beneath the ground. Trying to make themselves as small as possible, the two hunters curled up and held their breath. They knew that if found, those fanatics would have strangled them both, two more victims for their bloodthirsty goddess.

Three minutes had not yet passed, when they heard someone forcing his way through the bamboo trees. A man appeared in the darkness, wielding a noose and a dagger. He shot through the bushes like an arrow and quickly disappeared into the jungle.

"Did you see him, Kammamuri?" whispered Tremal-Naik.

"Yes, master," replied the Maratha.

"They think we've run off, I wouldn't be surprised if they all come after us. Soon we won't have a single man at our backs."

"I wouldn't be too trusting, master, those men frighten me."

"Don't worry, I'll protect you. Now keep quiet and be ready for anything."

Another Indian armed like the first ran past an instant later, disappearing among the bamboo like his companion before him. They heard cries off in the distance, followed by several whistles, perhaps signals of some kind, then silence returned once again.

Half an hour passed. The Indians they had spotted were probably a good distance away. The time had come to head back toward the shore.

"Kammamuri," said Tremal-Naik, "Time to go. Those men must all be searching for us by now. They're probably scouring the jungle as we speak."

"Are you sure, master?"

"I don't hear anything."

"Where shall we go? Back to the banyan tree?"

"Yes, they won't look for us there."

"Are we going to climb down it?"

"Not just yet; we'll return tomorrow night and try to shed some light on this mystery."

"Who do you think those men are?"

"I don't know, Kammamuri, but I'm going to find out. Did you hear what that old man said about the Guardian?"

"Yes, master."

"I'm almost certain he was talking about me. I suspect she's the woman that bewitched me so, Kammamuri. When the old man spoke of her, I felt my heart race; that only happens when I…"

"Shh, master!" Kammamuri whispered hoarsely.

"What?"

"Something's moving among the bamboo."

"Where?"

"Over there… thirty paces from us. Quiet!"

Tremal-Naik raised his head and carefully scanned the dark mass of bamboo, but could not see anyone. He held his breath and listened. A soft rustling sound emanated from where the Maratha had pointed, a hand was cautiously opening a path among the tangle of reeds.

"Someone's approaching," he murmured. "Don't move, Kammamuri."

The rustling was growing louder and slowly drawing nearer. Moments later, the bamboo parted and an Indian appeared before them. He bent towards the ground, put a hand to his ear and listened for a minute, then stood up and sniffed the air.

"Gary!" he whispered.

A second Indian stepped out from among the bushes, just six paces from the first.

"Hear anything?" asked the newcomer.

"No."

"I swear I heard someone whispering."

"You were probably mistaken. I've been here for the last five minutes, I haven't heard a sound. We're looking in the wrong place."

"Where are the others?"

"They've all gone back. They fear those men may attack the pagoda."

"What? Why?"

"Fifteen days ago, the Guardian of the Sacred Temple met a man. One of our men spotted her signalling to him."

"What kind of signals?"

"They believe the man wants to free her."

"Sacrilege!" exclaimed the Indian named Gary.

"Yes. The man we strangled earlier was probably one of his spies."

"Who would dare look the Guardian in the face? Do you know who he is?"

"A formidable man, Gary, capable of anything: Tremal-Naik, the Hunter of the Black Jungle."

"He must die."

"He will, Gary. We'll track him down and strangle him, no matter where he goes. You go back to the river; I'll go to the pagoda and protect the Guardian. May the goddess protect you."

The two Indians parted ways, each taking a different path. Once silence had returned, Tremal-Naik jumped to his feet.

"Kammamuri," he said excitedly, "It's best we split up. You heard them, they know I've landed and they're looking for me."

"I heard every word, master."

"Follow the Indian heading towards the river and make your way off the island at the first opportunity. I'm going to follow the other man."

"Why not come with me?"

"I'm going to find that pagoda."

"Don't, master!"

"There'll be no discussion. They're keeping that woman there."

"What if they catch you?"

"They'll kill me and I'll die happily by her side. Now go, Kammamuri, get back to the hut."

The Maratha sighed and got up.

"Master," he said sadly, "Where are we going to meet?"

"At the hut, provided they don't kill me first. Now go!"

The Maratha headed into the jungle, following the Indian's tracks towards the river. Tremal-Naik remained behind, watching him go, arms crossed over his chest, a deep frown forming upon his brow.

"And now," he said, raising his head proudly, once the Maratha had disappeared into the night, "Let's go challenge death!"

He slung his carbine over his shoulder, took one last look around and silently went off, following the second Indian's tracks.

A thick forest of bamboo stretched out before him, as far as the eye could see. A man unaccustomed to those places would have undoubtedly gotten lost among those giant plants or found it impossible to advance undetected, but, Tremal-Naik, who had been born and raised in the jungle, could move through that vegetation without making a sound.

He advanced like a serpent, slithering among the trees, never stopping, always certain of his path. Every now and then he would stop, place an ear to the ground, and listen for his quarry's movements.

He had gone about a mile, when the Indian came to a sudden halt. The hunter put his ear to the ground three or four times, but could not hear anything stirring among the reeds. Slightly uneasy, he stood up and listened, but the jungle had fallen silent.

"What happened?" he wondered, looking about. "Could he have heard me?"

He crawled forward another three or four metres, raised his head then quickly drew it back. He had bumped against something soft that had instantly retreated.

"Ah!" he said.

A terrible thought flashed through his mind. He immediately jumped to one side, unsheathed his dagger and looked up, but saw nothing but bamboo.

He had been standing there for several minutes, when a soft rustling sound suddenly reached his ears. He turned his head and spotted a long glistening mass descending from above. A monstrous python, more than seven metres long, was advancing towards him, its coils winding through the reeds. It hissed as it drew nearer, showing its fangs, its bright eyes shining sinisterly in the darkness.

Tremal-Naik dove to the ground.

"If I move, I'm dead," he murmured.

The python's head had reached the ground. It slithered towards the hunter, who dared not move, hovered over him for a while, licking his skin as it prepared to wrap him in its coils. Three times it attacked, and three times it retreated, hissing angrily as it writhed among the bamboo.

Though horrified by its touch, Tremal-Naik forced himself to lie still. Once the shifting coils had drawn back, he hurriedly crawled away. He had gone five or six metres when a menacing voice cried out:

"Who goes there?"

Tremal-Naik immediately sprang to his feet, clutching his knife. A tall thin Indian armed with a dagger and a noose had suddenly appeared about seven or eight metres from him, standing close to the python's lair. His chest bore the tattoo he had seen on the others: Sanskrit letters encircling a Nagi, that mysterious snake woman with a coiled serpentine body.

"Who goes there?" the Indian repeated menacingly.

"Who's asking?" Tremal-Naik replied with icy calmness. "One of those wretched murderers?"

"Yes, and you'll be my next victim."

Tremal-Naik laughed and cast a glance at the python undulating just above the Indian's head. It had begun to uncoil its rings.

"I'd say your hours are numbered," said the hunter.

"You'll die before I do!" yelled the Indian, as his silk rumaal began to whistle above his head.

He was about to cast his noose when an angry hiss made his blood turn cold. He raised his head and spotted the python directly above him. He tried to back away but tripped and fell to the ground.

"Help, help!" he yelled desperately.

The python lunged toward the Indian, quickly wrapping him in its coils.

"Help, help!" repeated the poor wretch, his eyes widening in horror.

Tremal-Naik quickly leaped towards them and cut the python in two with a slash of his blade. It hissed angrily as it sprayed its victim with blood and spittle. He was about to deal it another blow, when he heard the bamboo rattle furiously.

"There he is!" thundered a voice.

Several men rushed towards him, while the python, despite being sliced in two, fought to keep a grip on its prey, drawing blood as its coils squeezed ever tighter. Aware of the danger before him, Tremal-Naik tore off through the jungle.

"There he is! There he is!" repeated the same voice, "Fire at him!"

A rifle shot thundered through the trees, then a second, then a third. Having miraculously escaped those bullets, Tremal-Naik turned with a roar.

"Wretches!" he howled, enraged.

Daggers between their teeth, nooses whistling in the air, his attackers advanced, preparing to strike. Tremal-Naik levelled his carbine. A light flashed among the reeds followed by the sound of a discharge. An Indian let out a horrible cry, brought his hands to his head and fell among the grass. Before his companions could reply, the hunter rushed off, tore through a grove of bamboo trees and disappeared into the jungle.

He ran for fifteen minutes, stopping only for a moment to catch his breath at the edge of a field. He looked about then raced off like a madman, barrelling through marshland until he reached open ground. Heart pounding, lungs burning, he continued on his run, diving among bushes, wading through ponds and canals, straining every muscle to gain distance from his attackers.

How far he ran he did not know. When he finally came to a halt, he found himself standing before a large pond ringed with ruins, two hundred paces from a beautiful pagoda.

Chapter 5
The Guardian of the Temple of the East

The pagoda was the most beautiful the hunter had ever seen. Built entirely of grey granite, it was more than twenty metres high and almost fifteen metres across. It narrowed slightly as it rose, ending in a large dome capped by a giant metal sphere that rested beneath a bronze statue of a Nagi. Large pillars adorned the base, framing exquisite carvings of gods and monsters that covered every inch of its imposing walls.

Tremal-Naik paused for a moment, surprised at finding such a structure in the midst of the jungle.

"The pagoda!" he exclaimed. "I'm done for!"

He quickly glanced about; a vast clearing spread out before him, he would have to run a half mile before he reached the trees.

"I'm done for!" he repeated irately. "They'll be here in minutes and they'll strangle me if I don't find a place to hide."

The idea of running back into the jungle flashed through his mind for an instant, but the trees were too far off, he would not make it before his enemies reached the clearing. He scanned the ruins about the pond, but did not spot anywhere to hide.

"How about up there?" he murmured, looking at the top of the pagoda.

It would not be easy, but a man of his great strength and agility was more than capable of climbing up to the dome, scaling the pillars and sculptures that adorned the temple walls.

He unloaded his carbine, slung it around his shoulder and ran towards the pagoda. He stopped and listened for a few minutes, then reassured by the silence, began his arduous climb.

He advanced with surprising speed, swinging from carving to carving as he made his way up that pantheon of gods. His heart raced with each new step, his muscles filling with strength as if some mysterious force were drawing him ever higher.

It was just past two when he reached the top, unfazed by that arduous climb, even though he had risked falling at least a dozen times. With one last effort he reached out for the large metal ball and pulled himself up beneath the statue of the Nagi.

To his surprise he found himself looking down over a wide dark hole, a bronze bar lay across it on which he managed to rest his feet.

Moving slowly, he grabbed onto the metal bar and looked down into the darkness below. Not a sound reached his ears; the pagoda was empty. A thick rope hung from the bar and disappeared into the opening. He grabbed it and tried to pull it towards him, but it was heavier than he thought; metal tinkled faintly as he tried to draw it near.

"Must be a lamp," mumbled Tremal-Naik.

A sudden thought froze him where he stood.

"Those two men spoke of a pagoda!" he exclaimed excitedly. "Yes... of a Guardian... Great Vishnu, could it be..."

His heart pounded wildly. Though he did not know what awaited him below, he tightened his grip and began to make his way down into the darkness. Several minutes later his feet struck a round object, and a soft metallic sound echoed throughout the temple.

He was about to bend down to see where he was, when the squeak of a hinge reached his ears. He looked down and spotted a shadow moving silently through the darkness.

"Who could that be?" he whispered, shuddering.

He drew his pistol, determined not to surrender without a fight.

A deep sigh reached his ears.

His heart leaped.

"I've gone mad," he murmured.

The shadow stopped before a large dark mass just beneath the rope.

"Here I am, wretched goddess!" exclaimed a feminine voice that shook Tremal-Naik to the depths of his soul.

31

Surprised, the hunter watched in silence, listening to the sound of liquid pouring on the floor and breathing in the delicate perfume slowly filling the air.

What monstrous people! he thought. Yet that shadow's voice sounded as sweet as the notes of a sarangi.[8]

"I hate you, wretched goddess!" the voice continued bitterly. "You've destroyed everything I loved and condemned me to a life of martyrdom! Vile assassins! May you be cursed in this life and the next!"

The young woman began to sob. Tremal-Naik shivered a second time. Then that man, the son of the jungle, hunter of tigers and serpents, for the first time in his life felt deeply moved.

For a moment he considered jumping to the ground, but caution held him back. Besides, it was too late, the shadow had disappeared into the darkness; a short while later, he heard the hinge squeak once more then the sound of the door closing behind it.

"What's the meaning of this?" murmured Tremal-Naik. "Who are these monsters? Why do they need so many victims? Who is that frightening goddess? And that woman? Curse them all… who is she? They strangle, she weeps; they disgust me, she moves me… I must see her, talk to her, have her tell me all she knows. I'm sure I've seen her before, I can feel it… she's… it's like…"

He stopped, breathless, almost afraid to utter another word. A sudden shock had bathed his brow in perspiration.

"My vision!" he said, his voice trembling slightly. "As I scaled the temple, my heart beat wildly; my limbs shook as I descended the rope. If it were true? Best to take a closer look."

He slid down the rope until his feet struck something hard. It echoed metallically as if made of bronze. He had landed upon that dark mass, before which the tormented woman had poured her offering.

"What's this?" he murmured.

He bent down, felt his way forward then slid to the ground, almost slipping as he stepped onto the smooth wet surface.

---

[8] Similar to a violin but smaller and with more strings

32

"Perfume," he said. "I'll get my bearings with the morning light."

He crept six or seven paces forward in the darkness, then, still clutching his pistols, curled up into a ball and waited.

Several hours passed in deepest silence. Through the opening the sky grew lighter and the stars faded with the first rays of the dawn. Not daring to move, Tremal-Naik waited patiently, eyes open, ears straining to catch the slightest sound.

Towards four, the sun suddenly appeared on the horizon, illuminating the great bronze sphere atop the pagoda as a ray of light projected through the wide opening. Tremal-Naik jumped to his feet, surprised and stunned by the wondrous sight before him.

He was standing in a large vault; the lofty walls adorned with paintings depicting Vishnu's many incarnations. Sculptures of devas and asuras, gods and demons, peered down from great heights as the sun slowly lit up the interior.

A large bronze statue of a woman stood in the centre of the pagoda. She had four arms, one held a sword, another bore a severed head. A girdle of hands rested about her hips, a long garland of skulls stretched down to her feet. Skulls adorned her ears and a blood red tongue peered from between fierce lips. She stood upon a giant, who at first glance appeared to have been slain in battle.

A small basin of white marble rested upon the bright stones of the temple floor. It was filled with clear water and housed a small red fish.

Tremal-Naik had never seen anything like it.

He stopped before the enormous statue and gazed at it with a mixture of fear and amazement.

Who was that sinister figure standing before him? What connection did it have to those men, their strange tattoo, and that fish swimming in the basin?

"Could this be a dream?" he murmured, rubbing his eyes repeatedly. "None of this makes any sense."

The hunter had not yet finished uttering those words, when the soft squeak of a hinge reached his years.

He turned around, carbine in hand, and immediately stepped back, retreating to the monstrous goddess, barely able to restrain a cry of joy and amazement.

There in the doorway stood a young woman of incredible beauty, a look of terror upon her face.

She was perhaps fifteen years old, in the flower of her youth[9]. She was elegant, attractive and graceful with delicate, rosy skin, large black eyes, and a small thin nose. Her coral red lips had parted in a melancholy smile, revealing small white teeth. Long black hair fell to her shoulders, a few sciambaga flowers braided among her curls.

"Ada! The vision!" he whispered as his back struck the base of the statue.

Words failed him; he remained rooted to the ground, silent, breathless, dazed and uncertain, eyes fixed upon the beautiful young woman whose face had filled with terror.

As she stepped forward a dazzling light met the hunter's gaze so intense he was forced to look away.

The young woman was covered in riches. A long white silk shawl spread behind her like a cape, revealing a golden breastplate inlaid with large diamonds from Golconda and Gujarat set about a large Nagi engraved in its centre. Necklaces of diamonds and pearls hung about her neck, thick bracelets inlaid with precious stones adorned her arms. White silk pantaloons came down just above her ankles, a pair of red coral anklets resting above her small bare feet.

The sun had struck that exotic attire, bathing the young woman in a harsh golden light.

"The vision! The vision!" repeated Tremal-Naik. "How beautiful she is!"

The young woman looked about in bewilderment, raised a finger to her lips, and drew up before him.

"Fool!" she said, her voice failing to hide her fear. "What are you doing here? What folly dragged you to this horrible place?"

---

[9] Indian women are considered marriageable by age 10. They are considered old by the time they turn 30.

Despite himself, the hunter had fallen to his knees, arms outstretched in supplication, but the young woman backed away even more frightened than before.

"Don't touch me!" she whispered.

Tremal-Naik let out a sigh.

"You're beautiful!" he exclaimed passionately.

"Be quiet, Tremal-Naik!"

"You're beautiful!" replied the hunter.

She put a finger to her lips.

"Don't make a sound," whispered the young woman. "We're in grave danger."

"Danger!?! Who threatens you? Tell me and I'll slay him!"

"Don't talk like that, Tremal-Naik."

"I'm yours to do with as you please. The night you appeared in that mussenda bush, bathed in the light of the setting sun, I thought you were a goddess descended from the heavens and I burned with adoration."

"Quiet, Quiet!" repeated the young woman, burying her face in her hands.

"I cannot, rare flower of the jungle!" exclaimed Tremal-Naik, his passion mounting with every word. "When you disappeared, you took my heart with you; since then visions of you danced before my eyes and my heart beat ever faster. You've bewitched me!"

"Tremal-Naik!" murmured the young woman.

"I could not sleep that night," continued the hunter. "I was obsessed; I had to see you once again. Why? I do not know. I could not explain it. I'd never felt that way before.

"Fifteen days passed. Every night at sunset, I saw you behind the mussendas, and I was filled with great delight! We did not speak, but when our eyes met I knew that you…"

He fell silent, eyes riveted on the young woman, her hands still pressed to her face.

"Ah!" he exclaimed, his voice marked with pain. "You do not wish to hear this."

The young woman raised her head; her eyes were wet with tears.

"Why speak of this," she murmured, "it can never be! You shouldn't have come and stirred my heart! It's a false hope, nothing more. This place is cursed, deadly to those I love."

"Those you love!?!" Tremal-Naik exclaimed with joy. "Repeat, those words, rare flower of the jungle! You love me? Is it true? Did you come to the mussenda bush each night because you loved me?"

"You're putting our lives at risk, Tremal-Naik!" exclaimed the young woman, her voice filled with anguish.

"Fear not, my sweet. Am I not here to defend you? I'll tear down that monster if need be, raze this very temple to the ground. You'll never be forced to making offerings to her again."

"Make offerings! You saw me?"

"Last night, when you came with that perfume."

"You were in the pagoda?"

"Yes, up there, clinging to that rope."

"But, how did you find it?"

"I chanced upon it while trying to hide from those men that live on this wretched island."

"Did they see you?"

"They chased me."

"Ah, poor soul, you're done for!" the young woman exclaimed desperately.

Tremal-Naik rushed towards her.

"What goes on here?" he asked, barely able to contain his fury. "Why so much terror? Why do you pour perfume before that monstrous statue? Who is she? Why's there a fish swimming in that basin? Why is there a Nagi engraved on your armour? Why do these men live underground? Who are they? I must know, Ada! Tell me!"

"Don't ask me any questions, Tremal-Naik."

"Why not?"

"I cannot escape my fate!"

"I'll fight your captors; I'll show them no mercy!"

"They'll snap you like a reed. Do they not challenge the power of England? They're strong, Tremal-Naik, and merciless! No one can resist them. Legions of men have fallen before their invincible might."

"Who are they?"

"I cannot tell you."

"Even if I begged you?"

"I'd still refuse."

"Then you... don't trust me!" Tremal-Naik exclaimed angrily.

"Tremal-Naik! Tremal-Naik!" the young woman murmured, her voice filling with agony.

The hunter crossed his arms.

"Tremal-Naik," continued the young woman, "Only death can free me from my fate. I love you; I love you, but..."

"You love me!" exclaimed the hunter.

"Yes, I love you, Tremal-Naik."

"Swear it on that monster before us."

"I swear it!" said the young woman, stretching her hand towards the bronze statue.

"Swear to me you'll be my bride!"

"Tremal-Naik," she murmured sadly, "I'll be your bride if it's ever possible!"

"Possible? Is there another man?"

"Death alone may claim me."

Tremal-Naik took two steps back, reeling slightly.

"Death!" he exclaimed.

"Yes, Tremal-Naik, death. The day a man places a hand upon me, an avenger's noose will take my life."

"Is this a dream?"

"No, you're awake, talking to your beloved."

"What a mystery!"

"A terrible mystery, Tremal-Naik. No one can bridge the abyss between us. By the heavens! What have I done to be so unlucky? What crime have I committed to deserve such a fate?"

A sob stifled her voice as tears rolled down her cheeks. Tremal-Naik roared with rage.

"How can I help?" he said, moved to the very depths of his soul. "Your tears fill me with pain, rare flower of the jungle. Tell me what I must do! I'll obey your every command! Do you wish me to take you from here? I will, even if it costs me my life."

"No, no!" exclaimed the young woman. "It would bring death to us both."

She fell silent as tears streamed down her cheeks. Tremal-Naik gently drew her towards him. He was about to speak when the sharp notes of a ramsinga sounded from outside.

"Go, Tremal-Naik, get out of here!" the young woman exclaimed, terrified. "Go, or all is lost!"

"Wretched trumpet!" howled Tremal-Naik, gritting his teeth.

"They're coming," sobbed the young woman. "If they find us, they'll sacrifice us to that wretched goddess. Get out of here! Escape! Hurry!"

"Never!"

"They'll kill us!"

"I'll defend you!"

"Go you fool! Get out of here!"

Instead of replying, Tremal-Naik picked up his carbine and loaded it. The young woman quickly realized the hunter was determined to stand and fight.

"Have pity on me!" she said with anguish. "They're coming."

"I'll be waiting," replied Tremal-Naik. "The first man who dares raise a hand to you will meet his death."

"Fine, stay. Since there's no convincing you, I'll save you."

She turned about and headed towards the door.

Tremal-Naik rushed after her and attempted to hold her back.

"Where are you going?" he asked.

"To meet the man walking towards the pagoda and prevent him from entering this chamber. I'll come back at midnight. Then if the gods are willing... we'll escape."

"I still don't know your name."

"Ada Corishant."

"Ada Corishant! What a beautiful name! Go now, Ada, I'll see you at midnight!"

The young woman drew her cloak about her, cast one last look at Tremal-Naik, stifled a sob and left.

Chapter 6
Condemned to Death

Having left the pagoda, her face bathed in tears, but her eyes sparkling with pride, Ada entered a small room. Elaborate murals stretched from floor to ceiling, each wall depicting a battle between gods and demons. A bronze statue similar to the one in the pagoda stood in the centre, a small fish swimming in a white marble basin resting at its feet.

A man awaited her, pacing impatiently. He was a tall Indian, as thin as a reed, with a fierce energetic face framed by a short black bristling beard. He was clad in a yellow silk dhoti heavy with gold embroidery. His arms were scarred and marked by strange symbols that even a scholar would have struggled to read. Spotting Ada, he immediately came to a halt and fixed his eyes upon her as an evil smile spread across his lips.

"Greetings, Guardian of the Temple of the East," he said, bowing before the young woman.

"Greetings, Great Leader, Favourite of the Goddess," replied Ada, her voice trembling slightly.

They locked eyes and fell silent, each attempting to read the other's thoughts.

"Guardian of the Sacred Temple," said the Indian after a brief silence, "You're in grave danger."

Ada shuddered. The Indian's voice was dark and menacing.

"Where were you this evening? I've been told you entered the pagoda."

"That's true. You sent me some scented oils and I offered them to your goddess."

"Our goddess."

"Yes, our goddess," said the young woman, stifling a grimace.

"See anything unusual in the pagoda?"

"No."

"Guardian of the Sacred Temple," replied the Indian, his voice even more menacing. "Do not lie to me, I have learned the truth!"

Ada stepped back, letting out a cry of terror.

"Yes," continued the Indian, barely able to contain his anger, "I know all! Your heart has beaten with love for a man you met in the jungle. Last night he landed on our island, murdered one of our men and vanished before we could take him. We tracked him through the night and just when we thought we'd lost his trail, we discovered he'd been hiding in the pagoda."

"That's a lie!" exclaimed the young woman.

"Guardian of the Sacred Temple, you know your duty. You cannot love that man. Fortunately, he dared not touch you!"

"That's a lie, that's a lie!" repeated the young woman.

"He will not leave here alive," the Indian said coldly. "The fool dared challenge our power; we who make mighty England tremble. The snake has entered the lion's den, but the lion will tear it to pieces."

"You'll do no such thing!"

The Indian chuckled.

"Who dares oppose the will of our goddess?"

"I do."

"You?"

"Yes, you wretch!"

With one quick movement, Ada cast back her cloak, drew her dagger, and pressed the tip of its serpentine blade to her neck.

Knowing the blade had been dipped in poison, the Indian froze.

"What is this foolishness?" he asked, dismayed.

"Suyodhana!" the young woman howled defiantly, "If you so much as touch a hair on that man, your goddess will lose her Guardian."

"Put down that dagger!"

"Suyodhana! Swear on your goddess that no harm will come to Tremal-Naik."

"Impossible. He's already been condemned, the goddess awaits his blood."

"Swear it!" Ada said menacingly.

Suyodhana drew back as if to attack then hesitated, unsure if he would succeed.

"Listen, Guardian of the Sacred Temple," he said, attempting to regain his composure, "we'll spare that man, but only if you swear you'll never love him."

A moan of agony escaped Ada's lips.

"It would kill me!" she exclaimed with a sob.

"You serve the Goddess, chosen one."

"Monstrous wretch, why must you destroy the only joy my poor heart has known these many years? No, it's not possible. My love for him is too strong."

"Swear it and he'll live."

"Are you that cruel? Is there no other hope? I renounce your loathsome goddess, I've cursed her from the day fate hurled me into your clutches."

"We are that cruel," said the Indian.

"Have you never been in love?" she asked, as angry tears rolled down her cheeks. "Have you never had your heart broken?"

"No," said the inflexible Indian. "Give me your word, Guardian of the Sacred Temple, or I'll have that man killed."

"Wretch!" she said.

"Swear it!"

"Very well then," exclaimed the unhappy young woman, her voice barely a whisper, "I... I swear... I will not love... that man."

She let out a last desperate cry, brought her hands to her heart and fainted. The Indian roared with laughter.

"You've sworn not to love him," he said with satanic joy, picking up the dagger the young woman had let fall. "But I haven't sworn to spare his life. Smile with joy, sublime goddess, for we'll soon offer you a new sacrifice!"

He put a gold whistle to his lips and blew a sharp note.

An Indian entered and knelt before Suyodhana. He was dressed in a loincloth; a dagger peered from the silk rumaal fastened about his waist.

"At your service, Son of the Sacred Waters of the Ganges," he said.

"Karna," said Suyodhana, "Take the Guardian below. Watch her closely."

"It shall be done, Son of the Sacred Waters of the Ganges."

"She may attempt to kill herself. If she dies, so will you."

"I'll guard her with my life."

"Assemble fifty of our men and have them ring the pagoda. That man must not escape."

"There's a man in the pagoda?"

"Yes, the hunter, Tremal-Naik. Now, see to my orders. I'll await you at midnight."

The Indian gathered poor Ada in his arms and left. Once silence had returned, Suyodhana, the Son of the Sacred Waters of the Ganges, walked towards the centre of the room and knelt before the white marble basin.

"Father..." he said.

At the sound of that voice, the fish swam to the surface.

"Father," continued the Indian, "A man, a wretch, has cast his eyes upon the Guardian. He's in our hands; what is your wish? Should he live or die?"

The little fish submerged and swam about with great speed. Suyodhana shot to his feet, a sinister light in his eyes.

"The Goddess has condemned him," he said menacingly. "He'll die."

Left alone, Tremal-Naik sat at the base of the statue, hands resting upon his pounding heart. Never had such emotions taken hold of his soul; never in his life had he felt such joy.

"Beautiful! Beautiful!" he exclaimed, without stopping to consider that perhaps a hundred ears were listening to his every word. "You'll be my bride, rare flower of the jungle! I'll escape from here; I'll summon my brave friends and take you from this island. Your captors may be strong and ruthless, but I'll defeat them and make them pay for every tear you've shed for me. Love will give me strength, you'll see."

He stood up and began to pace, his fists clenched nervously, a frown upon his brow.

"My poor sweet Ada!" he continued tenderly. "What fate weighs so heavily upon you? What could keep you from loving me? You fear you'll die the day you become my bride, but I'll protect you. I'll solve this great mystery and on that day your enemies will tremble!"

He halted suddenly, the sharps notes of a ramsinga tearing him from his thoughts.

"That trumpet always heralds a murder," he murmured. "Have I been discovered or have they found and killed Kammamuri?"

He shuddered at the thought, held his breath and strained his ears. Several voices were whispering outside. A crowd was gathering, a large one by the sound of it.

Feeling slightly uneasy, he scanned every corner of the pagoda. His eyes soon rested upon the door, but to his relief found it was still closed.

"Any minute now," he murmured, "if they want a fight, I'll give them one."

He checked his pistol and carbine, drew his dagger, then crouched behind the monstrous statute, making himself as small as possible. Forced to fast and unable to move, he waited patiently as the day crept towards dusk.

As night fell, shadows slowly invaded the darkest recesses of the pagoda, gradually climbing towards the dome; by nine, Tremal-Naik could not see more than a foot in front of him, even though the moonlight reflected off the bronze sphere atop the temple.

The ramsinga's solemn notes had not been heard again, and the buzz of whispers had long since fallen silent.

Tremal-Naik had not moved, save to place his ear against the cold stone floor in an attempt to catch the slightest sound.

An inner voice told him to stay alert; his instincts were quickly proven correct, for towards eleven, a soft hiss reached his ears. Something had entered the pagoda, slithering down the rope fastened to the lamp. The hunter cast his eyes upward but could not make out what it was. He drew his pistol and silently got to his knees.

"It begins," he mumbled.

A wave of anger flashed across his face.

"Death to those who enter!"

The lamp jingled.

Tremal-Naik could no longer bare the suspense.

"Who's there?" he yelled.

No one replied; all fell silent once again.

Wondering if he had been mistaken, he stood and looked up. The moonlight reflected off the bronze sphere, lighting part of the rope: no one was there.

"Strange," said Tremal-Naik, his uneasiness increasing.

He crouched down once again and looked about.

Twenty minutes passed then the lamp jingled once more.

"Who's there?" he thundered menacingly, "Show yourself, Tremal-Naik awaits you."

Silence returned. Determined to end the suspense, Tremal-Naik slowly made his way up the statute. When he got to the top, he grabbed the lamp and shook it furiously.

A roar of laughter echoed in the pagoda.

"Ah!" exclaimed Tremal-Naik, flushed with anger. "Playing games, are we? Just wait!"

He gathered his strength and pulled. The rope snapped and the lamp crashed to the ground, filling the temple with a resounding clatter.

More laughter came in reply. Tremal-Naik rushed down the statue and hid behind it, drawing his pistols.

Seconds later the door opened and a tall Indian dressed in a silk dhoti entered the pagoda, a dagger clasped in one hand a torch burning in the other. Suyodhana had come to tend to this new victim, his bronze face beaming maliciously, a sinister light blazing in his eyes.

He stopped for a moment to gaze upon the giant goddess then took a few steps forward. Twenty-four Indians entered behind him, fanning out on either side.

"My sons," said Suyodhana, "It's midnight!"

The Indians readied their nooses, drew their daggers, and planted their torches in the brackets lining the stone walls.

"Vengeance!" they replied in unison.

"An infidel," continued Suyodhana "has desecrated the Sacred Temple. How shall he be punished?"

"Death," replied the Indians.

"That infidel has dared speak of love to the Guardian of the Temple of the East. How shall he be punished?"

"Death," repeated the Indians.

"Tremal-Naik," thundered Suyodhana, "Show yourself!"

A roar of laughter came in response then the hunter, who had heard every word, emerged from behind the giant statue.

His face was grim, his eyes flashed sinisterly and a ferocious smile slowly spread across his lips. The savage son of the jungle had reawakened, ready for battle.

"You wish to kill me?!" he exclaimed with a laugh. "You do not know the Hunter of the Black Jungle. Vile assassins, this is how I value your threats!"

He raised his pistols in the air, fired off the bullets and tossed them away. Then he emptied his carbine and grabbed it by the barrel, ready to use it as a club.

"Now," he said, "any of you wretches brave enough to challenge Tremal-Naik?"

He took a step back and let out a savage cry.

"Are there no men among you?" he thundered. "I'm fighting for the Guardian of the Temple of the East."

An Indian rushed towards him, his noose whistling in the air. Just as he was about to cast it, he slipped on the smooth stones, stumbled and landed before Tremal-Naik's feet. The hunter's club came down upon the Indian's head with lightning speed. Death was instantaneous.

"Step forward, step forward!" repeated Tremal-Naik. "I'm fighting for my Ada!"

The twenty-three Indians attacked simultaneously. Another Indian fell, as the carbine broke in the hunter's hands, unable to withstand a second blow.

"Death! Death!" howled the Indians, foaming with anger.

Tremal-Naik felt a noose tighten around his neck, but the hunter ripped it out of the strangler's hands, drew his knife, rushed towards the statue, and climbed up onto its head.

"Make way, make way!" he yelled ferociously.

He cast his eyes upon the door and leaped, flying over the Indians' heads. Two chords immediately tightened about his arms, knocking him to the ground.

He let out a terrible cry. The Indians were upon him in a flash. Though he resisted with all his might, he was quickly tied up and disarmed.

"Help! Help" he blurted.

"Death! Death!" howled the Indians.

He summoned his last remaining strength and sundered two of the chords. More nooses immediately took their place.

Suyodhana, having watched that desperate struggle with cold indifference, drew up before the hunter, an evil smile upon his lips.

Unable to move, Tremal-Naik spat at him.

"Infidel!" exclaimed the Son of the Sacred Waters of the Ganges.

He slowly drew his dagger and raised it over the prisoner. The hunter did not flinch.

"My sons!" said the leader, "How shall he be punished?"

"Death!" replied the Indians.

"Death it is."

Tremal-Naik let out one last cry.

"Ada! Ada!"

The priest's blade plunged into his chest, extinguishing his voice. The hunter's eyes widened, then closed; his limbs trembling slightly as a small pool of blood spread across the stones.

"Kali," said Suyodhana, turning towards the bronze statue, "You have been avenged."

He raised a hand and two Indians picked up the poor hunter's body.

"Throw him in the jungle, he'll make a fine meal for the tigers," concluded that terrible man. "This is the fate of all infidels."

Chapter 7
Kammamuri

After having left his master, Kammamuri had taken the path to the river, tracking the Indian that had run through the bamboo forest. He had done so reluctantly, each step forward increasing his uneasiness.

Knowing the hunter wanted to find the mysterious woman, he feared Tremal-Naik would do something rash. Though he had been ordered not to follow, he stopped every ten paces more inclined to go back than to go forward. How could he possibly return to the hut, knowing that his master was somewhere on this wretched island, where the enemy teemed like bamboo? It was madness to abandon him, almost criminal.

He had gone less than half a mile, when he decided to retrace his steps and risk angering Tremal-Naik.

"In the end," said the brave Maratha, "a friend will undoubtedly be of use to him."

He gathered his courage, turned about and headed west once again, without further thought to the Indian he had been tracking. He had not gone twenty paces, when he heard a desperate voice cry out: "Help! Help!"

Kammamuri jumped back.

"Help!" he murmured. "Who could that be?"

He fell silent and the night wind carried a sharp cry to his ears.

"Something's happening down there," the Maratha mumbled uneasily.

The cry had come from about a half mile away, from the direction his master had taken. Though he feared being captured, the possibility his master was in jeopardy quickly strengthened his resolve. He levelled his carbine and headed west, cautiously making his way among the bamboo.

Suddenly he heard a discharge.

The Maratha's blood turned cold. It was Tremal-Naik's carbine, he had heard it fired an infinite number of times in the jungle; he knew its sound too well to be mistaken.

"Great Shiva!" he murmured.

The thought Tremal-Naik was in danger infused him with courage. Casting aside every precaution, he began to run towards the source of the blast.

A quarter of an hour later he reached a clearing. A long dark silhouette writhed slowly in its centre, filling the air with hisses.

"A python!" exclaimed Kammamuri, who, familiar with those reptiles, did not feel the slightest fear.

He was about to move away, to avoid an attack, when he noticed that the python had been sliced in two and a body lay beside it.

The hair on the back of his neck stood on end.

"The master?" he murmured.

He grabbed his carbine by the barrel and slowly advanced towards the serpent. Blood gushed from its wounds as it writhed angrily upon the ground.

With one quick blow Kammamuri smashed in its head and rushed towards the man lying by its side.

"Vishnu be praised!" he exclaimed. "It's not the master."

The Indian that had attacked Tremal-Naik was little more than a mass of bleeding, twisted flesh. His mouth was covered with bloody foam, his eyes bulged from their sockets, bits of bone protruded from his chest and his limbs had been broken in ten different places.

Kammamuri knelt beside him and touched his arm; the body had grown cold.

The poor man had not been able to withstand those powerful coils. There was no doubt the Indian had been among those tracking them, his chest was marked by the mysterious tattoo.

He was about to leave when the soft rustle of bamboo reached his ears. He hit the ground immediately and lay among the grass, not daring to move. If he had not been spotted, he still had a chance for the reeds were tall enough to hide him from view. The rustling had stopped almost immediately, but that did not mean he was out of danger. Indians are as patient as Native Americans and can spy upon their prey for hours, even days, and Kammamuri was no exception. He lay silently for a long while, then slowly raised his head and looked around.

Instantly a noose hissed through the air and tightened about his neck.

He held in a cry of surprise, clutched at the rope with both hands, and fell among the grass, moaning in agony.

His plan worked perfectly.

Believing his victim was on the verge of death, the strangler, who had been hiding in a grove of wild sugar cane, jumped out to finish the task with his dagger. But Kammamuri had drawn one of his pistols and aimed it at him.

"You're dead!" he yelled.

A flash of light tore through the darkness. The strangler brought his hands to his chest, swayed slightly, and fell heavily among the grass. Kammamuri was upon him in an instant, his second pistol aimed and ready.

"Where's Tremal-Naik?" he asked.

The strangler attempted to get up, but immediately fell back to the ground. A stream of blood trickled from his mouth; he rolled his eyes and let out a final moan. He was dead.

Realizing the others would be drawn by the sound of the blast, the Maratha jumped to his feet and ran off, heading back towards the river. The dead man must have been the Indian his master had been tracking. Perhaps Tremal-Naik had escaped and found someplace safe to hide. He ran more than a mile, heading ever deeper into the jungle, planning to reach the shore. Once there he would await his master's return.

It was midnight when he found himself on the outskirts of a forest of coconut trees.

The Maratha did not dare advance any further; he climbed up a tree and quickly hid among the leaves.

He tied himself to a branch with the noose he had taken from the strangler then closed his eyes, reassured by the deep silence reigning over the jungle.

He had been sleeping for a few hours, when he was awakened by an infernal noise. A large band of jackals had gathered about the tree and were honouring him with a frightening serenade.

Kammamuri would have loved to scare them off with a blast of his rifle, but fear of attracting the Indians, a greater threat than those beasts, held him back. Resigned to his fate he watched them leap about, their angry howls filling the air.

The concert ended just before dawn and shortly after he finally managed to fall asleep. He rested for longer than he would have wanted, for when he reopened his eyes; the sun was rapidly setting in the east. He split open a large coconut, devoured its sweet pulp then bravely set off once again, intent on finding Tremal-Naik.

He spent several hours making his way through the forest of coconut trees, re-entered the jungle and headed south. He walked until midnight, stopping from time to time to examine the ground in hope of finding his master's tracks. Desperate to discover any clue or sign, he was about to look for a tree in which to spend the night, when two dull blasts, fired in rapid succession, reached his ears.

"Well!" he exclaimed, surprised.

A third shot, still louder, tore through the air.

"The master!" he yelled. "This time he won't escape me!"

He ran south with the speed of a horse, and half an hour later reached a large clearing, in the middle of which, bathed in splendid moonlight, stood a grandiose pagoda. He took several steps forward then dove back in among the bamboo. Two men had appeared in the clearing and were heading towards the jungle, carrying what appeared to be a body.

"What are they up to?" murmured the Maratha, his surprise increasing with each passing minute.

He retreated even further, heading back into the thick bushes, attempting to find a place where he could spy on the men without being seen. The two Indians rapidly crossed the clearing and came to a stop close to the bamboo.

"Ready, Sonephur," said one of the two. "We'll swing him and throw him into the middle of that bush. There'll be nothing but bones by tomorrow."

"Think so?" asked the other.

"Tigers love fresh meat. This Indian could feed a pack of them."

The two wretches roared with laughter.

"Get a good grip on him, Sonephur…"

"One, two…"

The two Indians swung the body and tossed it into the jungle.

"Good luck!" yelled one.

"Good night!" yelled the other. "We'll come visit you in the morning."

And the two men walked away laughing.

Kammamuri had not missed a single gesture. He waited until the two Indians were far off, then left his hiding place and drew up beside the body. A soft cry escaped his lips.

"The master!" he exclaimed in agony. "The wretches!"

Tremal-Naik lay before him, eyes closed, face horribly twisted, a dagger buried in his chest. Blood flowed from the deep wound, dying his clothes a dark red.

"Master, my poor master!" sobbed the Maratha.

He placed both hands upon the hunter's chest and started. Had he felt a heartbeat?

Holding his breath, he put an ear to his master's chest. He had not been mistaken. The hunter's heart beat weakly, Tremal-Naik was still alive.

"There may still be a chance," he murmured, trembling with emotion. "Remain calm, Kammamuri, there's no time to waste."

Slowly, carefully, he peeled back Tremal-Naik's dugbah. The dagger had been inserted between the sixth and seventh ribs, just missing his master's heart.

It was a grave wound, but not necessarily a fatal one. Kammamuri, who knew more about wounds than any doctor, could still hope to save his poor master. He grabbed the dagger gently and slowly drew it out of the hunter's chest. A tiny stream of blood gushed from Tremal-Naik's lips. It was a good sign.

"He's going to be okay," murmured the Maratha, sighing in relief.

He tore a strip from his kurti and staunched the flow of blood. Now it was just a matter of finding some water and several yuma leaves to squeeze onto the wound to quicken the healing.

He had to get him to a pond at all costs. Fortunately, Tremal-Naik was strong enough to withstand the journey.

Kammamuri gathered his strength, gently took the hunter in his arms, and slowly walked off into the jungle, heading east, towards the river.

Streaming with perspiration, barely able to stand, resting every hundred paces to catch his breath and check on his master, the good Maratha walked for more than a mile until finally he came to rest by a pond surrounded by rows of Indian fig and coconut trees. The water was incredibly clear.

He placed his master on a thick layer of grass and applied several wet cloths to the wound. At every touch Tremal-Naik moaned softly.

"Master, master!" called Kammamuri.

The hunter's hands shook and his eyes, swimming in circles of blood, opened and rested upon Kammamuri. A ray of joy lit up the Maratha's bronze face.

"Do you recognize me, master?" he asked.

Tremal-Naik nodded affirmatively and moved his lips as if to speak but could manage little more than a grunt.

"Don't try to talk," said Kammamuri, "You'll tell me everything later. Rest assured, master, we'll take our vengeance upon those wretches."

Tremal-Naik's eyes blazed darkly as his fingers clawed at the grass beneath him. He had understood.

"Try to relax, master. I'm going to look for some medicinal herbs. You'll be strong enough to return to the hut in four or five days."

He urged the hunter to remain still and quiet then pounded the nearby grass to ensure they did not conceal any snakes. Once assured, he silently crept away.

He had gone a few paces when his eyes fell upon a patch of yuma plants, its sap would make an excellent balm for his master's wounds. He picked a large amount and turned to head back, but after a few steps he stopped suddenly, resting his hands on the butt of his pistols.

A familiar scent had reached his nose, the strong smell of wild game.

"Careful, Kammamuri," he murmured. "There's a tiger nearby."

He put his dagger between his teeth and advanced towards the pond, cautiously looking about. Though he expected to find the ferocious carnivore before him at any moment, he reached the trees without catching sight of it.

Tremal-Naik had not moved. The hunter was sleeping quietly, much to the Maratha's relief. He knelt down, laid the carbine and the pistols by his side, within reach, then chewed the bitter leaves and applied them to his master's wound.

"There, that's good," he said, rubbing his hands happily. "You'll be better tomorrow and we'll be able to get out of here. In a few hours those brigands will probably head into the jungle to look for your remains. I'd love to see the expression on their faces when they discover you've disappeared; they're sure to start looking for you. We can't let them find…"

A formidable roar cut off his words. He turned his head quickly and reached for his weapons.

There, just fifteen paces from him, ready to pounce, stood an enormous tiger, its steel-blue eyes watching his every move.

Chapter 8
A Terrible Night

The tiger's roar had awakened Tremal-Naik; his arm moved slightly as if reaching for his dagger. Like a soldier hearing the call to battle, the wounded man had found new strength.

"Kammamuri…" he whispered, trying to get up.

"Don't move, master!" said the Maratha, his eyes trained upon the beast.

"The, Tiger! The ti…" repeated the hunter.

"I'll take care of it. Don't move!"

The Maratha drew his pistol and pointed it at the tiger. Fearing he would not kill it in one shot, he dared not fire, not wanting to draw his enemies' attention with the sound of the blast.

The barrel glinted in the moonlight; the tiger did not move. It beat its sides with its tail three or four times, let out a second roar, louder than the first, then slowly withdrew, its eyes locked on the Maratha.

"Kamma…muri… the ti…ger!" stammered Tremal-Naik, propping himself up with his arms.

"It's going away, master. We're safe."

The tiger paused suddenly, pricked up its ears, let out one last roar then rapidly turned about and disappeared into the jungle.

Kammamuri got up and looked about uneasily.

"What could possibly have scared off the tiger?" he mumbled anxiously. "Someone must be approaching."

He rushed towards the trees and came to a halt about a hundred paces from the jungle. He slowly scanned his surroundings, looking for signs of life, but, not spotting anything, he hurried back to Tremal-Naik, who lay upon the leaves once again.

"The tiger?" whispered the wounded man.

"It's disappeared, master," replied the Maratha, hiding his uneasiness. "My pistol frightened it off. There's no need to worry, try to sleep."

The hunter moaned softly.

"Ada!" he stammered.

"What is it master?"

"How beautiful she was… bea…u…ti…ful!"

"Who was beautiful?"

"The wret…ches kid…napped her."

He gritted his teeth and dug his fingernails into the ground.

"Ada…" he repeated.

"He's delirious," said the Maratha.

"Yes, they kid…napped her," continued the wounded man. "But… I… will… find… her… again… yes… I… will… find… her!"

"Don't speak, master, we're still in great danger."

"Danger?" stammered Tremal-Naik. "What danger? I'll go back there, yes, I'll go back, wretches… Darma will make a quick meal of them!"

His arms shook; he rolled his eyes and fell still.

The hunter had fallen asleep.

So much the better, thought Kammamuri. At least his master's cries would not give them away. Fearing the tiger was still nearby, he decided to chew some betel to stay awake.

He sat down, crossed his legs, laid his carbine across his knees and patiently waited for dawn, eyes open, ears straining to catch the slightest sound.

One, two, three hours passed uneventfully. No tiger's roar, no jackal's cry, not even a serpent's hiss broke the silence reigning over the jungle. From time to time, however, a gust of wind would caress the reeds and a soft rustling sound would fill the air.

It must have been past three o'clock, when a loud whistle broke the silence. Surprised, the Maratha held his breath, stood up and strained his ears. The mysterious noise sounded again, but this time it was louder, whatever was making it had drawn nearer.

"That's not a tiger…" murmured Kammamuri.

He armed his carbine, crept towards the trees and looked about. Thirty paces away stood a large heavy beast with a long sharp horn above its nose and thick grey skin that resembled plates of armour. It must have been at least three metres long.

Kammamuri's heart shrank with fear.

"A rhinoceros!" he exclaimed, his voice barely a whisper. "We're done for!"

He did not bother to raise his carbine, knowing the bullet would have had no effect against that thick armour-like skin. He could have struck the monster in an eye, its only vulnerable spot, but the fear of missing his mark and being torn apart by its horn or crushed beneath its powerful legs, forced him to remain still, hoping not to be spotted.

The rhinoceros seemed irritated. With surprising agility it suddenly rushed forward, shattering the bamboo, opening a wide path among the trees.

From time to time it would come to a halt, panting heavily. It would roll on the ground like a wild boar, shake its stubby legs wildly and drive its horn among the grass, then get back up and attack the bamboo once again.

Holding his breath so as not to make a sound, nervous sweat dripping from his brow, Kammamuri's grip instinctively tightened about his carbine even though the weapon was now as useless as a bamboo pole. He feared the beast would attack the nearby trees, make his way towards the pond, and stumble upon Tremal-Naik.

He studied it for a while then withdrew to his master's side, gathered several reeds and built a wall around the wounded man, trying to hide the hunter as best he could. Then he picked up his weapons and rushed off towards a large banyan tree, planning to draw the beast's attention with a blast from his rifle.

The rhino continued to barrel through the jungle, its hoarse breathing filling the air. He could feel the ground trembling as it moved, bamboo snapping and breaking before it.

Suddenly, Kammamuri heard a tiger roar. He rushed towards the pond and looked about in fear.

Within seconds he spotted the beast on the branches of the tree he had just abandoned; its eyes shining like a cat's, its claws scratching at the bark. He aimed his rifle, and the tiger, dismayed, jumped down, planning to disappear into the jungle, but found the rhino blocking its path.

The two formidable animals locked eyes and studied each other for several minutes. Realizing it would gain nothing by battling that brutal colossus, the tiger tried to escape, but before it could move the rhino let out a cry, lowered its head, presented its horn and attacked.

As it drew near the tiger leaped and landed on the colossus' back. The rhino ran forward thirty or forty paces then fell on its stomach, knocking the tiger to the ground.

"Well done rhino!" murmured Kammamuri.

The two enemies sprang to their feet, rushed towards each other for a second attack. The rhino struck first, driving its horn into the feline's chest and hurling it into the air.

The tiger roared in pain as it struck the ground. It tried to get to its feet, but the colossus attacked again, hurling it even higher, its blood spattering the battlefield. As it came down, the rhino thrust its horn through the tiger's stomach then cast it to the ground and quickly trampled it beneath its feet. Within minutes all that remained of the great cat was a mass of bleeding flesh and broken bones.

The battle was over in seconds. The colossus whistled triumphantly then returned to the jungle and began to attack the bamboo once again. Unfortunately, it was still close to the pond.

His retreat was well timed, for Tremal-Naik, in the grips of delirium and violent fever, had awakened and begun to call for Kammamuri.

The situation was growing extremely dangerous for the two Indians; that stubborn beast could have heard the hunter's cries at any moment and suddenly reappeared among the trees. The Maratha had no illusions of escape, knowing they had no chance against the rhino's speed.

He hurried to his master's side and began to remove the reeds and branches.

"Shhh," he said, putting a finger to his lips. "If it hears us, we're done for."

But Tremal-Naik, in the grips of delirium, was shaking wildly; a string of nonsensical words spewed from his lips.

"Ada... Ada!" he yelled, opening his eyes in fear. "Where are you? Yes... Yes, I remember. Yes, midnight! Midnight!... They came, armed... so many of them... Nagis tattooed on their chests... but I was not afraid, no; I did not tremble! I'm a hunter, Ada! I saw their leader. The wretch! He tried to stab me... They do not frighten me. Afraid of them? Me? Tremal-Naik? Ha! Ha!"

Tremal-Naik roared with laughter, making the Maratha tremble nervously.

"Quiet, master!" begged Kammamuri, hearing the rhinoceros charging at the bamboo groves along the outskirts of the jungle.

The hunter, delirious, looked at him through half-closed eyes and continued even louder, "It was dark, very dark; I climbed down into the pagoda, below me the vision moved about... I heard perfume splash upon the stone floor. Why do you adore that goddess? Don't you love me?... You laughed, I trembled. The Hunter of the Black Jungle loves you! Woe to those that keep you from me!... Look, the wretches draw near... they're laughing, mocking me... threatening me... away, away, assassins, away! They still have their nooses, they're hurling them... wait until I return... I'll avenge you! Murderers! Assassins! Kammamuri! Kammamuri! They're strangling me!"

Tremal-Naik sat up, his eyes bulging, his lips awash in foam. He clenched his fists, turned towards the Maratha and yelled: "You want to strangle me? Kammamuri, give me my pistols, I'll kill him."

"Master, master..." stammered the Maratha.

"Wretches!... Do you know who I am? Kammamuri, they're strangling me!... Help!... Help..."

Rapidly placing a hand over his mouth, the Maratha stifled the hunter's cries and laid him back upon the ground. The wounded man struggled furiously, roaring like a wild beast.

"Help!..." he howled.

A loud grunt sounded from the other side of the trees. Limbs shaking, the Maratha spotted the rhino's menacing face peering among the leaves. They were done for.

"Great Shiva!" he exclaimed, quickly reaching for his carbine.

The rhinoceros looked at the two men with its small shining eyes, more in surprise than in anger. There was not a moment to lose. That initial shock would not last long. The Maratha, emboldened by the imminent danger, coldly aimed his carbine at one of its eyes and fired, unfortunately the bullet missed its mark and smashed against the rhino's brow. The beast lowered its horn and prepared to attack. Within minutes, the two Indians would share the tiger's fate.

Fortunately, Kammamuri had not lost his cool. Realizing the animal was still standing, he dropped his useless weapon, rushed towards Tremal-Naik, gathered the hunter in his arms and raced into the pond, coming to a halt when the water touched his shoulders.

Mad with rage, the rhinoceros charged towards the shore and leaped into the pond, spraying the Indians with a shower of water.

Kammamuri tried to flee, but his legs had sunken into the mud; though he fought with all his strength he could not move. Trembling and pale, the poor man cried out, "Help! Help!"

Dull grunts came from behind him, he turned and saw the rhinoceros thrashing at the waters, thrusting its horn in all directions; the colossus, dragged down by its enormous weight, had sunk in up to its stomach.

"Help!" repeated the Maratha, struggling to keep his master above water.

A bark came in reply to that desperate call. Kammamuri started; though far off it was familiar, he had heard it a thousand times before. A mad hope flashed through his mind.

"Punthy!" he yelled.

A large black dog emerged from a thick mass of bamboo and ran towards the pond, barking furiously. It attacked the rhinoceros and attempted to rip off its ear.

Almost at the same instant they heard Aghur's voice.

"Hold on, Kammamuri!" yelled the brave young man.

61

"I'm here!"

The Bengali leaped over several thick bushes, disappeared among the bamboo and reappeared at the edge of the pond. He quickly loaded his rifle, went down on one knee and fired. Struck through the eye, the rhinoceros fell to one side, half its body disappearing in the water.

"Don't move, Kammamuri," continued the hunter. "I'm going to try and pull you out of there; but... what happened to the master?... Has he been injured?"

"Never mind the questions! Hurry, Aghur!" said the Maratha, still trembling. "Our enemies are still roaming about the jungle."

The Bengali quickly undid a rope fastened about his waist and threw it to Kammamuri, who grabbed onto it with all his might.

"Hold on tight," said Aghur.

The Indian gathered his strength and began to pull. The mud slowly gave way. Once he had reached the riverbank, Kammamuri quickly scrambled ashore.

"Well," asked Aghur, anxiously studying his master, "What happened to him?"

"They stabbed him."

"Who did?"

"The same men that murdered Hurti."

"When?... How?"

"I'll tell you later. We've got to hurry. Help me build a stretcher. We've got to get out of here; we're being followed."

Aghur needed no further explanation. He drew his dagger, cut down six branches, bound them together with two solid ropes and covered them with several handfuls of leaves. Kammamuri carefully picked up his master and slowly placed him upon it.

"Let's go, try not to make any noise," said Kammamuri. "Where's your gonga?"

"Just up the shore," replied Aghur.

"Are your pistols loaded?"

"Yes, both of them."

"Excellent, keep your eyes open."

"Are we being watched?"

"It's quite likely."

With Punthy scouting the way the two Indians picked up the stretcher and set off down a narrow path that led through the jungle. They reached the river fifteen minutes later and quickly found the canoe. They had just gotten aboard when the dog began to bark.

"Quiet, Punthy," said Kammamuri, picking up an oar.

Instead of obeying, the dog rested his paws on the side of the boat and began to bark even louder. The two Indians turned their eyes towards the jungle, but saw only trees. Yet Punthy must have heard something. They laid their pistols along the bottom of the gonga, grabbed the oars and set off, rowing upstream. They had gone less than three hundred yards when the dog began to bark once again.

"Halt!" commanded a voice.

Clutching a pistol in his right hand, Kammamuri turned about. There on the shore, in the very place their boat had been, stood a colossal Indian armed with a noose and a dagger.

"Halt!" he repeated.

Kammamuri fired. The Indian fell and disappeared among the bushes.

"Row, Aghur, row!" yelled the Maratha.

The gonga sliced through the waters, flying towards the floating cemetery as a menacing voice thundered: "We'll meet again!"

Chapter 9
Manciadi

Dawn had begun to break when the rowboat reached the shores of the Black Jungle. All was as they had left it. The hut still stood among the reeds, a dozen giant arghilah, hideous stork with long yellow legs, sat perched upon its roof as Darma slowly patrolled the clearing.

"Good," murmured Kammamuri, "The wretches haven't been here yet. Darma!"

At the sound of her name, the tiger stopped, raised her head, fixed her green eyes on the rowboat, roared softly and headed towards the shore.

Aghur and Kammamuri quickly disembarked, carried their master into the hut, and lay him in a comfortable hammock. The tiger and the dog remained outside, standing guard.

"Check his wound, Aghur," said Kammamuri.

The Bengali removed the crude bandage and carefully examined Tremal-Naik's chest. A frown spread across his brow.

"It's serious," he said. "The dagger cut deeply."

"Will he heal!?"

"It appears promising. Any idea why they stabbed him?"

"Something to do with the master's vision. You know how obsessed he was. Having landed on the island, he took it into his head to find her. He seemed to know where she was hidden; once we landed, he ordered me back to the hut and went off on his own. Twenty-four hours later, I found him in the jungle, lying in a pool of his own blood."

"Did you find out who those people were?"

"All I know is they live on that island and protect that woman."

"But why?"

"I don't know."

"Have you seen them?"

"Yes."

"Are they men or spirits?"

"Men. They attacked me and one of them tried to strangle me with a noose. Fortunately, I managed to kill a couple of them. Spirits don't die."

"That's strange," Aghur murmured thoughtfully. "What could those men be up to? Why do they murder those that set foot on their island?"

"The goddess they worship requires many sacrifices, but I don't know why."

"Do they frighten you, Kammamuri?"

"Yes, a little. We haven't seen the last of them."

"They won't take us easily. We're well armed and Darma will help keep them at bay."

"Nevertheless, we should keep our eyes open. We're in for quite a battle."

"Leave it to me, Kammamuri. I'll make preparations; you tend to the master."

While Kammamuri returned to the hunter's side to apply a new poultice of herbs, Aghur went and sat down in front of the hut; the tiger and the dog crouched down beside him.

The day passed uneventfully. At times, Tremal-Naik would mumble in his delirium, often crying out for Ada, the poor young woman he had left defenceless in the hands of those fanatics. Eventually he fell silent and, overcome by exhaustion, was soon asleep.

Once night had spread its dark mantle over the jungle, Aghur, armed to the teeth, took the first watch in front of the hut. Punthy had curled up at his feet, his eyes fixed on the south. Midnight arrived, but the river and the jungle remained deserted. However, the dog had gotten up repeatedly, sniffing the air uneasily as if someone or something were nearby. Aghur was about to wake Kammamuri for his turn at watch, when Punthy sprang to his feet and began to bark.

"Well!" exclaimed the Indian, surprised. "What could that mean?"

The barking grew louder as the dog pointed at the river. The tiger appeared in the doorway and roared dully.

"Kammamuri!" yelled Aghur, loading his carbine.

The Maratha, who had been sleeping with one eye open, was at his side in an instant.

"What is it?" he asked.

"Darma and Punthy have heard something."

"Did you?"

"No."

"Get Punthy quiet."

Aghur quickly obeyed.

A cry shot out from towards the river.

"Help! Help!"

The dog began barking furiously.

"Help!" replied the same voice.

"Kammamuri!" exclaimed Aghur. "Someone's drowning."

"Sounds like it."

"We've got to save him."

"We don't know who it is."

"It doesn't matter, come!"

"Draw your weapons and be ready for anything. Darma, stay and guard the master."

The tiger crouched down, eyes blazing, ready to attack the first person that dared approach the hut. With Punthy leading the way, barking furiously, the two Indians rushed towards the shore, their eyes fixed on the ink-black waters.

"See anything?" Kammamuri asked Aghur, who had knelt by the river.

"There's something out there."

"A man?"

"It looks like a tree trunk."

"Anyone out there?" yelled Kammamuri.

"Save me!" replied a weak voice.

"It's a castaway," said the Maratha.

"Can you reach the shore?" asked Aghur.

A moan came in reply. There was no time to lose; the poor castaway could drown at any moment. The two Indians jumped into the gonga and quickly rowed towards the voice. As they drew nearer, they spotted the silhouette of a man clinging to a tree trunk. Minutes later, they drew up beside it and reached for the castaway, who grabbed their arms with the strength of desperation.

"Save me!" he stammered once again, as he let himself be pulled into the canoe.

The two Indians leaned forward, curious to get a look at the man they had just rescued. He was a Bengali, of average height, dark skinned, thin, but muscular. Several bruises marked his face and his yellow tunic was stained with blood.

"Are you injured?" asked Kammamuri.

The man looked at him fixedly, his eyes shining strangely.

"I think so," he murmured.

"There's blood on your clothes. We should make sure it isn't serious."

"It's nothing," he said, raising his hands to his chest. "I hit my head on that tree trunk and got a bloody nose."

"Where are you from?"

"Calcutta."

"What's your name?"

"Manciadi."

The Bengali's limbs suddenly began to tremble.

"Who lives here?" he asked terrified.

"Tremal-Naik, the Hunter of the Black Jungle," replied Kammamuri.

"A ferocious man," he stammered nervously.

Aghur and the Maratha looked at each other in surprise.

"Are you mad?" said Aghur.

"Mad? His men have been tracking me."

"His men have been tracking you? That can't be! We're his men!"

Terrified, the Bengali sat up.

"You!... You!..." he repeated. "I'm done for."

He grabbed onto the side of the canoe and tried to plunge into the river, but Kammamuri quickly grabbed him by the arm and forced him to sit down.

"Why are you so afraid?" he asked menacingly. "We do not go about hurting people; however, if you don't explain yourself, I'll smash your head in with the butt of my carbine."

"You're going to murder me!" cried Manciadi.

"Only if you do not explain yourself. What are you doing here?"

"I'm a poor Indian, a hunter. A sepoy captain promised me a hundred rupees for a tiger pelt, so I came to the Sundarbans to catch one. I reached the jungle late last night and set off to explore the far shore, two hours later several men tried to strangle me."

"Ah!" exclaimed the two Indians. "With nooses?"

"Yes," confirmed the Bengali.

"Did you get a good look at them?" asked Aghur.

"Yes, I saw them clearly."

"Did they have strange markings on their chests?"

"Tattoos, I think."

"They're from Rajmangal," said Kammamuri. "Continue."

"I drew my dagger," continued Manciadi, quaking at the memory, "and got out of there. I ran with all my might, the men at my heels all the while, reached the river, and dove in head first."

"We know the rest," said the Maratha. "So, you're a hunter."

"Yes, a good one."

"Would you like to come with us?"

The Bengali's eyes blazed strangely.

"I ask nothing better," he said hurriedly. "I have no family."

"Very well then, you'll make your home with us. Come, we'll take you to our hut. Tomorrow morning, I'll introduce you to our master."

The two Indians took up their oars and rowed to shore. As soon as they had disembarked, Punthy rushed at the Bengali, barking angrily and bearing his teeth.

"Quiet, Punthy," said Kammamuri, holding him back. "He's one of us."

Instead of obeying, the dog began to growl menacingly.

"He doesn't seem to be very friendly," said Manciadi, forcing a smile.

"Don't be afraid, he'll befriend you soon enough," said the Maratha.

68

They moored the gonga then made their way to the hut. The tiger had not left her spot. At the sight of the Bengali she began to growl, eyeing him suspiciously.

"Oh!" exclaimed Manciadi, not hiding his fear. "A tiger!"

"She's tame. Stay here, I must check on the master."

"Your master! He's here?" asked the Bengali, surprised.

"Certainly."

"Still alive?"

"That's a strange question," exclaimed the Maratha.

The Bengali started and appeared confused.

"How did you know he'd been injured? Why did you ask such a question?" repeated Kammamuri.

"Didn't you tell me he'd been injured?"

"What?!"

"Yes, you must have."

"I don't remember."

"How else could I know? You or your friend must have told me."

"Must be."

Kammamuri and Aghur entered the hut. Tremal-Naik was sleeping soundly. He must have been dreaming for the odd word escaped his lips from time to time.

"It's not worth waking him," murmured Kammamuri, turning to Aghur.

"We'll make the introductions tomorrow," said the latter.

"What do you think of Manciadi?"

"He looks like a good man. He'll be of great help to us."

"I agree."

"We'll have him stand guard tonight."

Aghur filled a bowl with dal and rice and brought it to Manciadi. He instructed the Bengali to stand guard, remain alert, and to cry out at the first sign of danger, then went back into the hut, closing the door behind him as a precaution.

Left alone, Manciadi shot to his feet. His eyes sparkled as a satanic smile slowly spread across his lips.

He approached the hut and pressed an ear against the wall. He stood there silently and listened for a quarter of an hour, then took off like an arrow, coming to a halt after he had run a half mile. He put his fingers to his lips and whistled. Off to the south, a red flare tore through the trees and exploded, bathing the forest in an eerie light. Two cries reached his ears then the jungle fell silent once again.

Chapter 10
The Strangler

Twenty days passed. Thanks to his strong constitution and the assiduous care of his friends, the wound had closed and Tremal-Naik was healing rapidly. However, as his strength slowly began to return, the hunter grew more sullen and uneasy. His friends often found him with his head in his hands and his cheeks damp with tears. He rarely spoke and never mentioned the cause of his pain. At times he would erupt in anger, tear at his chest and attempt to throw himself from the hammock yelling, "Ada! Ada!"

He uttered the name repeatedly in his dreams and his delirium; it was his nightmare, his torment. In vain Kammamuri and Aghur tried to draw him out, hoping to learn the cause of those fits that threatened to reopen his wound.

Manciadi, the Bengali, assisted them from time to time, but only on rare occasions. It almost appeared he was avoiding the patient, as if he had something to fear. He only entered the room when the hunter was asleep, preferring to search the jungle for game, gather wood or fetch water.

Oddly, whenever he heard the master invoke Ada's name, his limbs would tremble and his face would turn pale.

Strangest of all, as Tremal-Naik's health improved, Manciadi grew sullen and ill-tempered. He almost seemed displeased the patient was recovering. Why? No one could say.

The morning of the twenty-first day began with a discovery that would have tragic consequences.

Kammamuri had awakened with the first rays of the dawn. Seeing that Tremal-Naik was sleeping quietly, he headed towards the door to awaken Manciadi who had spent the night keeping watch beneath a small bamboo lean-to. He raised the bar and pushed against the door, but to his dismay it did not open.

"Manciadi!" yelled the Maratha.

There was no answer. The thought that some misfortune had befallen the poor Bengali flashed through the Maratha's head. His enemies could have strangled him; a tiger could have crept in from the jungle and attacked him during the night. He peered through a crack in the door and spotted a body lying on the ground. It was Manciadi.

"Oh!" he exclaimed in horror. "Aghur!"

The Indian rushed to his friend's side.

"Aghur," said the dismayed Maratha, "Did you hear anything last night?"

"No, nothing strange."

"Not even a moan?"

"No, why?"

"Manciadi's been killed!"

"Impossible!" exclaimed Aghur.

"He's lying in front of the door."

"Darma and Punthy would have heard something. He can't be dead."

"He must be. He didn't answer my call, I caught a glimpse of him just now and I don't think he was breathing."

"We've got to open the door; push hard."

The Maratha placed his shoulder against the door and began to push with all his might. Manciadi's body moved slightly. Once the opening was wide enough, the two Indians slid outside.

The poor Bengali was lying face down. At first glance he appeared dead, but the Maratha did not spot any blood. Kammamuri put a hand on the hunter's chest; his heart was still beating.

"He's passed out," he said.

He drew a feather from a punya, a fan made of peacock feathers, hanging nearby, set fire to it and held it beneath the Bengali's nose. The hunter's chest stirred slightly, his arms and legs twitched then his eyes opened and he fixed them upon the two Indians in bewilderment.

"What happened?" Kammamuri asked kindly.

"You!" the Bengali exclaimed hoarsely. "What a shock! I thought I'd been killed!"

"What happened? Did someone try to kill you? Was it the same men that attacked you before?"

"Not men," said the Bengali. "An elephant."

"An elephant!" exclaimed the two Indians. "Here!"

"Yes, an enormous elephant with long tusks."

"It attacked you?" asked Kammamuri.

"It almost smashed in my skull. I was sleeping peacefully when I was awakened by a powerful blow; I opened my eyes and I saw it looming over me. I tried to escape, but before I could move it slammed its trunk down on my head and nailed me to the ground."

"And then?" Kammamuri asked anxiously.

"I don't remember anything after that. The blow knocked me out."

"What time did it happen?"

"I don't know; I'd been sleeping."

"Strange," said the Maratha, "Punthy didn't make a sound."

"What are we going to do?" asked Aghur, casting a worried look upon the jungle.

"We're not going to do anything. Best leave it be," replied Kammamuri.

"It'll come back," Manciadi added quickly, "and destroy the hut."

"That's true," said Aghur. "We should track it and try to kill it."

"I'll help," replied Manciadi.

"We can't leave the master unattended," observed Kammamuri. "Though his wound may have almost healed, he's still in danger."

"You'll stay with him, we'll go hunting," offered Aghur. "We'd never be safe with such a dangerous neighbour."

"Very well. If you're that determined, go ahead."

"Excellent!" exclaimed Aghur. "Leave it to us; we'll catch the elephant before noon."

He went into the hut and selected two heavy calibre carbines, carefully loaded them and offered one to the Bengali. Armed with guns, daggers and an abundant supply of ammunition, they set off determinedly into the jungle, taking a path through the bamboo. Aghur was happy and talkative; Manciadi, however, had grown sullen and often stopped to study his companion. At times he knelt down and listened, pretending to look for the elephant's tracks.

That sudden change, those looks and actions did not escape Aghur, and he began to think the Bengali was frightened.

"Take heart, Manciadi," he said happily. "It won't be difficult to kill our prey. A couple of bullets to the eye should bring it down."

"I'm not afraid," the Bengali replied, smiling uneasily.

"You seem nervous."

"I am, but it's not because of the elephant."

"What is it then?"

"Aghur," said Manciadi in a strange tone of voice, "Are you afraid of death?"

"Am I afraid of death? I've never feared anything… ever!"

"All the better."

"I don't understand."

"You'll understand soon enough; let's get moving."

"He's either mad or half numb with fear," mumbled Aghur. "Just as well; I'll take care of the elephant."

The two Indians picked up the pace, and an hour later, despite the hot sun and the many obstacles blocking their path, reached the forest of jack trees. The air was sweet, an extraordinary fragrance emanating from the large green fruit dangling from the branches about them. Manciadi, to his companion's great surprise, began to whistle a melancholy tune.

"What are you doing?" asked Aghur.

"Whistling," Manciadi replied calmly.

"You're going to scare off the elephant."

"Elephants love music; when they hear it, they come running."

"I've never heard that before!"

"Well known fact. Keep walking, Aghur, and keep your eyes open. Do you know where the pond is?"

"Near here."

"Let's go."

Though surprised by his friend's strange behaviour, Aghur obeyed. Making his way down a hidden path, he led Manciadi to a small pond ringed by large stones, the remains of an ancient pagoda.

"Stay here," said the Bengali. "I'll beat the forest and flush out the elephant, he's probably hiding somewhere nearby."

He shouldered his carbine and left without adding another word. Once Aghur was out of sight, Manciadi ran off into the forest, halting before a palm tree. A Nagi had been carved into its trunk.

"It's up to me now," he murmured. "These woods will be your tomb."

He drew himself up to his full height and whistled. A whistle came in reply a few minutes later then the sinister figure of Suyodhana emerged from between two bushes. He folded his arms across his chest, fixed his eyes upon Manciadi and gave him a piercing look.

"Welcome, Son of the Sacred Waters of the Ganges," said the Bengali, prostrating himself before the great leader.

"Well?" asked Suyodhana.

"There's a problem."

"What is it?"

"Tremal-Naik has recovered."

Suyodhana frowned.

"I missed," he growled. "I drove that dagger through his chest."

He lowered his head and fell silent.

"Manciadi," he said after a moment's contemplation, "He must die."

"I await your orders, Son of the Sacred Waters of the Ganges."

"The Guardian of the Sacred Temple has been deeply scarred by that man's poisonous tongue. The poor young woman still loves him. She'll love him for as long as he remains alive."

"Will she believe he's dead?"

"I'll give her proof."

"Should I poison him?"

"No, poison doesn't always kill; there are antidotes."

"Strangle him? I have my noose."

"One step at a time. Have you done what I asked?"

"Yes, Son of the Sacred Waters of the Ganges. Aghur is waiting for me near the pond."

"Excellent, you'll kill him then return to the hut and tell Kammamuri that Aghur's been murdered by the stranglers. He'll believe you and run to find him; you can figure out the rest."

"Any further instructions?" he asked with icy calm.

"That is all."

"What should I do after I've strangled Tremal-Naik?"

"Come find me on Rajmangal. Now go!"

Manciadi prostrated himself once more then quickly set off.

"The Son of the Sacred Waters of the Ganges is truly a great man!" mumbled the Bengali.

The fanatic did not give a second thought to the double murder he was about to commit. Suyodhana had ordered it, and Suyodhana spoke in the name of the great goddess to whom they had all pledged their lives. He crossed the forest of jack trees and reached the pond, his victim sat near it, his carbine resting on his knees.

"Did you see the elephant?" asked Aghur.

"No, but I found its tracks," said the strangler, his eyes flashing sinisterly.

"What's the matter, why are you looking at me like that?" demanded Aghur.

The Bengali kept his eyes fixed upon him and remained silent.

"Did you see something?"

"Yes," replied Manciadi. "Aghur, remember the conversation we had an hour ago?"

The Indian started.

"When you spoke of death?"

"Yes."

"I remember," replied Aghur.

"Doesn't it seem cruel to die at twenty when the future looks so promising? To go to your grave, descend into darkness on such a warm sunny day?"

"Have you gone mad?" demanded Aghur.

"No, Aghur, I'm not mad," said the assassin, drawing close enough to touch him. "Look!"

He opened his tunic and the Indian spied a Nagi tattooed upon Manciadi's chest.

"What's that?" asked Aghur.

"The call to death."

"I don't understand."

"You will."

The Bengali drew the noose he had kept hidden beneath his tunic and made it whistle about his head.

"Aghur," he yelled, "Suyodhana has condemned you and now you must die!"

The Indian understood immediately. He jumped to his feet and aimed his carbine, but did not have time to fire. The noose sliced through the air and tightened about the poor man's neck, the lead ball striking against the back of his head and knocking him to the ground.

"Murderer!" he shouted hoarsely, his voice choked by the noose.

"Farewell, Aghur," the strangler said sombrely, "your grave beckons."

"Kammamuri! Master!" stammered Aghur, gasping for air.

The fanatic grabbed the noose and stifled the hunter's voice with a violent jerk, then drew his dagger and stabbed Aghur through the chest.

"The goddess' will be done!" thundered Manciadi.

Aghur, his face ashen, his eyes bulging from their sockets, let out a dull moan and attempted to stand but instantly fell back to the ground.

"That's one," said the fanatic, casting a fierce look upon his victim.

He walked away rapidly as a storm of marabou descended upon Aghur's warm body.

Chapter 11
The Strangler Strikes Again

Kammamuri was starting to feel uneasy. Sunset was not far off, the two hunters had not yet returned, and not a single rifle blast had thundered in the jungle. Surprised by their prolonged absence he paced in and out of the hut repeatedly, carefully scanned the horizon, hoping they would soon appear among the endless sea of bamboo.

He made Punthy bark several times then led the tiger to the outskirts of the clearing, straining to listen for the slightest sound. He pulled down the hulola[10] and beat it repeatedly, even pulled out his carbine and fired a few shots into the air. His efforts were in vain. Not a voice, not a sound disrupted the silence reigning over the southern lowlands.

Discouraged, he sat before the hut, anxiously awaiting their return. He had been sitting there for a few minutes, when the tiger sprang to her feet with a dull growl. Almost simultaneously, Punthy began to bark.

Believing the hunters had returned, Kammamuri got up, but to his surprise no one appeared among the bamboo. He turned around, and there, standing upright, braced against the door, was Tremal-Naik.

"Master!" he exclaimed with amazement. "You're up!"

"Yes, Kammamuri," Tremal-Naik replied with a bitter smile.

"You shouldn't be, you're still convalescing and…"

"I'm stronger than you think," replied the hunter, his anger starting to rise. "I've suffered long enough in that hammock; it's time to put an end to it."

He took several steps forward, then sat down upon the grass, cradled his head in his hands, and fixed his eyes upon the setting sun.

---

[10] A type of drum.

78

"Master," said Kammamuri, after a few minutes of silence.

"Yes?"

"The hunters haven't returned. I'm afraid something bad has happened to them."

"What makes you think that?"

"Nothing in particular, just a feeling I have. The men that stabbed you could still be roaming about the jungle."

Tremal-Naik fell silent.

"Nearby?" he asked.

"Could be."

"It won't be long before I've healed completely, Kammamuri. Then we'll return to that wretched island and take our vengeance!"

"What?!" exclaimed Kammamuri. "We're going back to that island? Master, what are you saying?"

"Are you afraid?"

"No, but going back there, to that place, it's madness."

"Madness! Madness you say? I left her in their hands!"

"Who?"

"The Guardian of the Temple of the East."

"Who's that?"

"A beautiful young woman, Kammamuri; I love her, I'd set all of India ablaze for her."

"You left a woman there?"

"Yes, Kammamuri. Ada. My vision. I saw her. I talked to her. Ada! Ah, Ada. How I've suffered over her!"

"The vision?"

"The vision."

"How did she end up on Rajmangal?"

"It's a punishment of some sort, Kammamuri. I don't know the details, but those monsters have her in their grip. I watched her pour perfume at the base of a bronze statue in the pagoda."

"She made an offering! She's probably as fanatical as the rest of them."

"Do not repeat that insult, Kammamuri!" Tremal-Naik exclaimed menacingly. "Those men are forcing her to worship their goddess against her will! Fanatical? Hardly! Not my Ada!"

"Forgive me, master," babbled the Maratha.

"I forgive you, you could not have known. But woe to those men that have poisoned her young life. She's dying of sadness, forced to serve a goddess she despises. I'll exterminate them all, Kammamuri, to the last man! That dagger left a scar on my chest, a constant reminder of my vengeance! She won't remain in their hands for long, even if I must sacrifice my life to obtain her freedom. I'll put an end to her tormentors, Darma and I will kill them all!"

"You're scaring me, master. What if they killed you?"

"I'd gladly die for my beloved!" Tremal-Naik exclaimed passionately.

"When are we going to leave?"

"As soon as I can raise my carbine. I've regained much of my strength, but I'm not strong enough to attack them just yet."

At that instant, from the south, they heard a shot followed by two other discharges. Darma sprang to her feet with a roar. The Maratha and Tremal-Naik jumped to their feet as well, as Punthy began barking furiously.

"What's happening?" asked the Maratha, drawing his dagger from his belt.

"Kammamuri! Kammamuri!" yelled a voice.

"Who's calling?" asked Tremal-Naik.

"It's Manciadi!" exclaimed the Maratha.

The Bengali was running through the jungle at full speed, smashing through the dense wall of bamboo and waving his carbine about like a madman. He looked terrified.

"Kammamuri! Kammamuri!" he repeated hoarsely.

"Run, Manciadi, run!" yelled the Maratha. "Is someone after him? Careful, Darma!"

The tiger crouched down, claws ready to strike, lips parted, baring her sharp teeth.

Running at top speed, the Bengali reached the hut a few minutes later. The poor wretch's face and tunic were covered in blood; he had sliced a gash in his forehead to better play the part.

"Master! Kammamuri!" he exclaimed, crying desperately.

"What happened?" Tremal-Naik asked anxiously.

"Aghur's been stabbed! I still can't believe it. But it's not my fault, master... they attacked us... Aghur, poor Aghur!"

"They murdered him?" yelled Tremal-Naik, enraged. "Who? Who?"

"The men... the men with the nooses..."

"Damn! Quickly, tell us what happened, I want to know everything."

"We were sitting in a grove of jack trees," said the wretch, continuing to sob, "they attacked us before we could draw our weapons. Aghur fell. I grew frightened and ran off."

"How many of them were there?"

"Ten, twelve, I'm not sure. It's a miracle I managed to escape."

"Is Aghur dead?"

"I don't think so, master. They stabbed him then disappeared. As I was running, I heard him yell out, but I did not have the courage to go back."

"You're a coward, Manciadi!"

"Master, if I had gone back, they would have killed me," sobbed the Indian.

"When will it end?" yelled Tremal-Naik. "Kammamuri, Aghur may not be dead; go find him and bring him back here."

"What if they attack me?" asked Kammamuri.

"Take Darma and Punthy. Those two could fend off a hundred men."

"Who's going to lead me there?"

"Manciadi."

"And you're going to stay here alone?"

"I can defend myself. Now go, we can't waste any more time, Aghur's life is at risk. Manciadi, take Kammamuri to that grove."

"Master, I'm frightened."

"I said take Kammamuri to that grove; refuse and I'll have the tiger tear you to pieces."

81

Tremal-Naik's tone made it clear this was no idle threat. Feigning terror, Manciadi immediately went off to join the Maratha who had gone to retrieve a carbine and a pair of pistols.

"Master," said Kammamuri once he had made his preparations, "If we're not back in three hours, we'll probably have been murdered. The rowboat has been pulled ashore; get yourself to safety."

"Never!" exclaimed Tremal-Naik. "I'll avenge you on Rajmangal, end of discussion; now get going."

With the dog and the tiger leading the way, the Maratha and Manciadi rushed into the jungle.

The sun had already disappeared beneath the horizon, but the moon was rising, its soft blue light illuminating their way through the sea of bamboo.

"Be careful and try not to make any noise," Kammamuri instructed. "Those men could be hiding anywhere."

"Are you afraid, Kammamuri?" asked the Bengali, no longer trembling.

"A little. Fortunately, we have Darma with us. She'd face fifty armed men."

"I won't go back into that forest, Kammamuri. I can't!"

"You can wait for me wherever you wish, I'll leave Punthy with you if you like; he's a good dog and can hold his own against a half dozen attackers. Now lead the way and try not to make any noise."

Having already formulated every detail of his plan, Manciadi led the Maratha to the path he had taken that morning. They followed it for three quarters of an hour and came to a stop on the outskirts of the grove of jack trees.

"Here?" asked Kammamuri, anxiously scanning his surroundings.

"Yes, here," Manciadi replied mysteriously. "Follow this small trail into the forest and you'll soon reach the pond where Aghur was stabbed. I'll hide in those bushes and await your return."

"Take Punthy with you."

"I'm fine. The Indians won't find me."

"I'll be back in half an hour. Darma, Punthy, attack the first man that shows his face."

The two beasts immediately drew up before him, the tiger roaring softly, the dog bearing its teeth.

"Excellent," said Kammamuri, as he watched the Bengali head into the thicket. "No one would dare attempt to get past these two."

They entered the dark silent forest and advanced up the path without making a sound. Kammamuri stopped several times, hoping to hear a cry from Aghur, but not so much as a whimper reached his ears.

"That's strange," he murmured, wiping away the sweat forming upon his brow. "If Aghur were still alive, he'd be groaning and crying for help. It's too quiet."

He had gone three or four hundred paces when a melancholy tune suddenly reached his ears.

It was the same tune Manciadi had whistled before he had killed Aghur. The tiger growled and cast her eyes back along the path; the dog growled as well, looking about uneasily.

The moon disappeared behind a cloud and it grew darker beneath the trees.

The Maratha came to a halt, torn between advancing and turning back. He drew his pistols and decided to go forward.

"Kammamuri!" yelled a voice.

"Kammamuri!" repeated a second.

"Kammamuri!" added a third.

The tiger growled again, waving her tail from side to side. Twice she attempted to rush to the edge of the path, but the Maratha quickly summoned her back.

"Relax, little one, relax," he said. "Let them call. They're not spirits, just men trying to frighten me. If I make it back to the hut, I'll thank Vishnu for having protected me."

He picked up his pace, training his pistols on either side of the path. Minutes later he arrived within sight of the pond, the waters glimmering in the moonlight. Barely able to contain his fear, Kammamuri spotted a group of marabous buzzing excitedly about a body lying on the ground.

Punthy rushed towards it, howling mournfully, scattering the ravenous birds.

"Aghur! My poor, Aghur!" repeated Kammamuri, drawing the body to his chest. "Ah! Wretches!"

He let out a terrible cry as his eyes fell upon the stone, against which Aghur's head had rested.

Trembling in that pale moonlight, he read the following words written in blood: Manciadi killed m...

The Maratha jumped to his feet. His master was in grave danger.

"Darma! Punthy!" he yelled hoarsely, "Back to the hut! They're killing the master!"

With the tiger leading the way, he rushed through the forest, Punthy bringing up the rear, barking furiously.

While Kammamuri was running like a deer through the dark mass of vegetation, the Bengali was already racing back towards the hut. Once alone, he had immediately jumped out of the thicket and run off at full speed, determined to strangle his second victim. He knew he had at least a quarter of an hour's advantage on the Maratha; but, nevertheless, he barrelled down the trail with the speed of a cannonball, afraid of being surprised by the tiger and the dog, a pair of enemies he knew he could not defeat.

He crossed the jungle in less than half an hour, reached the outskirts of the plantation and stopped to prepare a second noose.

"The master must be keeping his guard up," he murmured. "If he sees me, he'll think I've abandoned Kammamuri and crack my head open with a bullet."

He slowly peered through the bamboo trees and spotted the hut four hundred paces from him. Tremal-Naik was standing beside it, carbine in hand.

"It won't be easy to kill him," muttered the wretch. "Best to use a little caution."

He ran towards the east, galloping furiously for six or seven minutes then headed onto the plain. The hut was on his right and Tremal-Naik had his back to him. With a bit of cunning, he could attack the victim from behind.

He quickly decided on his course of action. He began to crawl among the grass like a serpent, moving silently to avoid being heard.

Fortunately, the rustling of the bamboo trees was enough to mask his advance. Pausing at times to listen and study Tremal-Naik, who appeared oblivious to the threat, he slowly made his way to the hut. Once he reached the wall, he shot to his feet with the speed of a tiger. An evil smile spread across his lips.

"He's mine," he murmured, his voice barely a whisper. "Kali is protecting me."

He tiptoed along the wall of the hut and came to a stop ten paces from his prey. He looked towards the jungle one last time. Kammamuri was nowhere to be seen.

His eyes sparkled like a cat's as a second smile, crueller than the first, spread across his lips. In mere seconds the victim would fall, never to rise again.

He drew his noose, spun it three or four times and cast it as he lunged forward. Tremal-Naik fell to the ground, but fortunately, his hand had been caught as well.

"Kammamuri!" yelled the hunter, grabbing the rope with his free hand and pulling it towards him with desperate strength.

"Die, die!" yelled the assassin as he dragged the Bengali along the ground.

Tremal-Naik let out a second cry.

"Kammamuri, help!"

"Here I am!" thundered a voice.

Manciadi gnashed his teeth angrily. The Maratha had suddenly appeared on the outskirts of the plantation, Darma and Punthy running at his side.

A flash of light tore through the darkness, followed by a deafening discharge. Manciadi leaped away from the body and ran madly towards the shore. A second shot thundered and the Bengali fell into the river, disappearing into the waters.

Chapter 12
The Trap

Though disoriented, as soon as he felt the noose give way Tremal-Naik picked up his carbine and headed towards the river, determined to capture his assailant. He took several steps into the water, but could not spot a trace of the Bengali. Struck by a blast from the Maratha's rifle, Manciadi must have passed out and been dragged away by the current.

"Wretch!" Tremal-Naik exclaimed furiously.

"Master!" yelled Kammamuri, rushing towards him with Darma and Punthy. "Where's that scoundrel?"

"He's disappeared, Kammamuri, but we'll find him."

"Are you injured?"

"Nothing serious."

"Thank heavens! I was afraid I'd be too late. The scoundrel! Strangle my master! Traitor! If he falls into my hands, I'll cut him to pieces. To betray us like that, after we'd treated him like a brother! It's a miracle you're still alive."

"Where's Aghur? Did you find him?"

The Maratha fell silent and cast his eyes to the ground.

"Tell me, Kammamuri," said Tremal-Naik, expecting the worst.

"He's dead, master," murmured the Maratha.

Tremal-Naik's face turned ashen.

"Dead!" he sobbed. "Another friend murdered? Great Shiva! What did I do to deserve this? Am I cursed by the gods?"

He lowered his head as several tears rolled down his bronze cheek. Kammamuri could barely speak.

"Master..." he murmured.

Tremal-Naik was not listening. Eyes welled with tears he sat down on the shore, cradled his head in his hands and studied the jungle. A gentle breeze blew through the trees, filling the air with the sweet fragrance of jasmine and mussenda as it carried off the sobs rising from his chest.

"Master!" exclaimed Kammamuri. "There's no time for tears, you must be strong."

"Yes, you're right," Tremal-Naik said angrily. "We must avenge our friends. Poor Aghur! So young and intrepid! You're certain he's dead?"

"Yes, master. I found him near the pond. Manciadi strangled him then stabbed him through the heart. The dagger was still in his chest."

"Manciadi killed him?"

"Yes, master!"

"The scoundrel!"

"That'll be his last victim, I assure you. My bullet must've struck him; the fish are probably feasting on his remains as we speak."

"That monster did all this alone?"

"Yes, master. He murdered Aghur to draw me away from the camp. Luckily, I discovered his plan and arrived in time to thwart his attack."

"You had no suspicions?"

"None, master. He fooled us well. Why would he want to kill us?"

"He was probably from Rajmangal."

"You think so, master?"

"I'm certain of it. Did you see his chest?"

"No, he always kept it hidden."

"To hide his tattoo no doubt."

"It makes sense, but why try to kill you?"

"Because I love Ada."

"They're against it?"

"Yes, and they're trying to kill me."

"But why?"

"Because she's been condemned to serve them."

"Serve them? How? Why?"

"I don't know, but I'm determined to find out."

"Then those wretches are likely to try again?"

"I'd count on it, Kammamuri."

"They frighten me, master. Do you think we can keep fending off their attacks? "

Tremal-Naik did not reply, his eyes scanning the trees.

"See anything?" the Maratha asked nervously.

"Yes, Kammamuri. I think I saw a light flash near the outskirts of the jungle."

"Let's go back to the hut, master. It isn't safe here."

Tremal-Naik took a last look at the jungle and the river then turned and slowly walked back towards the hut, halting when he reached the door.

"Kammamuri," he said sadly. "This place was once full of laughter, now it feels like a grave. Poor Aghur."

He stifled a sob, went inside and lay down on the hammock, burying his face in his hands. Kammamuri leaned against the side of the door, his eyes fixed on the jungle.

Three long hours passed as the Maratha sat in silence.

The sharp notes of a ramsinga tore him from his thoughts. The warning had sounded; another attempt would be made.

He circled the hut several times and carefully searched among the grass, but not a soul appeared before him. He summoned Darma and Punthy and went back into the hut, barricaded the door and sat behind it, so he would be awakened by the slightest sound.

Though he tried to rest, Kammamuri could not close his eyes. Growing ever more uneasy, he got up repeatedly and cautiously peered out the hut's small windows.

The moon set towards midnight, blanketing the jungle in total darkness.

Without warning, Punthy got up and barked three times.

"Someone's approaching," murmured Kammamuri.

He entered the hunter's room; Tremal-Naik was sleeping soundly, dreaming of his beloved, her name softly escaping his lips.

Punthy growled three times and rushed toward the door. The tiger must have heard something as well, for she began to roar.

Drawing his pistols, Kammamuri checked each window, but saw

nothing. He pondered firing a warning shot to scare off the attackers, but decided against it, afraid Tremal-Naik would awaken and attempt to fight them off.

A few hours later, he saw a light flash in the south, followed by a discharge and a soft hiss, then all fell silent once again.

He stood guard for a few more hours, but then, overcome by exhaustion and fatigue, finally drifted off to sleep.

The Maratha awoke at first light and quickly went out, anxious to scout his surroundings. His eyes immediately fell upon a dagger sticking up from the ground a few paces from the hut. A light blue paper was wrapped about its hilt.

Surprised at how close his enemies had come, the Maratha took a few steps back.

He glanced about then cautiously walked toward the knife and picked it up, his arm trembling slightly. It was made of burnished steel, its blade marked with strange incisions.

He unfolded the paper and his eyes fell upon the drawing of a Nagi, several lines were scrawled beneath it, written in blood.

"What's this?" murmured the Maratha.

He summoned Darma and Punthy, had them stand guard and ran to Tremal-Naik. He found the hunter sitting at a window, his head resting in his hands, his eyes fixed on the cloudy southern horizon.

"Master," said the Maratha.

"What is it?" the Indian asked hoarsely.

"Look at this. Someone was here last night."

Tremal-Naik turned about with great difficulty. At the sight of the dagger, he started nervously.

"What's that?" he asked, shuddering. "Where did you get it?"

"I found it in front of the hut. Read the letter, master."

The hunter quickly tore it from his hand and read:

Tremal-Naik,

You have dared speak of love to the Guardian of our

89

most sacred temple. Such blasphemy cannot go unpunished! Your words have angered our goddess; only a life can appease her wrath. If you truly love the Guardian, you will make the ultimate sacrifice and use this dagger upon yourself. A scratch from its poisoned tip will speed you to your grave. Manciadi will await your body. Have your servant bring it to the outskirts of the jungle tonight at sunset.

Suyodhana

Tremal-Naik turned pale.

"My life!" he exclaimed. "My life to appease her wrath! Slay myself? Me!"

"Master," murmured Kammamuri, trembling from head to toe, "We're in grave danger."

"Don't be afraid, Kammamuri," said Tremal-Naik. "The wretches are trying to frighten us, but they won't succeed. They want my life? The goddess sends me a dagger and commands me to go to my grave? I won't be fool enough to use it…"

He stopped suddenly. A terrible thought flashed through his mind. He looked at the letter once again. A wave of pain swept across his face.

"Great Shiva!" he whispered. "Only a life can appease her wrath! Kammamuri!"

"Yes, master?"

"Their goddess requires a sacrifice… She's in their hands…"

"Your vision?"

"Ada!" exclaimed the poor Indian, not hiding his agony. "My poor Ada! Kammamuri! Kammamuri!"

"They wouldn't dare kill her, master."

"Wouldn't they? How can you be sure? The very thought of it fills me with horror! Shiva protect her! Protect my poor Ada!…What to do?" he sobbed, mad with fear. "Those monsters know of our love, if you don't deliver my body… they've already condemned her… she'll never be free

to love me… one of us must die… My poor Ada, so young, so beautiful! … I won't allow it!… Force me to die? So be it! I'll sacrifice my life
if need be!"

He sprang to his feet, a sinister light flashing in his eyes.

"The hour of vengeance has arrived!" he said darkly. "I'm coming,
Ada! Darma!"

The tiger rushed into the hut, announcing her presence with a formidable roar. Tremal-Naik pulled a carbine down from a nail and was
about to go out, but Kammamuri immediately moved to hold him back.

"Where are you going, master?" he asked, grabbing him by the waist.

"To Rajmangal, I have to save her."

"There are a thousand men on Rajmangal, all out for your blood!
You're sealing your fate, master! It's certain death! Once they realize
you're attempting to rescue your beloved, they'll kill her. You'll cause
her death!"

"What?!?"

"Yes, master! They'll kill that poor woman at the first sight of you."

"Great Shiva!"

"Let me take care of this and I promise we'll learn what their plans
are. Who knows, perhaps those men only wished to frighten you."

Stunned by the Maratha's reasoning, Tremal-Naik fell silent. Perhaps
Kammamuri was right.

"It's too soon for us to return to that wretched island; you haven't
fully recovered yet," continued the Maratha. "They want your corpse;
well, I'll deliver it, but you'll be alive and come the right moment you'll
attack the scoundrel that murdered poor Aghur. Leave it to me, master!
We'll soon learn all we need to know."

"What's your plan?" asked Tremal-Naik, slowly coming round.

"First we need a prisoner. We'll make him confess; once we know
what we're up against, we'll determine how to proceed. If necessary,
we'll leave for Rajmangal tomorrow."

"We need a captive?"

"Yes, master, we'll capture Manciadi. Now listen carefully. Tonight,
just after sunset, I'll take you into the jungle; you'll pretend to be dead.

91

Darma and I will hide in the bushes a few paces away to ensure that you're safe. Once Manciadi appears, we'll attack and take him prisoner. Then I'll force him to confess where they've hidden your beloved. He'll tell us all we wish to know, the number of men on the island, how they're armed. He'll keep no secrets from me."

Tremal-Naik took the Maratha's hands and squeezed them affectionately.

"You'll wait then?" Kammamuri asked joyously.

"Yes, I'll wait," said Tremal-Naik, sighing deeply. "But tomorrow, I'm going back to Rajmangal, alone if need be. Ada's in grave danger, I can feel it."

"You won't be alone," said Kammamuri. "Darma and I will accompany you. Now try to get some rest, but keep your eyes open. Manciadi will be in our hands by nightfall."

Kammamuri left his master, who preoccupied by dark thoughts and a thousand worries, had taken a seat by the door, and headed for the river to prepare the rowboat.

The day passed uneventfully. Kammamuri ventured into the jungle several times, armed to the teeth, hoping to spot someone, but not a soul appeared; all remained quiet.

At seven the sun was near the horizon. The moment to act had arrived.

"Master," said the Maratha, rubbing his hands happily, "Best not to waste any time."

Suddenly a ramsinga sounded off toward the south.

"The scoundrel's approaching," said Kammamuri. "Take heart, master, I'll carry you to the jungle. Not a word, not the slightest movement, or you'll ruin the trap. As soon as Manciadi appears, Darma will attack him."

He hid a couple of pistols beneath his large sash, picked up his master, slung him onto his shoulders, and, swaying slightly, headed towards the jungle.

The sun was disappearing beneath the giant plantations in the west when he reached the first bamboo groves. He placed Tremal-Naik upon the grass and knelt down by his side. The hunter did not move.

"Try to silence Manciadi as soon as Darma attacks," he whispered. "There could be others nearby."

"Leave it to me," whispered Tremal-Naik.

Kammamuri went off, eyes to the ground, appearing to stifle a sob. When he reached the hut, a second trumpet cry echoed through the bamboo forest.

"Manciadi's still far off," he said. "All is going as planned."

He entered the hut, armed himself with a pistol and a knife, then carefully scanned the river and the jungle.

"Come, Darma," he said.

With a single leap the tiger reached his side and the two headed into a small patch of mussenda and indigo bushes then raced off towards the south. They reached the bamboo grove less than five minutes later and set up an ambush just seven or eight paces from Tremal-Naik. A third trumpet cry broke the deep silence reigning over the Sundarbans. His prey was drawing nearer.

"Excellent," murmured Kammamuri, levelling one of his two pistols. "It shouldn't be long now."

He turned his eyes towards his master. Lying on one side with his head hidden under an arm, he looked just like a corpse. He would have fooled a marabou, even a jackal.

A peacock peered through the bamboo, looked about and raced off at the sight of them. Kammamuri glanced at the tiger. She was sniffing the air and waving her tail.

"Stay quiet, Darma," he whispered.

A second peacock appeared and shrieked with fear.

Manciadi was silently approaching, crawling like a serpent. Fearing an ambush, he advanced with a thousand precautions.

Kammamuri shot to his knees, clutching his pistol.

Opposite him, the bamboo moved imperceptibly, two hands appeared then a head.

Cold drops of sweat bathed Kammamuri's forehead.

It was Manciadi, Aghur's murderer.

"Darma…" he whispered.

The tiger had crouched down, waiting for the command to attack. Manciadi studied Tremal-Naik for a moment then laughed softly. The hunter did not move. Noose in hand, the Indian emerged from the bamboo and took several steps forward.

"Now, Darma!" exclaimed Kammamuri, jumping to his feet.

With lightning speed the tiger leaped more than fifteen paces and pounced upon the strangler, sending him crashing to the ground.

Tremal-Naik shot up, rushed at Manciadi and knocked him out with a formidable blow.

"Hold on, master!" yelled the Maratha, running towards him. "Break one of his legs so he can't escape."

"No, need for that, Kammamuri," said Tremal-Naik, holding back the tiger. "My blow almost killed him."

Struck in the face by the hunter's steel fist, the Indian no longer gave signs of life.

"There, that's better," said the Maratha. "Now we'll make him talk. He won't escape alive, master, Aghur will be avenged."

"Not so loud, Kammamuri," murmured Tremal-Naik, pulling Darma away from the strangler, the tiger wanting to tear the body apart.

"You think his accomplices are nearby?"

"It's possible. We should hurry back to the hut. It looks like we may be in for a hurricane."

Kammamuri took Manciadi by the legs, Tremal-Naik grabbed his wrists, and the two picked him up and left at a run. A few minutes later they entered their hut and barred the door behind them. Large black storm clouds had appeared to the south, advancing towards the hut with menacing speed.

Chapter 13
Torture

The hard part had been accomplished. Now it was just a matter of making the prisoner talk, not such an easy task, Indians being renowned for their patience and endurance. However, the two hunters possessed means powerful enough to loosen even the most obstinate tongues.

They laid the prisoner in the middle of the hut, lit a fire near his feet and patiently waited for him to regain consciousness.

It was not long before Manciadi began to stir. His chest heaved violently, his limbs shook and then his eyes opened and fell upon the hunter kneeling at his side.

His surprise quickly turned to spite, anger flashing across his face. He clawed at the ground and growled darkly, revealing teeth as sharp as a tiger's.

"Where am I?" he asked dully.

Tremal-Naik put his face close to the strangler's.

"Back in my hut; I'd say your plans have failed," he said, barely restraining his anger.

"I fell into your trap like a fool!" replied Manciadi. "I should have expected it. A setback, nothing more; you won't escape your fate."

"I wouldn't be so sure; your life is in my hands."

"Your words do not frighten me," the strangler exclaimed with a smile. "I fear no one but Kali."

"Kali! Kali? I've heard that name before."

"Yes, the night Suyodhana plunged his dagger into your chest. Ha! Ha! That was a beautiful thrust!"

"It missed its mark, I'm still alive."

"Unfortunately."

"True," said Tremal-Naik ironically. "If I were in my grave, I wouldn't be planning to return to Rajmangal to exterminate that band of murderers."

The strangler chuckled.

"You don't know Suyodhana," he said.

"I'll get to know him, Manciadi, sooner than you think."

"Why should I believe you?"

"I'm a man of my word."

"Ah!" said Manciadi, "As soon as you set foot on Rajmangal, you'll have a hundred nooses around your neck."

"Perhaps, but now let's talk of more serious matters."

"As you wish."

"I warn you, Manciadi, I can devise a thousand tortures to force an answer from you."

"I do not fear torture."

"You'll have the chance to prove it. Kammamuri, stir up the fire, we may need it."

The strangler's lips trembled slightly as he cast a look at the flames.

"Manciadi," continued Tremal-Naik, "Tell me about your goddess. Why does Kali demand so many sacrifices?"

"I have nothing to say."

"That's a bad start, Manciadi."

"I'm not afraid of your threats."

"Second question. How many men are there on Rajmangal?"

"Many, all loyal to our leader Suyodhana."

"Manciadi, do you know the Guardian of the Sacred Temple?"

"Naturally."

"Excellent, tell me about Ada Corishant."

Manciadi's eyes flashed ferociously.

"Tell you about Ada Corishant!" he sneered. "Never!"

"Manciadi!" Tremal-Naik howled furiously. "I will torture you if you refuse to speak. Where is Ada Corishant!?"

"Who knows! Rajmangal, Northern Bengal, afloat in the Ganges. She may be dying as we speak."

Tremal-Naik howled angrily.

"Dying!" he exclaimed. "What do you know!?! Tell me! Tell me, or I'll burn off your legs!"

"Burn off my arms if you like, I won't tell you a thing. I swear it upon my goddess."

"Wretch, have you never been in love?"

"I serve Kali, there is no other."

"Listen to me, Manciadi!" Tremal-Naik yelled wildly. "I'll set you free, I'll give you everything I own, I'll give you my weapons, I'll become your slave, just tell me where I can find poor Ada! Is she alive? Dead? Is there still time to save her? This suffering is unbearable, Manciadi! It's killing me! Speak!"

Manciadi gave him a dark look and remained silent.

"Speak, you monster, speak!" yelled Tremal-Naik.

"No!" exclaimed the Indian. "Never."

"You're that cold hearted?"

"I hate you."

"For the last time, Manciadi, speak!"

"Never!"

Tremal-Naik grabbed the strangler's wrists.

"Wretch!" he yelled. "I'll kill you."

"Kill me, you'll learn nothing."

"Kammamuri, it's time!"

He picked up the prisoner and hurled him to the ground. The Maratha grabbed his feet and drew them towards the fire. The acrid stench of burning flesh soon spread throughout the room. Manciadi started then roared like a tiger as his eyes filled with blood.

"Keep it up, Kammamuri," said Tremal-Naik.

The strangler howled in agony.

"Enough... enough..." shouted Manciadi, his voice choked with pain.

"Will you answer my questions?" asked Tremal-Naik.

Though the flames were unbearable, Manciadi bit his lip and adamantly refused. Two seconds passed then a second cry tore through the air.

"Enough!" he rattled, his voice filled with agony. "Enough!"

"Will you answer my questions?"

"Yes, I'll talk! Enough! Enough!"

With one violent jerk Tremal-Naik tore him from the brazier.

"Speak, you wretch!" he yelled.

Manciadi's eyes were wild, frightening. He tried to sit up, moaned softly and fell still, his face twisted in pain.

"Is he dead?" Kammamuri asked nervously.

"No, just unconscious," replied Tremal-Naik.

"We must be careful, master. We'll gain nothing if he dies before he confesses."

"He won't die, I assure you."

"You think he'll talk?"

"He must. You heard him, Ada may be dying... He'll tell me what he knows, even if I have to bleed him dry, drop by drop."

"You shouldn't believe him, master. The wretch could have lied."

"Pray to Shiva that it's so. If my Ada dies, I'll lose the will to live. Such a cruel fate! I love her, she loves me, yet we can't be together. I will free her; I swear it upon all the gods of India!"

"Master, our guest appears to be waking."

The strangler was regaining consciousness. His limbs trembled slightly as his expression began to soften. He opened his eyes and fixed them upon the hunter, then his lips parted as if to speak, but he remained silent, save for a dull moan that sounded from the depths of his throat.

"Speak, Manciadi!" said Tremal-Naik.

The prisoner did not reply.

"See that fire? We'll resume if you do not speak."

"Speak?" roared Manciadi. "You've ruined me... I can't walk... kill me if you must... I will not speak. I hate you... your Ada... the woman you love... will die! The joy I feel... knowing her fate... they'll torture her... I can almost hear her cries... almost see her... burning on the pyre... Suyodhana chuckling... Thugs dancing about her... Kali smiling... as flames envelope her... Ha! Ha! Ha!"

The wretch laughed satanically as a clap of thunder shook the hut to its foundations.

Tremal-Naik lunged at the Indian like a madman.

"You're lying," he howled. "I don't believe you!"

"It's true… your Ada will burn to death…"

"Tell me what you know!"

"Never!"

Overcome by anger and desperation, Tremal-Naik grabbed the Bengali and began to drag him towards the fire.

Kammamuri quickly intervened.

"Master," he said, blocking his path, "This man cannot withstand a second round of torture, he'll die. Fire failed, let's try steel."

"What do you mean?"

"Leave it to me, he'll speak, you'll see."

The Maratha went into the adjoining room and reappeared moments later with a gimlet. He grabbed the prisoner's right foot and rested the small drill's steel tip against his toe.

"Last chance, Manciadi."

The strangler did not reply.

Sharp metal pierced Manciadi's skin. The Maratha glanced at the prisoner; his face was bathed in cold sweat.

"Should I continue?" he asked.

Manciadi started but did not reply. Kammamuri pressed harder. The strangler, terrified, let out a desperate cry.

"Well?" said the Maratha.

"Stop… stop… I'll answer your questions…"

"I knew it was only a matter of time. Now be quick about it or I'll start on the other foot. Where is the Guardian of the Temple of the East?"

"In the caverns beneath the island," whispered Manciadi.

"Swear on your goddess that you're telling the truth."

"I swear it… on Kali."

"Is she in danger? Tell us everything you know."

"They ordered me… ah, you dogs…"

99

"Continue."

"Kali has condemned her to death... your master loves her... she loves him... well... one of the two... must die... they sent me here... to kill him... I failed..."

"Go on, go on!" exclaimed Tremal-Naik, not missing a single syllable.

"If I'm not back soon, they'll realize what happened... they'll know you... are still alive... one of the two... must die... Ada is in their hands... She'll die... burned alive... Kali has condemned her..."

"I'll save her!"

An ironic smile spread across the prisoner's lips.

"The Thugs are... powerful," he murmured.

"So am I. Listen to me, Manciadi. I know the sacred banyan tree leads to the caverns below; I have to know how to get down there."

"I've told you... too much already... Kill me if you wish... I'm dying... I won't... say another word. Let me die..."

"Shall I start on the other foot?" asked Kammamuri.

"I have all the information I need," said Tremal-Naik. "It's time to go!"

"Tonight?"

"Didn't you hear? There's no time to lose."

"There's a storm gathering."

"All the better; I'll land unseen."

"It could cost you your life, master."

"Nothing will stop me tonight, Kammamuri, not even a hurricane. Darma!"

The tiger, curled up in the adjoining room, got up with a growl and came to her master's side.

"We have quite the task before us, my good friend. Be ready for battle."

"What about me, master, what should I do?" asked Kammamuri.

Tremal-Naik fell silent for a few minutes then said, "Stay behind and guard the prisoner. Who knows, he may still prove useful."

"You're going without me?"

"One of us has to stay behind. Now help me get ready. Bring the oars; I'll wait for you by the canoe."

Tremal-Naik grabbed a carbine, a couple of pistols and a dagger, gathered a large amount of bullets and gunpowder then quickly left the hut. The tiger followed, jumping about, her roars mixing with the thunder and wind.

"The weather's against us," mumbled Tremal-Naik, studying the dark clouds, "But nothing is going to stop me. I just hope I'm in time!"

The sound of a gunshot tore him from his thoughts; Punthy howled dismally.

"What was that?" Tremal-Naik said, surprised. He cast his eyes at the hut and spotted Kammamuri running towards him. He was armed to the teeth and carrying a pair of oars on his shoulders.

"What happened?" asked the hunter.

"I avenged Aghur," replied the Maratha.

"You killed Manciadi?"

"Yes, master, with my pistol. He was becoming a hindrance; now I can go with you."

"We may never set eyes on our jungle again, Kammamuri."

"I know, master."

"We could both die on Rajmangal."

"I know, master. You're going to attempt to rescue the woman you love and I'm going with you. Better to die at your side than remain here alone."

"Well then, so be it. Come, my valiant Kammamuri! Punthy will stay behind and guard the hut."

Chapter 14
Rajmangal

The night was tempestuous. Massive storm clouds had risen in the south and descended upon the jungle with incredible speed, clashing and swirling violently as they raced across the sky.

Winds swept the Sundarbans, moaning through the bamboo forests, rattling the branches of the peepals and banyan trees as bands of peacocks and marabous rushed to find shelter.

At times bolts of lightning would slice through the darkness, illuminating the skies to the horizon, their loud roar echoing out to the Bay of Bengal.

It would not be long before the rains began.

Within minutes the two Indians and the tiger arrived within sight of the Mangal. The rain had swollen the river, the waters swirled and foamed as they raced between the banks, sweeping away large clumps of bamboo and fallen timber.

They remained hidden among the reeds, waiting for a flash of lightning to illuminate the opposite shore, then, once assured no one was watching, they hurried down to the river and pushed the rowboat into the water.

"Master," said Kammamuri, as Tremal-Naik jumped aboard, "Do you think those brigands will be out in this weather?"

"I'm sure of it, but it matters not. My love for Ada has given me the strength to battle a thousand men. Nothing can stop us."

"I know, master, but we must be cautious. If we're spotted, the sentries could sound the alarm and prevent us from landing."

"What do you propose we do?"

"Trick them."

"How?"

"Leave that to me, we'll pass unseen."

The Maratha steered the boat towards the shore, knocked down a large number of bamboo trees, each one no less than fifteen metres long, then carefully fastened them to the rowboat, making it look like a pile of reeds.

"That should do it," he said, as the three hid along the bottom of the boat. "It's getting dark. Who would suspect a large mass of reeds?"

"Let's get out of here," said Tremal-Naik, burning with impatience. "Every minute brings Ada closer to the pyre. They may already suspect something's happened to Manciadi."

"It's too soon, master," replied Kammamuri, steering the rowboat back in among the current. "They're probably still waiting for him to return."

"What if we're too late? Great Shiva, what a horrible thought! I couldn't survive such a catastrophe."

"You've got to remain calm, master. Manciadi may have been lying."

"True. Poor Ada, if only I could see her once again!"

"Be quiet now, master; try not to make any noise."

Tremal-Naik stretched out along the bow beside the tiger while Kammamuri lay down at the stern, oar in hand, trying as best he could to steer the tiny boat.

The wind grew stronger, roaring through the jungle as the hurricane intensified. Reeds and bushes swirled through the air, as jack trees and tara palms came crashing down. Lightning streamed from the clouds, the bright flashes drawing ever nearer.

Driven by the wind and current, the rowboat flew like an arrow, pitching wildly, bumping time and again against the multitude of islands and fallen timber floating among the water.

Kammamuri struggled to keep the canoe on course while Tremal-Naik attempted to quiet the tiger, who, frightened by the noise and dazzling light, roared ferociously, rocking the small craft and threatening to tip it over at any moment.

At ten o'clock, Kammamuri spotted a large fire burning on the shore less than three hundred paces from the rowboat's keel. A ramsinga sounded three times, three different notes reaching their ears.

"Stand ready, master!" he yelled.

"Spot someone?" asked Tremal-Naik, drawing his pistol as he held the tiger back.

"No, master, but I'd wager whoever's out there is probably hiding close to that fire. Keep your eyes open; the ramsinga may have sounded a warning."

"Grab your carbine. We may be in for a fight."

The canoe advanced rapidly toward the fire; a large mound of bamboo blazed brightly, illuminating both sides of the river as if it were day.

"Master, look!" whispered, Kammamuri.

"Quiet!" murmured Tremal-Naik, moving to prevent the tiger from roaring.

Two Indians had suddenly jumped out of a mussenda bush, carbines levelled, a Nagi marking each man's chest.

"Look down there!" yelled one of them. "See it?"

"Yes," replied the other. "It's just a mass of reeds being swept down the river."

"Look how big it is."

"So?"

"Someone could be hiding in there."

"I can't make out anything."

"Be quiet! I think I just heard…"

"A roar?"

"There could be a tiger in there."

"What of it?"

"The hunter has a tiger."

"I didn't know that. You think they could be hiding in there?"

"It wouldn't surprise me; he's a clever one."

"What should we do?"

"Flush him out with a couple of shots. Aim towards the bottom."

Having heard every word, Kammamuri and Tremal-Naik quickly rolled to the far end of the canoe.

The two stranglers raised their carbines.

"Don't fire, master," whispered the Maratha, "or all is lost."

The two carbines thundered in rapid succession, and bullets tore through the bamboo. The tiger jumped up with a furious roar.

"No, Darma!" said Tremal-Naik.

"May the goddess strike me down!" yelled one of the two Indians. "It's him."

"Give the signal, Huka!" commanded the other.

A brilliant flash of light tore through the air, stifling the ramsinga's notes, and knocking back the hunter and his servant as they moved to calm the tiger.

"Master," yelled Kammamuri, "Look!"

Though stunned by the blast, Tremal-Naik rose to his knees. A cry of rage escaped his lips.

"Damn! The boat's on fire!"

Struck by the lightning, the bamboo was burning rapidly.

"We're done for!" exclaimed Kammamuri. "Into the river! Into the river!"

"Don't move."

Tremal-Naik quickly severed the mass of reeds and pushed them away from the boat.

"It's him!" yelled a voice.

"Fire, Huka!"

Two more shots thundered through the air. Tremal-Naik heard the bullets whistle past his ears.

"Give the signal, Huka!"

"We're done for, master," yelled Kammamuri.

"Don't move," repeated Tremal-Naik. "Grab Darma…"

He rushed to the stern and aimed at the Indian placing the ramsinga to his lips. The shot was followed by a cry and a splash. Struck in the forehead by the hunter's infallible aim, Huka had fallen into the river.

After a brief hesitation, his companion ran off into the jungle at full speed, furiously playing the ramsinga he had picked up off the ground. Tremal-Naik fired his pistol, but to no avail.

"Missed!" he yelled, throwing his gun down in anger. "We've been discovered!"

"What are we going to do, master?" asked Kammamuri. "We've lost all hope of landing on Rajmangal undetected; the ramsinga will alert our enemies."

"We'll try just the same, Kammamuri. We'll fight them all if we have to. Grab the oars; we may be able to arrive before the wretches can prepare their defences. I'll keep an eye on both sides of the river and shoot anyone that comes within range of my carbine. Now let's go!"

Kammamuri wanted to add his thoughts, but Tremal-Naik was quick to cut him off.

"If you're frightened, you can stay behind," he said. "Darma and I will go alone."

"I'll go with you, master, may Shiva protect us."

He grabbed the oars, sat in the middle of the boat and began to row with all his might. Driven forward by those powerful strokes, the canoe descended the river with incredible speed, bouncing over the waves.

Tremal-Naik had reloaded his carbine and sat at the stern, his eyes scanning the shores; the tiger lay close to his feet, growling with each clap of thunder.

Ten minutes passed. The Indians sped past the shores, weaving through bamboo reeds and tara palms felled by the storm.

At one point, Tremal-Naik, his eyes riveted upon the river, spotted a flare soaring towards the sky. Within seconds a discharge sounded, rumbling darkly among the thunder and wind.

"A signal?" he murmured. "Row, Kammamuri, row!"

A second flare replied from the opposite shore.

"Master!" exclaimed the Maratha.

"Keep rowing, Kammamuri."

"We've been spotted!"

"Ada's in danger, we're going forward! Stand ready for battle, Darma!"

The river was beginning to narrow. Realizing they were approaching the floating cemetery, Tremal-Naik shuddered.

"Careful, Kammamuri. We're in danger, I can feel it."

The Maratha slowed their advance. The canoe entered a basin surrounded by a thick forest of tamarinds and mango trees. Branches tangled above them, blocking out the light. The darkness thickened quickly,
within minutes the two Indians could barely see more than five paces
ahead of them.

The rowboat struck something, there was a thud then a splash.

"Did you hear that, master?" asked Kammamuri. "Something dove
into the water."

Tremal-Naik leaned over the side to see if someone was swimming
towards the canoe, but saw only darkness.

The canoe struck something a second time.

"Someone's out there," said a voice that sounded close by.

"Could it be them?"

"Could be some of our men. It's almost midnight."

At those words, Tremal-Naik's heart began to race.

"Midnight!" he murmured nervously. "It's almost midnight! I have a
terrible suspicion!"

"Hey!" yelled one of the voices. "Who goes there?"

"Don't reply, master," Kammamuri whispered quickly.

"Quiet, I have a plan."

"You're going mad."

"Who goes there?" asked Tremal-Naik.

"Who goes there?" demanded the voice instead of replying.

"Brothers of Rajmangal."

"Hurry, it's almost midnight."

"What's happening at midnight?"

"The Guardian of the Temple of the East will be sacrificed to Kali."

Tremal-Naik stifled a cry.

"Shiva, Shiva, have pity on her!" he murmured. Then steadying his
voice he added, "Has Tremal-Naik been killed?"

"Probably not, brother, Manciadi hasn't returned."

"So we'll sacrifice the Guardian?"

"Yes, at midnight. The pyre has been prepared. The young woman
will soon join Kali in Paradise."

"Thank you, brother," Tremal-Naik replied hoarsely.

"One more thing. Did you hear the ramsinga?"

"No."

"Did you see Huka?"

"Yes, by the fire."

"Do you know where they're going to sacrifice the Guardian?"

"In the main cavern."

"Yes, in the Great Pagoda. Hurry, it's almost midnight. Goodbye, brother."

"Row, Kammamuri, row!" roared Tremal-Naik. "We've got to save Ada!"

He stifled a sob and fell silent.

Kammamuri manned the oars with desperate energy. The rowboat flew through the mass of floating corpses, heading towards the opposite shore.

"Hurry, hurry..." said Tremal-Naik, verging on insanity. "They're going to sacrifice her on the pyre at midnight... row, Kammamuri, row!"

The Maratha needed no encouragement. He rowed furiously, straining his muscles until they almost burst from his skin. The canoe crossed the basin and quickly entered the river. The isle of Rajmangal came within sight, its enormous banyan tree spreading out before them, its immense branches twisting in the wind.

A flash of lightning shattered the darkness, illuminating the barren shore.

"Shiva is with us!" exclaimed the Maratha.

"Forward, Kammamuri, forward!" said Tremal-Naik, who had rushed to the bow.

Advancing at full speed, the rowboat grounded on the shore, a third of it shooting out of the water. Tremal-Naik, Kammamuri and the tiger rushed to the main trunk of the sacred banyan tree.

"Hear anything?" asked Tremal-Naik.

"Nothing," replied Kammamuri. "They must all be underground."

"Are you afraid?"

"No, master," the Maratha replied firmly.

"Well then, into the tree. We'll either free Ada or die in the attempt!"

They grabbed onto the columns and reached the upper branches, drawing closer to the trunk's summit. With a leap the tiger was at their side.

Tremal-Naik looked down into the hole. A flash of lightning revealed steps leading below.

"Follow me, Kammamuri, and stay close."

Without making the slightest sound, he slowly climbed down into the hollow trunk. Kammamuri and Darma followed closely behind.

Five minutes later the two Indians and the tiger found themselves standing in a semicircular cavern carved out of the rock, six metres beneath the Sundarbans.

Chapter 15
In the Sect's Lair

Having entered the caverns undetected, they merely had to locate the Great Temple, attack the horde of stranglers, and then, taking advantage of the confusion caused by the tiger's unexpected attack, make off with the Guardian.

However, it would not be easy. The tunnels were dark and neither Tremal-Naik nor Kammamuri knew the way, nor were they sure of the temple's location. Not the type of men to abandon hope or retreat from danger, they ran their hands along the walls and began to move forward, keeping close to one another, testing the ground with each step. Realizing that guards could have been posted throughout the tunnel, they advanced cautiously, trying not to make a sound. It was not long before they reached a large opening.

They stopped for a moment and listened.

"Hear anything?" whispered Tremal-Naik.

"Just thunder."

"The ceremony must not have started yet."

"You're right, master. There'd be all kinds of noise."

"My heart's pounding, Kammamuri. Like it's about to burst through my chest."

"Your emotions are getting the better of you, master."

"We have to reach the pagoda in time!"

"We will."

"We could get lost in this maze of tunnels. Look at me, I'm trembling. Now that we're this close… you'd almost think I was afraid."

"Impossible! You afraid? You?!"

"I don't know what it is... a fever, my emotions... something's affecting me."

"Be strong, master, we'll advance slowly. The last thing we want to do is sound the alarm."

"I know, Kammamuri; here take Darma."

Tremal-Naik cautiously began to make his way down a set of stone steps, hands outstretched along the walls, feeling his way forward, ears straining to catch the slightest sound. Minutes later, he reached a tunnel that sloped downwards.

"See anything?" asked Kammamuri.

"Nothing; it's like I've gone blind."

"Could this be the way to the pagoda?"

"I don't know, Kammamuri. I'd give half my blood to light a small torch. What a frightening situation!"

"We've got to keep moving, master. Midnight can't be far off."

Tremal-Naik's skin crawled at those words and his heart began to pound even faster.

"Midnight!" he exclaimed hoarsely.

"Quiet, master, they might hear us."

Stifling a moan, Tremal-Naik fell silent and resumed his march, groping the walls as he felt his way forward.

As he advanced, a strange dizziness began to take hold of him. Blood hissed in his ears as his heart raced ever faster. His mind began to play tricks on him. He thought he heard cries of agony in the distance, believed he saw shadows swirling in the dark. Fists clenched, he began to run, his speed increasing with every step, tossing aside every precaution as if taken by delirium. Kammamuri begged him to slow down, to keep his cool, but the good servant's voice went unheeded.

Fortunately thunder continued to echo beneath the dark arches, its roar masking the sound of their footsteps.

Suddenly the hunter felt a sharp object press against his chest. He came to an immediate halt and took a few steps back.

"Who goes there?" he asked menacingly, drawing his dagger.

"What is it?" asked the Maratha, about to rush forward with Darma.

111

"There's someone here, Kammamuri. Stand ready."

"Did you see a shadow?"

"No, I walked into a spear. It almost put a hole in me."

"Darma doesn't seem worried."

"There's something in front of me."

"Are we going back?"

"Never. It may be close to midnight. Let's go, Kammamuri!"

He took another step forward and felt the same sharp point pierce his skin. He stifled a curse, stretched out his right hand, and grabbed onto a lance protruding from the wall at chest height. He tried to pull it towards him, but it resisted; he tried to twist it, but it did not move.

"What is the meaning of this?" he murmured in surprise.

"What is it, master?" asked Kammamuri. "Another obstacle?"

"A spear. It's imbedded in the wall; we have to make a detour."

He turned right, took a few more steps and brushed against a second spear embedded in the rock.

"Must be a type of defence," he said, "Or some kind of torture device. We'll go left. We'll find a way forward somehow."

He advanced a few more paces and struck his head against the ceiling. Slowly edging his foot forward, he felt a set of steps descending further into the ground. Hands still pressed against the walls, he cautiously made his way down them and soon arrived at the bottom, stopped, reached for Kammamuri's hand and squeezed it tightly.

"Hear that, master?" asked the Maratha.

"Yes," Tremal-Naik whispered softly.

"What do you think it is?"

"I don't know; listen."

They held their breath and strained their ears. A low murmur emanated from above them, echoing throughout the cavern. Moments later, a light flashed off in the distance, followed by a thunderous roar.

Their nervousness increasing, Kammamuri and Tremal-Naik drew their pistols.

The light flashed again, another roar sounded in the distance.

"Make anything of that?" asked the Maratha.

"The walls have grown damp," replied Tremal-Naik. "that murmuring sound suggests we're somewhere beneath the river."

"What about that light?"

"Lightning reflecting off a mirror or a gong. That roar is probably just thunder. Whatever the cause, we're not going back. It's close to midnight."

"This is a terrible place, master. I can't stop trembling. The silence and darkness are playing tricks on my mind."

"Does Darma look uneasy?"

"No, master, not at all."

"Then there's nothing to worry about. We'll keep going."

They resumed their march through the cold damp darkness, advancing blindly, their heads often striking against the low ceilings. Darma brought up the rear.

Ten minutes dragged by. The two hunters had begun to believe they had taken the wrong path and were on the verge of turning about, when they spotted a large flame burning in the middle of a cave. Tremal-Naik spotted an Indian dressed in a loincloth standing next to it, leaning against a spear. A sigh of relief escaped his lips.

"Finally!" he murmured. "I was beginning to fear we'd taken the wrong path. Be careful, Kammamuri."

"Did you spot the enemy?"

"Yes, there's a Thug over there."

"Oh!" exclaimed the Maratha, shuddering.

"He's blocking our path; we'll have to kill him."

"There's no other way?"

"Only if we head back, and I'm not giving up now."

"We're going to make a lot of noise, he's going to yell and then they'll all descend upon us."

"He has his back to us and Darma can sneak up on him without making a sound."

"Be careful, master."

"I'll fight a thousand men if I have to."

113

He crouched beside the tiger. She was glaring ferociously at the Indian, baring her sharp fangs.

"See that man, Darma," said Tremal-Naik.

The tiger grumbled dully.

"Go tear him to pieces, my friend."

Darma's gaze went from her master to the Indian. Her eyes blazed darkly. She had understood. Drawing low to the ground, she gave Tremal-Naik one last look, then silently crept off towards her prey. Leaning on his spear, his back to the fire, the Indian appeared unaware of her approach.

Carbines in hand, Tremal-Naik and the Maratha anxiously followed Darma's every move, watching in silence as she advanced cautiously, eyes fixed on her victim, hearts pounding with fear. A cry from the Indian would sound the alarm throughout the cavern and put an end to their daring rescue.

"Do you think she'll succeed?" the Maratha whispered.

"Darma is intelligent," the latter replied.

"And if she fails?"

Tremal-Naik shuddered.

"Then we'll fight," he said firmly "Quiet now; stand ready."

Unaware of the tiger's approach, the guard had not moved. Suddenly Darma stopped and crouched closer to the ground. Tremal-Naik squeezed Kammamuri's hand. The tiger was only ten paces from the Indian.

Two seconds passed. Darma leaped. Man and beast fell with a dull crunch, bones breaking as they hit the ground.

Tremal-Naik and Kammamuri rushed towards the fire, pointing their carbines towards the tunnel.

"Well done, Darma!" said Tremal-Naik, stroking her strong back.

They reached the Indian and picked him up. The poor man was bathed in blood, his head crushed from the tiger's attack.

"He's dead," said Tremal-Naik, letting the guard fall to the ground. "I knew Darma would be invincible; just wait until we reach the cavern. She'll cause quite a stir among those fanatics."

"They'll flee for their lives at the sight of her."

"And we'll take advantage of the commotion to make off with Ada."

"Where do you plan to take her?"

"The hut for now, then we'll make plans. Perhaps Calcutta, maybe even further away."

"Shhh, master!"

"What?"

"Listen!"

A sharp note sounded off in the distance. The two hunters recognized it immediately.

"The ramsinga!" they exclaimed.

A dull roar thundered beneath the passageway similar to the one they had heard the night they had gone to Rajmangal to look for Hurti.

Tremal-Naik shook from head to toe then suddenly it seemed as if his strength had increased a hundred fold. He leaped like a tiger and raised his carbine.

"Midnight!" he exclaimed with a voice that no longer sounded human. "Ada!"

He stifled a cry and rushed into the tunnel, Kammamuri and the tiger quickly racing after him. Heart pounding, eyes aflame, he had drawn his dagger, ready to battle whatever appeared before him. He was fearless, determined; a thousand Thugs would not have stopped his mad run.

The hauk continued to thunder, echoing in the caverns and tunnels as it summoned Kali's devotees. Voices murmured, growing louder as the ramsinga's sharp notes sounded off in the distance. It would not be long now, midnight was at hand.

Tremal-Naik doubled his speed, not caring to mask his footsteps.

"Ada! Ada!" he rattled, barrelling through the winding tunnels with the fury of a bull.

A light appeared in the distance as a resounding cry echoed throughout the caverns.

"There they are!" Tremal-Naik yelled hoarsely.

Kammamuri gathered all his strength, rushed towards his master and knocked him to the ground.

"Not another step!" he said.

Tremal-Naik turned to face him, wild with anger.

"What!?!" the hunter yelled ferociously.

"If you value Ada's life, don't take another step," repeated the Maratha, holding him down.

"Let me go, Kammamuri, let me go! I can't bear it!"

"That's just it! You've lost your reason! If you rush into that cave, you'll give us away. Calm down, master, we'll save her, but we have to be cautious."

"My heart's pounding, my blood's boiling. I could tear down these walls and bury these monsters alive. Listen! Hear that?"

"What?"

"I thought I heard her voice."

"You're delirious. Master, if you wish to save her, you'll have to get a hold of yourself."

"I'll control myself, but we can't stop here, Kammamuri."

"We're not going to. Now come with me, and don't do anything rash or I'll leave you behind."

The two men got up and slowly headed towards the cavern. Minutes later they came to a halt behind an enormous pillar, from where they could spy on events unobserved.

A vast cavern spread out before them. The walls were of red granite, like the temples of Ellora; twenty-four pillars towered to the ceiling, adorned with elaborate carvings of elephants, lions and goddesses.

A large bronze statue stood in the centre, a terrifying woman with a long red tongue hanging down to her chin. She wore a garland of hands and a necklace of skulls, identical to the one Tremal-Naik had seen in the pagoda. Scenes from the Ramayana stretched out above her, vast murals of Rama's epic struggle to free his beloved Sita. Large bronze lamps hung from the ceiling, filling the room with a pale blue light.

Dressed in loincloths, forty Indians sat about the statue, daggers drawn, silk rumaals fastened about their waists, eyes fixed upon the goddess. A man sat next to a hauk, an enormous drum adorned with fur and blue feathers. He would strike it from time to time, filling the cavern with its thunderous echo.

Stunned by that sight, Tremal-Naik had not moved, his hands running instinctively to his weapons.

"Ada!" he murmured, scanning the cavern. "Where's my Ada?"

A flash of joy lit up the hunter's eyes.

"The sacrifice hasn't begun yet!" he exclaimed. "Shiva be praised."

"Not so loud, master," said Kammamuri, tightening his grip on the tiger's neck. "There are less of them than I thought; it shouldn't be difficult to rescue Ada."

"Yes, yes, we're going to save her, Kammamuri!" exclaimed Tremal-Naik excitedly. "We'll massacre the lot."

"Quiet…"

The hauk fell silent and the forty Indians rose to their feet.

Tremal-Naik's heart leaped.

"Midnight!" he murmured, barely managing to hold himself back.

"Remain calm, master," whispered Kammamuri, grabbing his arm.

A large door opened and a tall thin Indian dressed in an elegant yellow silk dhoti entered the cavern. His eyes sparkled darkly and his face was framed by a long black beard.

"Greetings Suyodhana, Son of the Sacred Waters of the Ganges!" the forty men exclaimed in unison.

"Greetings to Kali and her children!" the Indian replied darkly.

At the sight of that man, Tremal-Naik muttered a curse and tried to rush into the cavern, but Kammamuri quickly held him back.

"Don't move, master," he whispered.

"That man!" exclaimed Tremal-Naik through clenched teeth.

"Yes, I know; he's their leader."

"That's the man that stabbed me."

"So that's the wretch!"

Suyodhana advanced slowly, knelt down before the giant bronze goddess, turned towards the Indians and thundered, "Brothers, Manciadi is dead. The final hour has sounded for the Guardian of the Temple of the East."

A dark murmur filled the cavern.

"Sound the tarès," commanded Suyodhana.

Two men picked up long trumpets and began to play a melancholy tune.

A hundred Indians carrying bundles of wood marched into the cavern, built a giant pyre at the foot of the statue and doused it with torrents of fragrant oil.

A squadron of devadasis[11] pirouetted into the room, ringing tiny bells and sounding small silver gongs, the diamonds in their golden breastplates sparkling in the light as they advanced towards the goddess Kali.

At the sound of the hauk and the sombre tarè, they began to dance about the statue, their red silk saris swirling gracefully about their hips.

Then suddenly the dancing stopped. The devadasis bowed to the goddess and withdrew to one side.

Having retaken their seats during that performance, at a sign from Suyodhana, the Thugs rose to their feet. The sacrifice was about to begin.

"Kammamuri," babbled the poor hunter, leaning against the pillar, "Kammamuri!"

"Be strong, master," said the Maratha.

"My head is spinning, my heart is about to burst… Ada!… Ada!"

A drum roll sounded off in the distance. Tremal-Naik drew himself up to his full height, eyes flaming, fists tightening about his pistols.

"They're coming!" he roared with hatred.

The drums were drawing nearer, echoing through the dark tunnels leading into the cavern. Wild discordant voices soon filled the air, accompanied by the sound of the tom-toms.

"They're coming!" Tremal-Naik exclaimed a second time.

The tiger grumbled dully and waved her tail.

A large door opened and the procession entered the cavern. Ten stranglers led the way, sounding mrdangas, barrel-shaped, double-skinned terracotta drums. Twenty more followed a few paces behind them ringing large bronze bells, then another twelve playing ramsingas, tarè and tom-toms.

---

[11] Dancers.

118

The Guardian entered last, dressed in white silk, her golden breast-plate sparkling in the firelight. Her face had become deathly pale, exhausted by long fasts and numbed by the opiates she had been forced to swallow.

Two stranglers dressed in yellow silk dhotis helped her advance, another ten followed close behind, singing praises to her heroism and promising infinite happiness in Kali's paradise in reward for her virtue.

Suyodhana lit the pyre and the flames began to swell, stretching towards the cavern's ceiling. The stranglers, deafening her with a thousand cries, dragged her forward, the drums and the tarè heralding her death.

Suddenly, the victim regained her senses. She spotted the pyre flaming before her and quickly realized she was in danger. A cry of agony tore from her chest.

"Tremal-Naik!"

A fierce cry thundered from inside a dark tunnel.

"Now, Darma! Tear them to pieces!"

The great Bengal tiger had been waiting for those words. She rushed from her hiding place, let out a loud roar, and leaped among the stranglers. Cries of terror filled the air. Within seconds two men lay lifelessly on the ground.

"Attack, Darma! Attack!" her master's voice repeated.

Four blasts thundered, knocking four Indians to the ground and sending the others to their knees. The great Hunter of the Black Jungle suddenly appeared among the clouds of smoke, his face twisted in anger, a dagger clutched in his fist.

Smashing through those rows of terrified Indians, reaching the young woman who had fainted and fallen to the ground, gathering her in his arms and disappearing into the tunnel with Kammamuri and the tiger, took but a minute.

Chapter 16
The Caves

The caverns of Rajmangal were far vaster than the famous caves of El-lora and Mahabalipuram. Countless tunnels meandered beneath the ground, crisscrossing in a thousand directions, some rising ever upwards to the island's swampy surface, others descending into the very bowels of the earth. Some led to damp, dark caverns uninhabited for untold centuries, others to exquisite pagodas carved from the rock. The Thugs themselves had not explored every corner of those infinite caves.

His attack successful, Tremal-Naik had rushed into the nearest tunnel followed by Kammamuri and Darma. He did not know where it led and could not see very far in front of him, but for the moment, these were not grave concerns.

He had to flee, to gain distance from the stranglers before they recovered from the terror of the tiger's unexpected appearance and organized their pursuit.

Clutching the unconscious young woman in his arms, he ran at full speed, never stopping for a breath.

"We did it! We did it!" he repeated from time to time.

His excitement fed his strength and he raced forward at dizzying speed, his burden growing lighter with every step.

Kammamuri struggled to keep up, groping through the darkness, the faithful Darma at his side, growling dully as they tried to match the hunter's pace.

"Stop, master," repeated the poor Maratha. "I can hardly keep up."

Tremal-Naik, however, continued to increase his speed and invariably replied, "Keep running! We did it! It worked!"

They had been running for ten minutes, when the hunter collided violently against a wall and dropped to the ground.

He shot to his feet, the young woman still in his arms and collided with Kammamuri, who had been just a few paces behind.

"Master!" exclaimed the Maratha. "What happened?"

"It's a dead end!" exclaimed Tremal-Naik, looking about ferociously.

"We should pause to catch our breath, master."

Tremal-Naik was about to reply, when a frightening cry thundered off in the distance. He jumped back, letting out a cry of rage and desperation.

"The Thugs!"

"Master!"

"Run, Kammamuri, run!"

He turned to the right and ran off, but after going ten paces he found the path blocked before him. His hair stood on end.

"Damn!" he thundered. "We're trapped!"

He rushed to the left and struck a third wall. Darma roared in anger.

Tremal-Naik turned about. He pondered retracing his steps and finding another tunnel, but the fear of stumbling upon the stranglers held him back.

Had he been alone, he would not have hesitated to fling himself into the middle of that throng, no matter the cost. But the thought of attacking now, now that he had rescued the one he loved, filled him with fear.

They had to get out of the cavern; otherwise it would become their tomb.

"Am I cursed by the gods?" he exclaimed furiously. "Am I to parish now that I hold my beloved in my arms? No! No, Ada, you won't fall back into their hands again, we'll take our lives if we have to!"

He slowly began to retrace his steps; his eyes fixed on the tunnel ahead, his ears straining to catch the slightest sound. He knelt down, gently placed the young woman on the ground and quickly drew his pistols.

"Darma!" he said.

The tiger approached.

"Stay close to her," commanded Tremal-Naik. "Don't move until I call you. If anyone approaches, tear them to pieces."

"Do you have a plan, master?" asked the Maratha.

"We've got to find a tunnel out of here," said Tremal-Naik. "Come, Kammamuri."

The Maratha slowly groped through the darkness and soon reached his side. The sound of pistols being loaded quickly filled the tunnel.

"Time to go, my friend."

"What if we come across the Thugs?"

"We'll fight them if need be."

The two Indians reached the main tunnel and slowly made their way down it, their uneasiness increasing with every step. Tremal-Naik turned about and spotted the tiger's green eyes shining in the darkness.

"At least Ada is safe," he murmured.

He stifled a sigh and headed forward, walking on tiptoes, running his hands along the left wall. Kammamuri followed five paces behind him, feeling his way along the opposite wall. They advanced for a few minutes then halted, holding their breath. A soft rustling sound reached their ears. Someone was coming towards them, crawling along the ground.

Tremal-Naik moved to the opposite wall and collided with Kammamuri.

"Who goes there?" the Maratha whispered nervously, pointing a pistol at the hunter's chest.

"Did you hear that?" asked Tremal-Naik.

"Ah, it's you master. Yes, I heard it. The stranglers are crawling towards us."

Quaking from head to toe, Tremal-Naik turned to look at the cave. The tiger's eyes had disappeared. His uneasiness grew.

"What's happening?" he murmured.

He took a few steps back, but immediately came to a halt. A sigh had reached his ears. He grabbed Kammamuri's hand and squeezed it tightly.

"Anything?" murmured a voice.

"Nothing," whispered another.

"Are we lost?"

"I'm afraid so."

"Know where we are?"

"I think so."

"Any more tunnels?"

"No, it's a dead end."

"Hiding places?"

"There's a well nearby I think."

"Could they be down there?"

"We'd have to check."

"Shall we continue forward then?"

"I'd rather head back. The brothers at the mouth of the tunnel will make sure no one gets through."

"You're right, we should check the other exits; we'll come back later and check the well."

A soft rustling sound echoed down the passageway then all fell silent.

Tremal-Naik grabbed Kammamuri's hand once again.

"Did you hear that?"

"Every word, master," replied the Maratha.

"All the exits are blocked."

"We should go back, master."

"You heard them! They'll be back, they'll find us."

"I don't know what else we can do."

"What if we try to force our way through?"

"What about Ada?"

"I'll carry her; no one will dare touch her."

"The first rifle blast would draw the Thugs upon us. Sound travels quickly through these tunnels."

Tremal-Naik tore at his chest.

"Am I doomed to lose her?" he murmured desperately.

"What if we went down into the well?" said Kammamuri.

"Into the well?"

"It may lead to another tunnel, maybe even outside."

"Yes, that's possible!"

"Let's go back, master."

Tremal-Naik did not wait to be told twice. He ran his hand against the wall and followed it to the cavern. The tiger greeted him with a dull roar.

"Quiet, Darma," he said.

He knelt down beside the young woman.

"Ada! Ada!" he whispered excitedly.

She did not move; her body was cold. He put his hand to her heart and felt it beat. A sigh of relief escaped his lips.

"She'll be fine," he said.

"You think so, master?" asked Kammamuri.

"Yes, she should regain consciousness in a few minutes. The shock was great. Now, let's look for the well, Kammamuri."

"Leave it to me, master. Take care of Ada and make sure no one enters the cave."

He began his search, groping about blindly, advancing, retreating, often feeling the ground. Four times he bumped against the walls without having found anything and just as many times he returned to his master's side. He was beginning to doubt whether they would ever find the well when his hand brushed against a stone wall, which, according to his calculations, was right in the centre of the cave.

"This must be it," he murmured.

He stood up, ran his hands over the top, bent over it and looked down. More darkness met his eyes. He grabbed a bullet from his carbine and dropped it into the void. Two seconds later he heard a dull thud.

"Excellent, it's empty and it isn't very deep. Master!" he shouted.

Tremal-Naik carefully picked up the young woman and made his way toward him.

"Well?" he asked.

"We're in luck. We can climb down."

"Are there steps?"

"I don't think so. I'll go down first."

He fastened the rope around his waist, gave one end to Tremal-Naik and lowered himself into the well. Fifteen seconds later, Kammamuri's feet struck smooth polished stone.

"Stop, master," he said.

"Hear anything?" asked Tremal-Naik, bending over the parapet.

"Not a sound. Lower Ada then jump down, it's less than three metres to the bottom."

The rope was fastened about Ada's waist and she was slowly lowered into Kammamuri's waiting arms. Once she was safely below, Tremal-Naik jumped into the well, taking the rope along with him.

"Think they'll find us in here?" asked the Maratha.

"They might, but it'll be easy to defend ourselves."

"I wonder if this well connects to the other tunnels."

"I don't think so, but we can check. You remain here with Darma; I'll light the small torch I brought and try to revive Ada."

He picked up the young woman and carried her away from the opening; the tiger jumped down into the well and lay down beside the Maratha.

He removed his sash, spread it out on the ground, laid the young woman on top of it, knelt down beside her, and lit a small torch. A soft blue light filled the well's interior, revealing stone walls chipped with age. Gods and monsters had been carved into the rock, scenes from great battles stretching from floor to ceiling.

Pale and trembling, Tremal-Naik bent over the young woman and removed her golden breastplate. Her skin was as cold as marble; her face a deathly white, her eyes lined by dark blue circles. Not a sound came from her parted lips, she barely seemed alive.

Tremal-Naik gently brushed back her long black hair and studied her for several minutes, holding his breath. He stroked her forehead and she sighed softly.

"Ada! Ada!" exclaimed the Indian.

The young woman slowly opened her eyes and rested her gaze upon the hunter's face. A cry escaped her lips.

"Ada?" asked Tremal-Naik.

"You... Tremal-Naik..." she whispered weakly. "No... It's not possible... God, please don't make this a dream..."

She turned her head as several tears streamed down her cheeks.

"Ada!" the hunter murmured, frightened by that response. "Why are you crying? Don't you love me?"

"Is it really you, Tremal-Naik?"

"Yes, my love."

She turned to look at the proud Indian and squeezed his hands affectionately.

"This isn't a dream!" she exclaimed, laughing through her tears. "It is you!... You came! Where are we? Are we still in danger? I'm frightened, Tremal-Naik."

"You're safe now, Ada! There's no need to be frightened. No harm will come to you."

She looked at him fixedly then suddenly turned pale.

"Did I dream it?" she whispered.

"It wasn't a dream," said Tremal-Naik, guessing her thoughts. "They were about to sacrifice you to their goddess."

"Sacrifice me! Yes, yes, I remember. They drugged me and promised me happiness in Kali's paradise... yes, I remember! They dragged me into the tunnels... deafening me with their cries... The fire burned before me. They were about to throw me onto the flames... It was horrible! Oh! Tremal-Naik!"

"There's no need to worry, Ada. Kammamuri and I will defend you with our lives and I have yet to meet anyone that's a match for Darma's powerful claws," said Tremal-Naik, deeply moved.

"I'm not afraid, brave Tremal-Naik. But how did you get here? How did you arrive in time to save me? What happened to you that terrible night I was taken from the pagoda? How I've suffered since then, Tremal-Naik! So many tears, so many worries, so many torments! I feared the wretches had killed you!"

"They almost did. The wretch's dagger just missed my heart; it took me weeks to recover."

"They stabbed you?"

"Yes, but it's just a scar now."

"And you came back to this wretched island?"

"Yes, Ada, I would have come back no matter the cost. When I learned you were to be sacrificed to that goddess, I set out immediately. I raced down into these caverns and attacked the horde of fanatics, snatched you from their claws, and hid in here with my friends."

"We're not alone?"

"No, Kammamuri and Darma are with us."

"Ah, I want to meet these brave friends of yours!"

"Kammamuri! Darma!"

The Maratha and the tiger came to their master's side.

"This is Kammamuri," said Tremal-Naik, "A true warrior."

The Maratha fell to the young woman's feet and kissed her hand.

"Thank you, my good friend," she said.

"Mistress," replied Kammamuri, "My good mistress, I am your slave. Do with me as you wish. I will gladly sacrifice my life for your freedom and…"

He stopped suddenly and jumped to his feet. Despite his extraordinary courage, Tremal-Naik shuddered. A dark rumbling sound had just reached their ears and was rapidly growing louder.

"They're coming!" said Tremal-Naik, clutching the young woman's hand with his left and drawing a pistol with his right.

The tiger roared dully.

The sound grew louder. The ceiling shook as it passed over their heads, then, all fell silent.

"Master," murmured Kammamuri, "Put out the fire!"

Tremal-Naik obeyed and the four were cloaked in darkness. The sound resumed, drawing nearer until it came to a stop close to the well.

The hunter felt Ada tremble beside him.

"I'm here to defend you," he whispered. "We won't allow anyone to come down here."

"What was that?" asked Kammamuri.

"I've heard it before," whispered the young woman, "but I was never told what it was."

The tiger let out a second roar and fixed his eyes on the mouth of the well.

"Kammamuri," said Tremal-Naik, "Someone's coming."

"Yes, Darma noticed that too."

"Stay with Ada. I'm going to see if anyone's climbing down."

The young woman grabbed him, trembling with fear.

"Tremal-Naik! Tremal-Naik!" she pleaded, her voice barely a whisper.

"Don't be afraid, Ada," replied the hunter, who in that instant would have fought against a thousand men.

He slipped out of the young woman's arms and made his way to the centre of the well, carbine drawn, his dagger between his teeth. The tiger looked at him and growled. He had not gone ten paces when he heard a soft crackling sound a few feet above him. He placed his hand upon Darma's head to keep her quiet then advanced with even more caution, coming to a stop beneath the mouth of the well.

He looked up, but saw only darkness. Straining his ears, he heard faint whispers. Several people had gathered near the parapet.

"They know we're here," he murmured.

He had not yet finished that thought when a light flashed from above. Though it had only lasted for an instant, Tremal-Naik spotted six or seven Indians leaning over the side of the well.

He quickly aimed his carbine.

"They're down there," said a voice.

"We've found our man," said another.

Tremal-Naik fired. The blast echoed throughout the well. A dull thud followed then all fell silent. He threw down his carbine, drew one of his pistols and emptied it into the air.

"Wretches!" he yelled angrily.

Kammamuri and Ada rushed towards him.

"Tremal-Naik!" exclaimed the young woman, grabbing one of his hands, "Are you injured?"

"I'm fine," replied the Indian, forcing himself to speak calmly.

"What was that noise?"

"They sealed us in, but we'll find another way out, Ada, I promise."

He lit the torch and led the woman away from there, sitting her down on his sash.

"You must be tired," he said sweetly. "Lie down; we'll look for a way out. You're safe now, try to get some rest."

Though afraid the Thugs would descend upon them at any moment, the young woman, exhausted by all she had been through, decided to heed the hunter's advice and stretched out on the sash. Tremal-Naik and Kammamuri headed towards the walls and began to tap them carefully, hoping to find a passageway that led out of the well. Strangely, mysteriously, a dark rumble emanated from the other side of the wall from time to time, similar to the one they had heard just moments ago.

They had been searching for about half an hour, beating the rock with their blades, when they noticed the temperature begin to change; it was growing hotter. Tremal-Naik and Kammamuri began to sweat.

"What's happening?" the hunter asked uneasily.

Another half hour passed; the temperature continued to rise, it would not be long before the heat became unbearable.

"They're going to roast us alive!" said the Maratha.

"How's this possible?" replied Tremal-Naik, removing his dugbah.

"Where's this heat coming from?"

"Keep looking."

They resumed tapping the walls, making their way around the entire cavern, but did not find a single passageway. However, in a corner, the rocks sounded as if they were hollow. If they could pry them loose, there was a chance they would find a tunnel.

The two Indians returned to the young woman's side and found her asleep. They grabbed their knives and vigorously attacked the rock, but soon had to stop. The heat had become unbearable. Dying of thirst, they searched the ground for water, but the stones were dry and barren. The first pangs of fear crept into their bones.

"Are we destined to die in this cavern?" Tremal-Naik asked, casting a desperate look upon the scorching walls.

A strange murmur reached their ears then an enormous rock dropped from the ceiling and crashed noisily to the ground. Instantly a stream of water gushed through the opening.

"We're saved!" yelled Kammamuri.

"Tremal-Naik," murmured the young woman, awakened by the sound of the downpour.

The Bengali rushed to her side.

"What is it?" he asked.

"I'm suffocating. I can't breathe. It's so hot! A drop of water. Tremal-Naik... some water."

The hunter gathered her in his arms and carried her to the waterfall, where Darma and Kammamuri had quickly gone to drink.

He cupped his hands, filled them with water and put them to the young woman's lips. When she had drunk enough he bent down and quickly quenched his thirst.

Suddenly the tiger roared softly and fell to the ground, her mouth foaming, her legs shaking violently. Frightened, Kammamuri rushed to her side but his strength gave way and he fell on his back, eyes bulging, hands trembling, lips covered in bloody foam.

"Ma...ster!" he exclaimed, his voice barely a whisper.

"Kammamuri!" yelled Tremal-Naik, "Great Shiva! Ada! Ada!"

Like the tiger and Kammamuri, the young woman's eyes bulged open, and her lips were covered in foam. Her hands trembled as she tried to grab the hunter's neck. She opened her mouth, tried to speak, then closed her eyes and grew stiff. Tremal-Naik howled with agony.

"Ada! Help! Help!"

They were the last words to escape his lips. His vision clouded and his muscles stiffened as a violent spasm raced through his body. He swayed forward, sat up then fell to the ground, still clutching his beloved. Moments later, the stone seal slid back and a throng of Indians jumped down into the well.

Part II

Tremal-Naik's Revenge

Chapter 1
Captain MacPherson

It was a magnificent August night. The air was warm, filled with the sweet fragrances of jasmine, sciambara, mussenda and nagatampi. Bathed in moonlight, the Hugli shone like a long silver ribbon as it meandered through the vast lowlands of the Bengali delta, flowing past the coconut, tamarind, jackfruit and banana trees gracefully lining its shores.

Bands of marabou circled above the river and the trees; from time to time a jackal would appear, roaming along the riverbanks, its sharp melancholy cry breaking the silence reigning over the jungle.

Despite the late hour, a man sat at the foot of a large tamarind tree, unfazed by the dangers lurking in the shadows. About forty years old, he was clad in the uniform of a sepoy captain, gold and silver medals adorned his jacket. He was tall, well built, with darkly tanned skin, a European that had lived in the tropics for many years.

He had a proud face, framed by a well-trimmed black beard and large sad eyes that sparkled daringly. From time to time he would raise his head, fix his eyes upon the great river and tap his fingers impatiently upon his knee.

He had been sitting there for a half hour when a shot thundered off in the distance. The captain reached for his carbine, a striking weapon inlaid with silver and mother-of-pearl, rose to his feet and walked down to the shore, making his way over the tangle of tamarind roots twisting along the ground. A black dot had appeared on the river and was slowly advancing towards him, the waters sparkling about it as it drew nearer.

"There they are," he murmured.

He raised his carbine and fired. A light tore through the darkness as a third discharge filled the air.

"So far, so good," continued the captain. "Let's hope they have some information this time."

A wave of pain flashed across his face.

He fixed his eyes on the black dot once again. It was approaching quickly; as it took form the captain made out a small boat driven forward by half a dozen oarsmen. She was carrying what appeared to be seven or eight armed men.

In less than ten minutes, the boat, a sleek murpunky under the command of a sepoy sergeant and manned by six Indians wielding long oars, arrived to within a few cable lengths of the shore. Minutes later, she drew up along the grass.

The sergeant quickly jumped ashore and saluted.

"Take the murpunky to the stream," the captain ordered. "Bhárata, come with me."

The murpunky rowed off. The captain led the Indian beneath the tamarinds, and the two men sat down among the grass.

"Are we alone, Captain MacPherson?" asked the sergeant.

"Yes," replied the captain. "You may give your report."

"Negapatnan will be here within the hour."

The captain started.

"They captured him?" he exclaimed excitedly. "I was afraid it was only a rumour."

"It's true, sir. They've been keeping him under guard at Fort William."

"And they're certain he's a strangler?"

"He's one of their most respected leaders."

"Has he confessed?"

"Not a word, Captain. They even tried to starve him, but to no avail."

"How was he captured?"

"The scoundrel had been plying his trade about the fort. Six soldiers had already fallen beneath his noose; their bodies had been found stripped of their clothing, the cult's mark branded on their chests.

"Seven days ago, Captain Hall assembled a squadron of sepoys and set out to find the assassin. After searching unsuccessfully for two hours, he decided to have a short rest beneath a borax tree. Suddenly, he felt a

134

noose tighten about his neck. He grabbed the rope, jumped to his feet, attacked the strangler, and called for help. The sepoys were close by. They rushed to his aid and tackled the Indian to the ground."

"And the prisoner will be here within the hour?" asked Captain MacPherson.

"Yes, Captain," replied Bhárata.

"Finally!"

"You plan to question him?"

"Yes," declared the captain, his voice barely a whisper.

"You're hiding something, Captain," said the sergeant.

"Yes, Bhárata," MacPherson replied hoarsely.

"You can confide in me, sir. I may be able to help."

The captain did not reply. He had grown sullen; his face was bathed in perspiration.

"Captain," said the sergeant, moved by that sudden change, "I didn't mean to intrude. Forgive me, I did not know."

"There's nothing to forgive, my good Bhárata," replied MacPherson, pressing the sergeant's hand, "You should know the full story."

He stood up, took four steps forward, eyes on the ground, arms crossed tightly, then sat back down beside the sergeant. A tear silently rolled down his bronzed cheek.

"My wife passed away several years ago..." he began, struggling to keep his voice steady, "taken by an attack of cholera. We had a young girl, as lovely as a rose, with long black hair and eyes like diamonds. I can still see her, playing in the park, chasing butterflies, or sitting with me beneath our tamarind tree, playing the sitar or singing old Scottish tunes. The joy she gave me... my poor Ada!"

A flood of tears stifled his voice. He buried his face in his hands as sobs tore from his chest.

"Be strong, Captain," said the sergeant, after a few minutes had passed.

"Yes," murmured the captain, wiping the tears away in anger. "It's been a long time since I've cried, sometimes it does me good."

"Please continue... if it isn't too painful."

The captain remained silent for a few minutes as he struggled to compose himself, then continued:

"One morning, in 1848, I awoke to find the inhabitants of Calcutta in a state of alarm. The Thugs had pasted leaflets on every wall and tree; their goddess needed a servant, a young woman for their sacred temple.

"A wave of terror ran through me; a premonition, something bad was about to happen. That night I sent my daughter to Fort William, hoping to keep her safe behind its walls, I was certain the Thugs would never have gotten to her there. But three days later, my Ada awakened with the strangler's mark on her arm."

"Ah!" exclaimed Bhárata, turning pale. "How did they get to her?"

"I never found out."

"A Thug managed to infiltrate the fort?"

"It's the only explanation."

"One of our sepoys?"

"The sect is huge, Bhárata. It has members throughout India, Malaysia, even as far as China."

"Please continue, Captain."

"Until that day I had never known fear. But that monstrous goddess had selected my daughter and I doubled my precautions. We ate our meals together; soldiers stood guard day and night in front of her door, I slept in the adjoining room. But despite all my efforts, one night, my daughter disappeared."

"How!?!"

"The stranglers broke through a window and abducted her. Someone must have drugged our food for no one heard or noticed anything."

The captain fell silent, visibly shaken.

"I searched for a long time," he continued, trying to steady his voice, "But I never found so much as a trace of her. The stranglers had taken her to their secret lair.

"To hide my identity, I changed my name to MacPherson and waged war against them. I was merciless. A hundred stranglers fell into my hands; I tortured every one of them, hoping for a confession that would lead me to my poor Ada, but nothing I did could make them speak.

Three long years have passed and my daughter is still their prisoner..."

The captain burst into tears a second time.

A trumpet blared off in the distance. The two men jumped to their feet and ran towards the river.

"There they are!" yelled Bhárata.

A dull roar escaped Captain MacPherson's lips, his eyes flashing with ferocious joy. He descended the riverbank and spotted a large canoe five or six hundred metres away, rapidly advancing towards him. Several sepoys were on board, armed with bayonets.

"Do you see him?" he asked through clenched teeth.

"Yes, Captain," replied Bhárata. "He's in chains, seated at the stern, between two sepoys."

"Quickly now!" yelled the captain.

The canoe doubled its speed and drew up to the shore a few feet from the captain. Six sepoys in red uniforms, their helmets, collars and cuffs embroidered with silver and gold thread, quickly disembarked. Two soldiers, clutching the strangler Negapatnan by the arms, came ashore immediately after them.

The prisoner was a thin, agile Indian about six feet tall. His bearded face was grim, and his small eyes sparkled like an angry serpent's. His chest was marked by a blue tattoo, a Nagi surrounded by several indecipherable symbols. He wore a turban of yellow silk, with a large diamond in its centre, a matching dhoti about his waist.

At the sight of Captain MacPherson he started, a deep frown forming upon his brow.

"You recognize me?" asked the captain, that reaction not having escaped him.

"You're Captain Harry Corishant."

"No, Captain Harry MacPherson."

"You changed your name."

"Do you know why I've brought you here?"

"To make me talk, I imagine. A waste of time."

"I wouldn't be so sure. Time to go, my friends; keep your eyes open. There could be Thugs nearby."

137

Captain MacPherson picked up his carbine, loaded it and led the small column of men up a path and into a forest of nagatampi trees. They had gone a quarter of a mile when suddenly a jackal's cry sounded from among the vegetation.

Negapatnan quickly raised his head and cast a rapid look about. The sepoys walking alongside him grunted a warning.

"Keep your guard up, Captain," said Bhárata. "The Thug senses something."

"Someone's watching us?"

"Could be."

The cry sounded again, louder than before. Captain MacPherson halted.

"By thunder!" he exclaimed. "That's not a jackal."

"Keep your eyes open," repeated the sergeant. "It's a signal."

"Double time, men."

The squad resumed their march, moving forward, their carbines trained on both sides of the path. Ten minutes later, they arrived on the outskirts of Captain MacPherson's farm.

Chapter 2
Negapatnan

Captain Harry MacPherson's villa stood on the left bank of the Hugli, by a small stream where several gongas and a couple of murpunkys rested at anchor. It was a small one-story bungalow with a brick cellar, a high sloping roof and a veranda that opened up onto a large terrace. Coconut mats hung from the eaves, sheltering the villa from the sun. Several huts and small buildings stood nearby: sheds, stables, kitchens, and barracks shaded by latanie, peepal and neem trees.

Having dismissed the sepoys, Captain MacPherson entered the villa, passed through a series of elegantly furnished rooms, and stepped onto a terrace overlooking the compound. Bhárata arrived minutes later, dragging the strangler Negapatnan.

"Sit down," said the captain, offering the strangler a bamboo chair.

Negapatnan obeyed, the shackles about his wrists rattling slightly as he settled in the chair. Bhárata stood by the prisoner's side, hands resting on his pistols.

"You claimed to know me," said Captain MacPherson, fixing his eyes on the Indian.

"You're Captain Harry Corishant," replied the strangler.

"Now what makes you say that?"

"I saw you several times in Calcutta. I even followed you one night. I'd hoped to strangle you, but I was unsuccessful."

"Wretch!" exclaimed the captain, turning pale with anger.

"You shouldn't let such trivial matters upset you," smiled the strangler.

"Trivial? The Thugs took my daughter!"

"Yes, I know. On the night of the 24th of August, 1848. I was there. I smashed through the window and kidnapped her."

"And you have the gall to say this to my face?"

"I do not fear my enemies."

"I'll snap you like a reed."

"The Thugs will have their revenge."

"We shall see."

"Captain Corishant," the strangler said gravely, "The British may rule over India, but there are other more powerful forces lurking in the shadows. Crowned heads bow before the might of the goddess Kali; you will not escape her wrath!"

"There are no cowards in this room, Negapatnan. No one will be frightened by your threats."

"Fine words. I wonder if you'll be brave enough to repeat them the day you feel a noose tighten about your neck."

"I wonder if a good flogging will help you shed some of that insolence."

"So you plan to torture me?"

"Yes, if you do not tell me all you know. Answer my questions and I'll spare your life."

"Ah, you seek information... What kind of information?"

"I'm Ada Corishant's father."

"So?"

"I have not given up hope of finding her."

"That matters little to me."

"Negapatnan," said the captain, his voice cracking slightly, "Do you have a daughter?"

"No," replied the strangler.

"Have you ever loved someone?"

"No one but my goddess."

"I love my daughter; I'd sacrifice my life for her freedom. Negapatnan, tell me where she is, tell me where I can find her."

The Indian remained silent.

"I'll spare your life, Negapatnan."

Again there was no answer.

"I'll shower you with gold; I'll send you to Europe where you'll be safe from Kali's vengeance. I'll arrange a commission in the British army, I'll help you rise through the ranks, just tell me where I can find my Ada."

"Captain MacPherson," the strangler said coldly, "Does your regiment have a flag?"

"Yes, of course."

"Did you not swear allegiance to that flag?"

"Yes."

"Would you betray that oath?"

"Never!"

"Well, I've sworn to serve my goddess. The gold, freedom and honours you've offered me will not cause me to betray her. I will not tell you anything!"

At those words Captain MacPherson picked a whip up off the floor. His face had turned crimson, his eyes seethed with anger.

"Monster!" he exclaimed, enraged.

"Do not touch me with that whip, I'm of noble birth!" yelled the strangler, wrenching his chains.

The captain cracked the whip. The strangler roared in pain as blood gushed from his cheek.

"Kill me," he howled savagely, "Kill me, if you do not, I'll peel the flesh off your bones."

"I'll kill you; you have my word, but not just yet. Bhárata, drag him to the cellar."

"Shall I torture him?" asked the sergeant.

Captain MacPherson hesitated.

"No," he said. "Let him fast for twenty-four hours."

Bhárata grabbed the strangler by the waist and dragged him off, the prisoner not putting up any resistance.

Captain MacPherson tossed the whip aside and began to pace along the terrace.

"Patience," he murmured, gritting his teeth. "He'll confess everything

141

he knows. I'll rip out every word with a branding iron if I have to."

A formidable blare interrupted his thoughts. He stopped and quickly raised his head.

"Bhagavadi must have seen something!" he exclaimed.

He leaned over the railing. The dogs had started barking and the elephant's trunk was peering over the fence. It trumpeted once again, louder than before. Almost simultaneously, a shadow jumped through the air, dropped to the ground and disappeared among the grass three hundred metres from the bungalow.

The darkness prevented the captain from making out what it was.

"You there!" he yelled.

The sepoy on watch approached the terrace; his carbine at the ready.

"Captain…" he said, raising his head.

"Did you see anything?"

"Yes, Captain. Some kind of animal, but I couldn't get a clear look at it."

The shadow jumped up once again. The sepoy let out a cry of terror.

"A tiger!"

The captain fired at the beast as it leaped towards the jungle.

"Damn!" he exclaimed angrily.

At the sound of that blast, the feline came to a stop, roared menacingly and headed off into the bamboo with even greater speed.

"What's happening?" asked Bhárata, rushing towards the terrace.

"There's a tiger out there," replied the captain.

"A tiger! Impossible!"

"I saw it with my very eyes."

"There haven't been any around these parts for months; I thought we'd killed them all!"

"It appears we missed one."

"Did you hit it?"

"I don't think so."

"That beast could prove quite troublesome, Captain."

"It won't have the chance."

"We're going to hunt it down?"

The captain looked at his watch.

"It's three o'clock. Have them prepare Bhagavadi, we'll set off in an hour, within two we'll have that tiger's pelt."

Chapter 3
The Rescue

Dawn was colouring the eastern sky when Captain MacPherson and Bhárata descended into the courtyard armed with heavy-calibre carbines, pistols and double-edged, wide-bladed swords. A sepoy accompanied them, carrying two spare carbines and several pikes. Minutes later, they reached the enclosing wall, Bhagavadi stood at the gate, trumpeting loudly, surrounded by a half dozen mahouts.

Bhagavadi was one of the largest and most beautiful cumareà on the banks of the Ganges. Though not as tall as a merghi elephant, she was more energetic, with incredible strength; she had short stout legs, sharp tusks and a long powerful trunk. A hauda, or carriage, had been fastened to her back with thick chords and chains.

"Is everything ready?" asked Captain MacPherson.

"Yes, sir," replied the head mahout.

"And the scouts?"

"They've taken the dogs to the outskirts of the jungle."

One of the most skilled mahouts took his place astraddle Bhagavadi's neck; he was armed with an ankusa[12], and several long pikes.

Weapons in tow, Captain MacPherson, Bhárata and the sepoy climbed up into the hauda. Once the sun had risen above the Palmyra palms, the captain gave the signal to depart.

Excited by the mahout's voice the elephant quickly set off, grinding roots and barrelling through bushes, knocking down the trees and bamboo reeds blocking her path with vigorous swings of her trunk.

---

[12] An elephant goad, a short pole with a spike and a hook at one end.

Seated at the front of the hauda, carbine in hand, Captain MacPherson carefully scanned his surroundings; the tiger could have been anywhere.

A quarter of an hour later, they arrived at the outskirts of the jungle; masses of thorns and groves of bamboo trees stretched out before them.

Six sepoys armed with long poles, axes and rifles, awaited them with a pack of small hunting dogs.

"Anything to report?" asked the captain, leaning over the hauda's side.

"We've just found the tiger's tracks," replied the scout leader.

"Are they fresh?"

"Very; I'd guess the beast passed this way about half an hour ago."

"We'll head into the jungle. Unleash the hounds."

The dogs rushed in among the bamboo, following the tiger's tracks, barking furiously. Bhagavadi sniffed the air three times then headed into the jungle, smashing through the sea of vegetation with her chest.

"Keep your eyes open, Bhárata," said MacPherson.

"Seen anything, Captain?" asked a sergeant.

"No. The tiger could have retraced its steps and hidden among the bamboo. They're clever beasts; some are even brave enough to attack an elephant."

"Bhagavadi's no easy prey. She's trampled more than one tiger to death."

"Did you get a look at the beast?"

"Yes, it's huge. I can't remember the last time I saw a tiger as large or as agile."

"Oh!" exclaimed the Indian. "Then it could easily jump into the hauda."

"If we let it get close enough."

"Hear that, Captain!?!"

The dogs had started barking; they heard a roar followed by a whimper.

Bhárata shivered.

"The dogs have found it," he said.

"Sounds like they're not doing too well," added the sepoy, picking up his carbine.

Five hundred metres from them a flock of peacocks flew off, cawing in terror.

"Uzaka!" yelled the captain.

"Careful, sir!" replied the head scout. "The tiger's in a mood to fight."

"Sound the retreat."

Uzaka placed his bansi, a type of flute, to his nose and blew a sharp note. Moments later, the sepoys rushed back at full speed and took refuge behind the elephant.

"Be careful," said the Captain, "We'll advance cautiously. Bhárata, watch our left; I'll watch our right. We may be dealing with more than one beast."

The barking grew louder and more savage. Bhagavadi quickened her pace, advancing intrepidly towards a large thicket of bamboo.

When they had arrived to within a hundred metres of it they spotted the remains of a hunting dog strewn about the ground; it had been disembowelled with a single blow. The elephant halted and began to swing her trunk nervously.

"Bhagavadi senses it nearby," said MacPherson. "Make sure she doesn't retreat."

"Leave it to me, sir," replied the mahout.

A formidable roar thundered from the bamboo.

"Forward!" yelled Captain MacPherson, his fingers resting against the trigger of his carbine.

The mahout kicked the elephant with his foot. She snorted, rolled up her trunk and presented her sharp tusks.

She advanced ten or twelve paces then came to a stop. A giant tiger leaped from the bamboo with a formidable roar.

Captain MacPherson fired.

"Damn!" he yelled, annoyed.

The tiger had escaped the blast. It jumped up twice more then disappeared.

Bhárata fired into the thicket, but the bullet struck a wounded dog limping through the grass.

"Is that tiger possessed?" the captain asked, irritated. "That's the second time it's escaped my bullets."

Bhagavadi resumed her march, cautiously feeling her way forward with her trunk, pulling it back whenever she sensed danger. She advanced another hundred metres, following the dogs as they searched for the feline's tracks, then came to a stop, planting her legs down firmly. She began to tremble, puffing noisily.

A grove of sugarcane spread before her, less than twenty metres away. A blast of air heavy with the scent of wildlife reached the hunters' noses.

"Look!" yelled the captain.

The tiger had rushed out from among the sugarcane, racing towards the elephant with lightning speed. Bhagavadi immediately presented her tusks.

Having escaped the hunters' carbines, the tiger leaped at the elephant's forehead and tried to swipe at the mahout, who immediately jumped back in terror.

Just as it was about to lunge at his throat, a ramsinga sounded off in the distance. Without warning, the tiger jumped down and rushed towards the thicket.

"Fire!" yelled Captain MacPherson, emptying his carbine at the beast. The tiger let out a tremendous roar, fell, got back up, vaulted over the thicket and landed on the other side with a thud.

"It's not moving!" yelled Bhárata.

"Well done!" exclaimed the captain, putting down his carbine. "Lower the ladder."

The mahout obeyed. Once Captain MacPherson had reached the ground, he drew his knife and headed towards the bushes.

The tiger had not moved, but to his surprise, the captain did not spy any blood upon its fur.

Knowing that tigers often play dead to lure in their prey, he attempted to back away. It was too late.

The ramsinga sounded again. The tiger leaped to its feet, jumped at the captain and knocked him to the ground, its jaws open, ready to rip him apart.

Unable to move, Captain MacPherson cried out in desperation.

"Help!"

"Hold on!" thundered a voice.

An Indian rushed out of the thickets, grabbed the tiger by the tail and tossed it to one side.

A furious roar filled the air. The animal, crazed with rage, had immediately gotten up to attack the new enemy; but then suddenly without warning, it turned about and ran off at great speed, disappearing into the jungle.

Captain MacPherson, shaken but unharmed, immediately got to his feet, his face still pale from the attack.

An Indian stood five paces from him dressed in a yellow silk dugbah and a small turban embroidered with silver. A cashmere sash hung about his waist. Handsome, broad shouldered and well built, that man, who had so intrepidly faced the tiger, was completely unarmed. Arms crossed, a daring look in his eye, he studied the captain curiously.

"I believe I owe you my life," said the captain. "If you hadn't intervened, I'd be dead now."

"More than likely," smiled the newcomer.

"That was an incredible display of bravery; allow me to shake your hand."

Trembling slightly, MacPherson proffered his hand; the Indian shook it warmly.

"Your name, sir."

"Saranguy," replied the Indian.

"I shall never forget it."

A brief silence fell between the two men.

"How can I repay you?" asked the captain.

"There's no need, sir."

MacPherson drew a purse swollen with coins from his jacket and offered it to him. The Indian declined it nobly.

"I've no use for your money," he said.

"Are you rich?"

"Hardly. I hunt tigers in the Sundarbans."

"What brings you to this part of the jungle?"

"Tigers no longer prowl about the Black Jungle. I came north to look for others."

"Where are you headed?"

"I'm a wanderer; I go where I please."

"How would you like to work for me?"

The Indian's eyes flashed brightly.

"You've seen what I can do, I'd serve you well."

"Come, my friend, I think you'll enjoy my hospitality."

The captain was about to return to the elephant when he was struck by a sudden thought.

"What about the tiger?"

"It's probably a long way from here by now."

"You think we'll find it?"

"I doubt it. No matter, I'll kill it soon enough."

"Let's go back to the bungalow."

As they drew near the elephant, Bhárata, who had watched the rescue in stunned silence, rushed towards the captain.

"Are you injured, sir?" he asked anxiously.

"No, my friend," replied MacPherson. "But I wouldn't be alive if it weren't for this man."

"You're a good man," Bhárata said, addressing Saranguy. "I've never seen such bravery."

A smile was the Indian's only reply.

The three men climbed up into the hauda. They reached the bungalow a half hour later; several sepoys were waiting in front of the gate.

Saranguy frowned at the sight of those soldiers. He appeared uneasy and barely managed to suppress a look of displeasure. Fortunately, no one noticed that fleeting expression.

"Saranguy," said the captain, as Bhárata entered the villa, "If you're hungry, have them show you the kitchen; if you wish to sleep, choose whichever room takes your fancy, if you prefer to go hunting, you'll be given whatever weapons you desire."

"Thank you, sir," replied the Indian.

The captain entered the bungalow. Saranguy sat down next to the door. His face had grown serious, his eyes sparkled strangely. He appeared agitated, restless. Four times he got up to enter the bungalow, but always returned to his seat.

"Who knows what fate has in store for him," he murmured dully, "It's strange but my heart leaped at the sight of him. His voice... his face... he resembles... bah... best not to dwell on it..."

He fell silent.

"I wonder if the strangler's here," he murmured. "What if he isn't?"

He got up for the fifth time and set off for a walk, a deep frown forming on his brow. Passing by a tall wooden fence, he thought he heard several voices coming from the other side. He stopped and quickly raised his head. Still uncertain, he looked about to make sure he was alone then dropped to the ground and crawled towards the wall, straining his ears to listen.

"You'll see," said a voice, "Captain MacPherson will make that scoundrel talk."

"Impossible," said another voice. "Those wretched Thugs aren't afraid of death. I've seen a dozen of them face a firing squad without flinching."

"Captain MacPherson's methods are impossible to resist."

"Our prisoner's no coward. They could flay his skin layer by layer, and he wouldn't utter a single word."

Drawn by those words Saranguy placed his ear against the wall.

"Where's he being kept?" asked the first voice.

"In the cellar," replied the other.

"He'll try to escape."

"Impossible, the walls are too thick, besides he's well guarded."

"He won't do it alone, he'll probably have help."

"You think the Thugs are keeping an eye on us?"

"Last night the sepoys spotted something moving about the shadows."

"You're making me nervous."

"You're worried?"

"Their nooses are infallible."

"You won't have to fear them for much longer. Once Negapatnan reveals the location of their lair, we'll attack and destroy them all."

At the sound of that name, Saranguy jumped to his feet excitedly. A sinister smile spread across his lips as he fixed his eyes upon the bungalow.

"Ah!" he whispered. "Negapatnan is here! The wretches are going to be pleased."

Chapter 4
The Thugs' Request

Night had fallen.

Captain MacPherson had not appeared throughout the day and nothing of importance happened at the bungalow.

Having explored the grounds, casually attempting to eavesdrop on every conversation, Saranguy stretched out behind a thick bush fifty paces from the main house and pretended to fall asleep.

From time to time, however, he cautiously raised his head and rapidly scanned the surrounding countryside, as if expecting someone to appear.

An hour passed. The moon rose over the horizon, casting its dim light upon the jungle and the river, the waters murmuring dully as they crashed against the shores. A jackal cry broke the silence. Saranguy shot to his feet and looked around uneasily.

"Finally," he murmured, shuddering.

Two bright green dots appeared in a thicket a hundred paces away.

Saranguy placed his fingers to his lips and whistled softly. The two dots drew nearer, a growl filled the air.

"Darma!" said the Indian.

The tiger lowered her head, crouched down and silently crept forward. She halted before the hunter, purring softly.

"Are you injured?" he asked tenderly.

The tiger opened her mouth and licked the Indian's hands and face.

"My poor, Darma, you ran a great risk," Saranguy continued affectionately.

He placed a hand beneath the tiger's neck and removed a small roll of red paper fastened to her neck by a thin silk thread.

Hands trembling, he opened it and quickly scanned its contents. A single line of Sanskrit met his eyes.

Come, the messenger has arrived.

He shivered as several drops of sweat formed upon his brow.

"Come, Darma," he said.

He cast one last glance at the bungalow, crawled three or four hundred metres forward, and headed into the forest, followed by the tiger.

Taking a narrow path hidden among the vegetation, he walked quickly for twenty minutes then came to a sudden stop and summoned the tiger to his side.

A man jumped up from behind a bush twenty paces before him, training his rifle on the Indian's chest.

"Who goes there?" he shouted.

"Kali," replied Saranguy.

"Advance."

As Saranguy drew near, the guard studied him carefully.

"Yes?"

"I've come to see Kugli."

"Follow me."

The Indian shouldered his carbine and went off without another word. Saranguy and Darma followed.

"Did you see Captain MacPherson?" the guide asked a short while later.

"Yes."

"What's he up to?"

"I don't know; I haven't seen him since this morning."

"Did you learn anything about Negapatnan?"

"Yes, he's the captain's prisoner."

"Do you know where he's being held?"

"In the bungalow's cellar."

"The captain's a cautious man."

"So it would seem."

"You'll find a way to free him."

"What!?!" exclaimed Saranguy. "Who told you that?"

"Never mind, keep walking."

The Indian fell silent and headed into a grove of bamboo trees. Every few paces he would stop and examine the tara palms dotting the path.

"What are you looking for?" Saranguy asked, surprised.

"Notches to point the way."

"Kugli's moved?"

"Yes, the British found his hut."

"Already?"

"Captain MacPherson has excellent bloodhounds. Keep your eyes open, Saranguy; they may turn on you when you least expect it."

He stopped, put his hands to his lips and howled like a jackal.

A similar howl came in reply.

"The way is clear," said the Indian. "Follow this path to the hut, it's not far. I'll wait for you here."

Saranguy set off. As he made his way forward, he spotted numerous Indians hiding among the trees, rumaals about their waists, carbines at the ready.

"We're certainly well protected," he murmured. "No one will disturb us."

He soon arrived before a large wooden hut. Several openings had been carved into the walls, just wide enough for the barrel of a carbine. The roof was thatched with latanie leaves and crowned by a statue of the goddess Kali.

"Who goes there?" asked an Indian, guarding the entrance, armed with a carbine, dagger and noose.

"Kali," Saranguy replied.

"Pass."

The hunter entered. A torch burned brightly, filling the room with its smoky light.

An Indian as tall as the grim Suyodhana lay on a mat, Kali's mark proudly born on his chest. His hard cruel face was the color of brass and framed by a thick black beard. His eyes sparkled darkly.

"Hello, Kugli," said Saranguy upon entering, a trace of sadness lining his voice.

"Ah, it's you, my friend!" replied the Thug, rising to his feet. "I was beginning to grow impatient."

"The bungalow is quite a good distance from here."

"I know, my friend. How did it go?"

"It couldn't have gone better! Darma played her role magnificently. Had I not been there, the captain would not have survived."

"A clever beast that tiger of yours."

"Yes."

"So, now you're in the captain's service..."

"Yes."

"In what capacity?"

"As a hunter."

"Does he suspect anything?"

"No."

"Does he know you've gone into the jungle?"

"I don't know. He told me I could come and go as I pleased."

"Keep your guard up at all times. That man has a hundred eyes."

"I know."

"Tell me about Negapatnan."

"They brought him to the bungalow last night."

"I know. We've been monitoring the captain's every move. Where are they hiding him?"

"In the cellar."

"Have you been in it?"

"Not yet, but I will. The walls are thick and the door is guarded by an armed sepoy at all times."

"You've obtained more information than I expected. Allow me to congratulate you; you're cleverer than I thought."

"Thanks," Saranguy replied, keeping the irony out of his voice.

"Do you know if Negapatnan has given them any information?"

"I have no idea."

"If he talks, we're done for."

"Don't you trust him?" asked Saranguy, a light trace of sarcasm lining his voice.

"Negapatnan is a great leader, he would never betray us; however, Captain MacPherson is no stranger to torture. Now, to business."

Saranguy shuddered.

"You have my undivided attention," he said as they sat down.

"Do you know why I've summoned you?"

"To discuss…"

"Ada Corishant."

At the sound of that name, the sullen look on Saranguy's face disappeared; his eyes sparkled as a heavy sigh escaped his lips.

"Ada! My Ada!" he exclaimed hoarsely. "Tell me all you know, Kugli, if you knew how I've suffered!"

The Thug looked at the distraught Indian. He chuckled darkly as an evil smile spread across his lips.

"Tremal-Naik," he said sinisterly, "do you remember the night you hid in that well with your Ada and the Maratha?"

"Yes," Saranguy, or more precisely, Tremal-Naik the hunter, replied hoarsely.

"We took you prisoner. Suyodhana held your fate in his hands."

"I know. Why remind me of this now?"

"I'll be brief. The Thugs had sentenced you to death; you and Kammamuri were to be strangled, the Guardian sacrificed on the pyre. Suyodhana, however, stayed that sentence. You had proven your resourcefulness on several occasions and he pardoned you, provided you agreed to serve us."

"I know all this."

"You loved our Guardian. We promised no harm would come to her in exchange for you loyalty. Our goddess Kali now offers her to you."

Tremal-Naik jumped to his feet, transfigured.

"Is that true?" he asked.

"It's true," said Kugli, marking each word.

"She'll be my bride?"

"She'll be your bride. But only if you accept certain conditions."

"Whatever they are, I accept. I'd set India ablaze for her."

"You'll have to kill."

"I'll kill."

"You'll have to arrange an escape."

"I will, even if I have to attack a garrison."

"Excellent."

He drew a piece of paper from his sash, unfolded it and carefully studied it for several minutes.

"As you know," he said, "the Thugs love Negapatnan. He's a brave leader. You'll free him then... Suyodhana has one final request."

"Consider it granted," said Tremal-Naik, shuddering unexpectedly.

Kugli remained silent, his eyes fixed on the hunter.

"Well?" stammered Tremal-Naik.

"If you wish to obtain Ada's hand, you must kill Captain MacPherson."

"Captain..."

"MacPherson," said Kugli, his lips parting in a cold smile.

"A high price."

"The only price."

"And if I refuse?"

"You'd never see her again. She'd be burned alive, sacrificed to Kali; Kammamuri would be tortured and strangled. What's your answer?"

"My life is Ada's. I accept."

"Excellent. Remember, you must free Negapatnan first."

"I will."

"We'll keep our eyes on you. If you need any help, contact me."

"I'll manage on my own."

"As you wish; you may go."

Tremal-Naik did not move.

"You wish to add something?" asked Kugli.

"May I see my beloved?"

"No."

"Are you that cold hearted?"

"Bring me the captain's head then… the Guardian… will be your bride. Now go, Tremal-Naik."

Hiding his uneasiness, the hunter turned and walked out of the hut.

Chapter 5
The Escape

The stars were beginning to fade when Tremal-Naik, still shaken by the conversation with the strangler, reached Captain McPherson's bungalow. Sergeant Bhárata was leaning against the door, yawning from time to time as he took in the fresh morning air.

"Hey, Saranguy!" he yelled. "Where've you been?"

That cry abruptly tore Tremal-Naik from his thoughts. He turned about to see if Darma had followed him, but the clever tiger had stopped at the outskirts of the jungle and disappeared among the bamboo.

"Where've you been, my friend?" Bhárata repeated, advancing towards him.

"The jungle," replied Tremal-Naik, composing himself.

"At night, alone?"

"Why not?"

"Tigers?"

"I'm not afraid of them."

"Snakes? Rhinos?"

"Didn't see any."

"You're a brave man, my friend..."

"So I've been told."

"Anything to report?"

"A couple of tigers, but they kept their distance."

"Any men?"

Tremal-Naik started.

"Men!" he exclaimed, feigning surprise. "Who could possibly be out roaming the jungle in the middle of the night?"

"Ever heard of the Thugs?"

"The stranglers?"

"Yes."

"They're nearby?" asked Tremal-Naik, feigning terror.

"Yes, and they'll kill you if you fall into their hands."

"Why are they here?"

"It just so happens that Captain MacPherson is their most ruthless enemy."

"Really."

"He's vowed to destroy them."

"I'll join you. I hate those wretches."

"We won't turn away a man as brave as you. You can help us patrol the jungle, I'll even assign you to guard the strangler we're holding prisoner."

"Ah!" exclaimed Tremal-Naik, unable to hide the joy in his eyes. "You've captured one of them?"

"Yes, one of their leaders."

"What's his name?"

"Negapatnan."

"And you want me to guard him?"

"Your strength will be of great service to us."

"My fist will keep him in check," said Tremal-Naik.

"Come. We're going to interrogate Negapatnan; we may have need of your strength."

"What for?" Tremal-Naik asked uneasily.

"The captain may need to get tough with him."

"So, I'll be his jailer and, if need be, his torturer."

"You catch on quickly, Saranguy. Follow me."

They entered the bungalow and walked up to the terrace. Captain MacPherson was lying in a hammock, smoking a cigarette.

"Any news, Bhárata?" he asked.

"No, Captain, but I found a new ally; he's ready to join us."

"Saranguy?"

"Yes, Captain," replied Tremal-Naik, speaking with natural hatred.

160

"Welcome. Be warned though, you'll be risking your life."

"If I can risk it tracking tigers, I can risk it fighting Thugs."

"You're a good man, Saranguy."

"Thank you, Captain."

"How did Negapatnan spend the night?" asked MacPherson, turning to address the sergeant.

"He slept like someone whose conscience is at rest. That devil of a man is made of steel."

"We'll break him. Bring him here; we'll start the interrogation immediately."

The sergeant turned and left. A short while later he returned with Negapatnan. Though his arms were bound tightly, the Thug appeared at ease, a smile upon his lips. His eyes immediately fell upon Tremal-Naik, who had gone to stand behind the captain.

"Well, my dear friend," Captain MacPherson said sarcastically, "How did you sleep last night?"

"Like a rock," replied the strangler.

"Have you decided to cooperate?"

"You'll get no information from me."

The captain's hand raced to the hilt of his sabre.

"You snakes are all the same!" he yelled.

"It would appear so," said the strangler.

"I wouldn't have made up my mind so quickly. I possess some terrible means of persuasion."

"I do not fear them."

"I'll make you beg for death."

"You can try."

"We'll see if you still feel that way when you're writhing in pain."

"You may begin at your leisure."

The captain turned pale then a wave of blood rushed to his face.

"You refuse to speak?" he asked, his voice choked with anger.

"Not a word."

"That's your final decision?"

"Absolutely."

"Very well then, we'll begin. Bhárata…"

The sergeant approached.

"Tie him to the pole in the cellar."

"Yes, Captain."

"When he starts to fall asleep, jab him awake with a needle. If he still hasn't spoken in three days, take a whip to him. If his stubbornness persists, boil some oil and pour it over his wounds."

"It shall be done, Captain. Give me a hand, Saranguy."

The sergeant and Tremal-Naik dragged the strangler away. Negapatnan had listened to those instructions without flinching.

They descended a long spiral staircase and entered a large, arched cellar, lit by a small window defended by thick iron bars. Once the strangler had been tied to a pole in the centre of the room, Bhárata pulled out four long needles and placed them on the ground.

"Who's going to stand guard?" asked Tremal-Naik.

"You'll take the first watch. A sepoy will come to relieve you this evening."

"Very well."

"If he closes his eyes, jab him hard."

"Understood," replied the hunter.

The sergeant went back upstairs. Tremal-Naik watched him disappear. Once all was silent, he sat down before the strangler. Negapatnan had been studying him with great interest.

"Listen," said Tremal-Naik, lowering his voice.

"Do you have something to say as well?" Negapatnan asked mockingly.

"Do you know Kugli?"

The strangler started.

"Kugli!" he exclaimed. "Never heard that name before."

"You're cautious, that's good. Do you know Suyodhana?"

"Who are you?" asked Negapatnan, a look of terror spreading across his face.

"A Thug."

"You're lying."

162

"It's the truth; I'll prove it to you. Rajmangal."

The prisoner barely suppressed a cry.

"You're one of us?" he asked.

"Haven't I just proven it to you?"

"Why did you come here?"

"To rescue you."

"To rescue me?"

"Yes."

"How?"

"Leave it to me; you'll be free by midnight."

"Are we escaping together?"

"No, I have to remain behind. There's something else I must do."

"A vendetta?"

"Perhaps," Tremal-Naik said bleakly. "That's enough talk for now, we'll wait for it to get dark."

He sat down at the foot of the staircase and patiently began to wait for nightfall.

The day passed uneventfully as the sun slowly made its way across the sky. Once it disappeared beneath the horizon, darkness quickly filled the cellar. The moment to act had arrived; the sepoy would relieve him in less than an hour.

"And now to work," said Tremal-Naik, drawing two steel files from his sash.

"What's the plan?" Negapatnan asked excitedly.

"We're going to cut through those bars," replied Tremal-Naik.

"Won't they realize you helped me escape?"

"Not if we follow my plan."

He untied the prisoner's bonds then vigorously set to work, trying not to make any noise.

Two of the three bars had already been cut away, when Tremal-Naik heard footsteps coming towards the stairs.

"Stop!" he said quickly. "Someone's coming."

"The sepoy?"

"Must be."

"We're done for."

"Not yet. Are you good with a noose?"

"I never miss."

Tremal-Naik pulled out a rumaal he had kept hidden in his dugbah and gave it to the Thug.

"Stand by the door," he said, drawing his dagger. "Kill whoever appears."

Negapatnan quickly fashioned the noose and the two took position on opposite sides of the door. The footsteps were drawing nearer. Light fell upon the stairs as the sepoy appeared, hand resting on the hilt of his scimitar.

"Careful, Negapatnan," whispered Tremal-Naik.

The Thug's face darkened. His eyes flashed sinisterly as his lips parted in an evil smile.

The sepoy halted on the landing.

"Saranguy!" he yelled.

"Come down," said Tremal-Naik. "I can't see you."

"Okay," he replied and entered the wine cellar.

Negapatnan was ready for him. The noose whistled through the air and tightened around the soldier's neck. The sepoy fell without a sound.

"Should I strangle him?" asked the Thug, resting his foot on the fallen man's chest.

"We have no choice," Tremal-Naik said coldly.

Negapatnan tightened the noose. The sepoy's eyes bulged and his tongue shot out of his mouth as his skin turned a pale brown. His arms trembled then stiffened. He was dead.

"May the goddess Kali accept this sacrifice," said the fanatic, drawing back the noose.

"Hurry, before someone else comes down."

The two men returned to the window and quickly cut away the last bar.

"Is the hole large enough?" asked Tremal-Naik.

"I've squeezed through tighter."

"Excellent. Now tie me up."

The Thug looked at him in surprise.

"Tie you up? Why?" he asked.

"So they don't suspect I'm in league with you."

"Yes, of course."

Tremal-Naik sat down beside the sepoy's body; Negapatnan quickly bound and gagged him.

"You're a good man," said the Thug. "If you ever need a favour, do not hesitate to ask."

He picked up the sepoy's pistol, rushed towards the opening, climbed through it and disappeared.

Within seconds a rifle thundered and a voice yelled out, "To arms! The prisoner's escaping!"

Chapter 6
Yuma

At that cry, Tremal-Naik shot to his knees. A second blast sounded, then a third, then a fourth. A loud cry thundered from the bungalow; the hunter grew uneasy.

"There, towards the jungle!" yelled a voice.

"To arms!" yelled another.

"Ready the elephant!"

"Everyone to arms!"

A trumpet blared above the cacophony of neighing horses and rushing footsteps.

His brow beaded with sweat, Tremal-Naik listened, holding his breath.

"Run, Negapatnan, run!" he murmured. "If they catch you, we're done for."

With a desperate effort he got to his feet and tried to jump towards the window, struggling against the ropes. The sound of rushing footsteps stopped him.

"They're coming down," he murmured, dropping to the ground. "I've got to remain calm. Negapatnan may be able to reach Kugli."

He began to writhe, pretending to struggle against the rope, filling the air with muffled cries. And just in time.

Within seconds, Bhárata came racing down the steps four at a time, rushed into the cellar, and let out a frightening cry.

"Escaped!?! Escaped!?!" he yelled, his eyes racing to the pole.

He leaped towards the window. A second cry erupted from his quavering lips.

"The wretch!"

He cast a despairing look about the room and spotted Tremal-Naik twisting on the ground. He was beside the hunter in a flash.

"Alive!" he exclaimed, removing his gag.

"Wretched Thug!" Tremal-Naik yelled hoarsely. "Where's that dog? I'll rip out his heart!"

"What happened? How did he escape? Why are you tied up?" shouted Bhárata, crazed with anger.

"We've been tricked, Great Shiva! I fell into that trap like an idiot!"

"What happened? How did he manage to escape? Who cut through those bars?"

"Them."

"Who?"

"Thugs."

"Thugs?!?"

"Yes, they helped him escape."

"Impossible! No Thugs could have gotten this close."

"And yet they did. I saw them with my very eyes; it's a miracle I wasn't strangled like that poor sepoy."

"They strangled a sepoy?"

"Yes, the man you sent to relieve me."

"Tell me everything, Saranguy, what happened?"

"The sun had set," said Tremal-Naik, "I'd been sitting opposite the prisoner for three hours, neither one of us had moved a muscle, his eyes locked on mine. Suddenly, I felt my eyelids grow heavy and my mind turn numb. I battled the drowsiness for a long time, but despite my efforts, I fell asleep. When I awakened, I discovered I'd been bound and gagged; the bars from the window were on the floor. Two Thugs were strangling a poor sepoy. I tried to writhe free, to yell out, but it was impossible. Once their victim was dead, the Thugs climbed through the window and disappeared."

"And Negapatnan?"

"He was the first to escape."

"What caused you to fall asleep?"

"I have no idea."

"Did they drop anything through the window?"

"I didn't see anything."

"They must've used some kind of sleeping potion."

"It seems likely."

"We've got to recapture Negapatnan."

"I'm a very good tracker."

"I know; you'll set off immediately. He must not escape."

"I'll go."

Bhárata finished untying the rope. They walked up the stairs and went out of the bungalow.

"Which way did he go?" asked Tremal-Naik, grabbing a rifle.

"He headed towards the jungle. Follow that path; you'll spot his tracks. There's no time to lose, that scoundrel must be a good way off by now."

Tremal-Naik slung the rifle strap around his shoulder and ran off towards the jungle. Bhárata watched him disappear into the trees then frowned, disturbed by a sudden thought.

"What if his story isn't true?" he wondered aloud. "Nysa! Nysa!"

An Indian studying the ground near the window rushed to his side.

"Yes, Sergeant," he said.

"Did you examine the tracks?" asked Bhárata.

"Yes, sir."

"How many men came out of the cellar?"

"Just one, sir."

Bhárata started.

"You're sure?"

"Positive, Sergeant. Negapatnan left alone."

"Very well. See that man heading towards the jungle?"

"Yes, that's Saranguy."

"Follow him; I want to know where he goes."

"Leave it to me," replied the Indian.

He waited for Tremal-Naik to disappear into the forest, then set off, hiding as best he could among the bamboo trees. Satisfied, Bhárata went back into the bungalow and found the captain pacing nervously about the terrace, venting his rage with deafening imprecations.

"Well?" he asked, his eyes resting upon the sergeant.

"We've been betrayed, Captain."

"Betrayed! By who?"

"Saranguy."

"Saranguy! Impossible! He saved my life!"

"I have proof."

"Tell me everything!"

Bhárata quickly related all he had learned. Captain MacPherson could not contain his surprise.

"Saranguy a traitor!" he exclaimed. "But why didn't he go off with Negapatnan?"

"We'll know soon enough, Captain. I've ordered Nysa to keep an eye on him. The scoundrel won't escape."

"If what you say is true, I'll have him shot."

"I won't allow it, Captain."

"Pardon me!?!"

"We're going to make him talk. He'll know as much as Negapatnan."

The captain fell silent and fixed his eyes on the jungle once again. Bhárata cast his eyes towards the river, straining his ears to catch the slightest sound.

Three long hours passed, but not a cry or a discharge broke the silence. Impatient for news, Captain MacPherson was about to leave the terrace and head into the jungle, when Bhárata cried out triumphantly.

"What is it?"

"Look down there, Captain," said the sergeant.

"One of our men is rushing towards us."

"It's Nysa."

"But he's alone. Could Saranguy have escaped?"

"I don't think so. Nysa would not have returned."

The Indian was racing towards the bungalow with the speed of an arrow, looking back over his shoulder from time to time.

"Up here, Nysa!" yelled Bhárata.

"Hurry, hurry!" yelled the captain, no longer able to contain himself.

The Indian ran up the stairs and quickly reached the terrace, panting heavily. His eyes shone with joy.

"Well?" asked the captain and the sergeant, rushing to meet him.

"I've learned the truth. Saranguy's a Thug!"

"You're certain?" asked the captain, his voice trembling slightly.

"Yes, sir. I have proof."

"Tell us everything you saw. That wretch will pay for Negapatnan's escape."

"I followed his tracks to the jungle," said Nysa. "Once there they disappeared, but it didn't take me long to find them again a hundred metres further on. I increased my pace and a short time later I spotted him. He was walking quickly but cautiously, often looking back and stopping to place an ear to the ground. Twenty minutes later, he let out a cry and an Indian jumped out of a bush. It was a Thug; I saw the tattoo on his chest and the rumaal about his waist. I couldn't hear their conversation, but before they parted, Saranguy yelled out: 'Tell Kugli I'm going back to the bungalow, he'll have the head in a few days.' I'd learned enough and I ran back here. Saranguy cannot be far behind."

"What did I tell you, Captain?" asked Bhárata.

MacPherson did not reply. Arms crossed, grim faced, he appeared deep in thought.

"Who could this Kugli be?" he said after a few minutes had passed.

"I don't know," replied Nysa.

"Undoubtedly a Thug leader," said Bhárata.

"Whose head do you think those wretches were referring to?"

"I don't know, Captain. He did not give details."

"One of ours?"

"It's probable," said the sergeant.

The captain became even more sullen.

"I'd wager he was talking about mine," he murmured. "What do you suggest we do with Saranguy?"

"Make him speak."

"Do you think we'll succeed?"

"You'd be amazed what fire can do."

170

"Thugs are more stubborn than mules."

"It'll be easy to make him talk, Captain," said Nysa. "I'll do it."

"What?"

"All we need is some lemonade."

"Lemonade! Have you gone mad, Nysa?"

"No, Captain!" exclaimed Bhárata. "Nysa is quite correct. I've heard of that concoction."

"It can make anyone talk," said Nysa. "And it's simple to make. A few drops of lemon juice and a small quantity of opium mixed with the sap of a yuma plant."

"Go prepare this lemonade," said the captain. "If it works, I'll give you twenty rupees."

The Indian did not wait to be told twice. A few minutes later he returned with three large glasses of lemonade resting on a tray of Chinese porcelain. One of the glasses contained the mixture.

His timing was excellent. Tremal-Naik had appeared at the edge of the jungle accompanied by four trackers. Their expressions made it clear Negapatnan had not been found.

"No matter," murmured the captain. "Saranguy will tell us all we need to know. Best keep our guard up, Bhárata; we don't want that rascal to suspect anything. Nysa, have someone replace the bars on the cellar window. We're about to have a new guest."

As the guard was leaving, Tremal-Naik arrived before the bungalow.

"Hey Saranguy!" yelled Bhárata, leaning over the railing. "How did it go? Did you find the rascal?"

Tremal-Naik shook his head.

"No, Sergeant," he said. "We lost his tracks."

"Come up and give us your report."

Not suspecting anything, Tremal-Naik did not wait for the invitation to be repeated and was soon standing before the small group.

Captain MacPherson had taken a seat by the small table that bore the tray of lemonade.

"Well then, my friend," he said with a good-natured smile, "No sign of the rascal?"

"No, Captain. We looked everywhere."

"Any luck finding his tracks?"

"We followed them for quite a distance; but suddenly lost all trace of them. It's almost as if that damned Negapatnan crossed the forest swinging from tree to tree."

"Has everyone returned?"

"Four sepoys are still out searching the jungle."

"How far did you go?"

"All the way to the outskirts of the forest."

"You must be tired. Have some lemonade."

He offered a glass; Tremal-Naik emptied it in one shot.

"Tell me, Saranguy," continued the captain, "Are there any Thugs in the forest?"

"I don't think so," replied Tremal-Naik.

"You've never seen any lurking around?"

"Never!" exclaimed Tremal-Naik.

"Yet one of my men told me he saw you speaking with a suspicious looking Indian."

Tremal-Naik looked at him, but did not reply. The hunter's eyes had begun to shine and his face had grown darker.

"You wish to say something?" asked Captain MacPherson.

"Thug!" stammered the hunter, waving his arms crazily and roaring with laughter. "Talk to a Thug? Me?"

"The lemonade's beginning to take effect," Bhárata whispered into the captain's ear.

"Yes, you talked to a Thug!" urged the captain.

"Yes, I remember, I spoke to a Thug at the edge of the forest. Ha! Ha! They thought I was looking for Negapatnan. What fools! Ha! Ha! To think I'd chase after Negapatnan! After I worked so hard to help him escape… Ha! Ha!"

Overcome by an almost feverish joy, Tremal-Naik began to laugh uncontrollably.

"It won't be long now, Captain!" exclaimed Bhárata.

"It's like he's gone mad," said the captain.

"There's no need to worry, sir, since he's in the mood to talk, let's chat with him."

"You're right. Saranguy, what…"

"Saranguy!" interrupted the prisoner, continuing to laugh. "My name's not Saranguy, I… you're so stupid, my friend… my name's Tremal-Naik… Tremal-Naik, the Hunter. Ever been to the Black Jungle? It's beautiful. What fools you are!"

"I am a fool," said the captain, "So your real name is Tremal-Naik? Why did you change it?"

"To avoid suspicion. I wanted to enter your employ."

"Why?"

"The Thugs wanted me to. They spared my life… Do you know the Guardian of the Temple of the East? No? She's beautiful, very, very beautiful… She'll be my bride… Brahma, Shiva and Vishnu will go mad with envy."

"And where is this Guardian of the Temple of the East?"

"Far from here, very far."

"Where?"

"I won't tell you. You might steal her from me. The Thugs have promised her to me… she'll be my bride… I'm strong… courageous… I'll do whatever they ask to have her. I freed Negapatnan… like they asked…"

"You have another mission to complete?"

"Mission? Ha! I have to… bring them a head… Ha! Ha! It makes me laugh like a fool."

"Why?" asked MacPherson, his surprise increasing with each revelation.

"Because it's yours!… Ha! Ha!…"

"Mine!" exclaimed the captain, jumping to his feet. "My head?"

"Yes… yes…"

"Who do you have to deliver it to?"

"Suyodhana!"

"Who?"

"What? You don't know him? He's the leader of the Thugs."

173

"And you know where his lair is?"

"Yes, of course."

"Where?"

"On... on..."

"Speak, tell me!" yelled the captain, jumping towards the hunter and grabbing his wrists tightly.

"Curious?"

"Yes, I must know!"

"What if I didn't want to tell you?"

The captain, his anger getting the best of him, grabbed the hunter by the waist and raised him in the air.

"If you don't tell me, I'll throw you into the river," he said.

"You're joking. Ha! Ha!..."

"Tell me where Suyodhana is!"

"What a fool you are! Where else but Rajmangal?"

"Say it again, say it again!"

"Rajmangal! Rajmangal!"

Captain MacPherson let out a cry, dropped the hunter and fell back into his chair murmuring, "Finally..."

Chapter 7
Flowers

When Tremal-Naik awoke he found himself locked in the cellar, his wrists shackled to the pole in the centre of the room. The small window had been repaired, and light filtered through a double row of thick iron bars. At first he thought he was having a bad dream, but quickly realized he was in fact a prisoner. He vaguely remembered Negapatnan, his escape, and the lemonade, but nothing more. Despite his courage, he felt a sudden pang of fear.

"Who could have betrayed me?" he murmured, shuddering.

Though still groggy he tried to stand up, lost his balance and fell back to the ground.

The sound of a door opening reached his ears.

"Who's there?" he asked.

"Bhárata," replied the sergeant, drawing near.

"Finally!" exclaimed Tremal-Naik. "Why have you imprisoned me?"

"You're a Thug."

"What?"

"Yes, Saranguy."

"You're lying!"

"No, you talked, you confessed."

"When?"

"A little while ago."

"Have you gone mad, Bhárata?"

"No, Saranguy, you drank some yuma and confessed."

Tremal-Naik's eyes widened with fear. He remembered the lemonade the captain had offered him.

"Wretches!" he exclaimed, as a slight feeling of desperation crept into his bones.

"Interested in saving your life?" said Bhárata, after a brief silence.

"Make me an offer," Tremal-Naik replied hoarsely.

"Tell us everything you know about the Thugs and perhaps the captain will spare you."

"I cannot, they'll kill the woman I love."

"What story is this? Tell me."

"It would be of no use!" Tremal-Naik exclaimed savagely. "Curse the wretches!"

"Listen to me, Saranguy. We know the Thugs' secret lair is on Rajmangal, but we don't know how to find it or how many men we'll have to fight. If you tell us, the captain will spare you."

"What do you plan to do to the Thugs?" Tremal-Naik asked hoarsely.

"We'll shoot them all."

"Even if there are women among them?"

"They'll be the first."

"Why? What fault do they have?"

"They're worse than the men. They serve the goddess Kali."

"You're wrong, Bhárata! You're wrong!"

Tremal-Naik's face had become extremely pale, almost ashen, his chest heaved mightily.

"I'll tell you all I know if you promise to spare one of those women."

"Impossible! Taking them alive would cost us torrents of blood. We'll drown them all in their cavern."

"My fiancée is in there!" Tremal-Naik exclaimed desperately. "Let her die? No! No! I will not tell you anything. Kill me, torture me, hand me over to the British authorities; do with me as you wish, but I will not utter a single word. The Thugs are powerful, they'll defend my beloved."

"Who is this woman?"

"I cannot tell you."

"Saranguy," said Bhárata his voice louder, "tell me who she is."

"Never."

"Is she Indian or European?"

"Not another word."

"She's probably a fanatic like the others."

Tremal-Naik did not reply.

"Fine," repeated the sergeant. "We'll take you to Calcutta in three or four days."

The prisoner started. He watched the sergeant leave the room then quickly fixed his eyes upon the window.

"I must escape tonight," he murmured, "Or all is lost."

The day passed uneventfully, his only visits from guards bringing him his meals.

Once the sun had disappeared behind the jungle and darkness had grown thick in the cellar, Tremal-Naik began to feel at ease. Fearing someone would enter unexpectedly, he did not move for three long hours, then, reassured by the silence, he began to prepare for his escape.

Indians are expert knot makers; it takes a lot of practice to acquire the skills to undo them. Fortunately, Tremal-Naik had good teeth and prodigious strength.

With a powerful jerk he loosened the chord restraining his head, then, patiently drew his right wrist to his mouth and, ignoring the pain, began to gnaw at the rope. Once he had freed his arm, the other bindings were severed in minutes.

He got up, stretched his numb limbs, then quietly walked to the window and peered outside. The moon had not yet risen, but the sky was full of stars. Gusts of fresh air, carrying the rich fragrances of a thousand different flowers, swept through that small opening. All was quiet; the grounds appeared deserted.

The prisoner grabbed one of the bars and pulled; it bent slightly, but did not give way.

"Escape appears impossible," he murmured.

He quickly searched around for something he could use to remove the bars, but not a single tool had been left behind.

"I'm done for," he murmured nervously.

He silently approached the door, but a growl stopped him in his tracks. It had come from outside.

177

He turned his head towards the window; two bright green dots sparkled between the bars.

"Darma!" he murmured, barely containing his excitement.

The tiger growled again. Tremal-Naik approached the window and reached for her paw.

"Well done, Darma, I knew you'd come to visit your master!" he exclaimed. "There's still a chance."

He ran to a corner where he had spotted a scrap of paper. He tore a splinter from the pole, bit one of his fingers until it bled, and quickly wrote the following lines:

> I've been betrayed. They've imprisoned me in Negapatnan's cell. Help me immediately or all is lost.
>
> Tremal-Naik

He rolled up the paper, returned to the window and fastened it to the small rope about the tiger's neck.

"Quickly, Darma, find the Thugs," he said. "Your master is in great danger."

The great cat shook her head and ran off with the speed of an arrow.

"Run," said the Indian, his eyes fixed upon her. "The Thugs will help me escape."

A long hour passed. Tremal-Naik convulsively grabbed at the bars, anxiously awaiting Darma's return. Suddenly, he spotted the tiger on the outskirts of the field, bounding towards the bungalow.

"What if they see her?" he murmured, nervously.

Fortunately, Darma reached the window undetected. She carried a large bundle round her neck; so large that Tremal-Naik struggled to pull it through the bars.

It contained a letter, a dagger, a revolver, a rumaal, some ammunition and some flowers carefully sealed in two crystal jars.

"What could these flowers be for," he murmured surprised.

He opened the letter, held it up to the moonlight streaming through the window and read:

> We're surrounded by several battalions of sepoys, but we've sent one of our men to assist you. You must escape; we're in grave danger. I've enclosed two bunches of flowers. The white ones induce sleep; the red ones counter the effect. Sedate your guards and keep the red ones close at hand. Once you're free, make your way into the bungalow and cut off the captain's head. Nagor will signal his presence once he arrives.
>
> Hurry,
>
> Kugli.

Another man would probably have been frightened by those words, but not Tremal-Naik. Now that the moment to act was at hand, he felt strong enough to attack his enemies even without Nagor's assistance. Love would give him the strength and courage to complete his mission.

He hid the weapons and ammunition beneath a mound of dirt and returned to the window.

"Go, Darma," he said. "You're running a great risk."

The tiger went off. She had not gone more than twenty paces when he heard one of the sentries yell, "A tiger! A tiger!"

A rifle thundered.

A second blast rang out, but the smart beast had doubled her pace and quickly disappeared.

The sound of rushed footsteps reached his ears then several men stopped before the window.

"Hey!" exclaimed a voice that Tremal-Naik recognized as Bhárata's. "Where's that tiger?"

"It's escaped," replied the guard on the veranda.

"Where was it?"

"Near the cellar window."

"A hundred rupees says it's one of Saranguy's friends. Hurry, two men into the cellar before the scoundrel escapes."

Tremal-Naik had heard every word. He picked up the two jars, smashed them open, threw the white ones into the darkest corner, hid the red ones in his sash and lay back against the pole, fastening the ropes to his limbs as best he could. He finished just moments before two armed sepoys entered the cellar.

"Ah!" exclaimed one, carrying a torch. "Still here, Saranguy?"

"Leave me be, I want to sleep," said Tremal-Naik, feigning annoyance.

"By all means, my friend, rest easy, no one will disturb you; we'll stand guard."

Tremal-Naik shrugged, leaned back against the pole and closed his eyes. The sepoys, having placed the torch in a bracket in the wall, sat on the ground, resting their carbines between their knees. Several minutes later, a sharp, sweet fragrance reached the hunter's nose. Despite the red flowers concealed in his sash, he began to feel drowsy. The two sepoys began to yawn.

"Do you feel strange?" asked one of the soldiers, after a few minutes.

"Yes," replied his companion. "I feel like I'm…"

"Drunk?"

"Yes, my eyes feel heavy."

"What could be causing this?"

"I don't know."

"A manzanilla bush?"

"There aren't any in the garden."

The conversation ended there. Eyes riveted upon the guards, Tremal-Naik watched as they slowly closed their eyes, opened them three or four times, then closed them once again. They struggled to stay awake for a few more minutes then fell heavily to the ground, snoring loudly.

Assured they would not awaken, Tremal-Naik quickly unfastened the rope and quietly got to his feet. He bound the sleeping soldiers, grabbed one of their revolvers and rushed towards the stairs.

Chapter 8
The Sergeant's Revelations

The landing was clear, not a guard in sight. Shaking with excitement and determined to regain his freedom, Tremal-Naik silently climbed the steps and reached a dark, deserted room. He paused to listen for a moment, levelled his revolver, slowly pushed the door open and cautiously peered into the room.

"No one," he murmured.

He opened a second door, went down a long, dark hallway and entered a third room.

It was vast. A lantern burned at the far end, casting a dull light over a dozen beds; their occupants were sleeping soundly.

"Sepoys!" murmured Tremal-Naik, halting at the sight of them.

He was about to turn back, when he heard footsteps in the corridor. He started and pointed his revolver at the door. Someone was approaching, his spurs jingling with every step. Tremal-Naik heard him pause for a moment, then continue on his way.

"The captain!" he whispered.

He slipped back into the hallway and spotted a dim shadow at the far end, its spurs jingling as it moved through the darkness. Trying not to make a sound, he followed it up a flight of stairs, walking on the tips of his toes. He had just reached another corridor when the footsteps stopped; he heard a key turn in a lock, then a door opened and the man disappeared.

The hunter silently crept forward and came to halt in front of the door. It had been left slightly ajar; he peered through the crack.

A lamp cast a dim light about the room. A man was sitting before a small table, in the shadow of a column, with his back to the door. At the thought it might be Captain MacPherson, Tremal-Naik trembled slightly. Pain tore through his chest, as if he had just been stabbed in the heart.

Strange, he thought. Could I possibly be afraid?

He gently pushed against the door and opened it without a sound. He crept towards the table, but though he moved silently, his prey sensed his presence and immediately jumped out of the chair.

"Bhárata!" exclaimed Tremal-Naik, rapidly training his revolver on him. "Don't move, don't make a sound, or you're dead!"

At the sight of the prisoner, the Indian had attempted to rush towards the pistols he had placed on a chair. But that harsh warning stopped him in his tracks. He roared like a panther caught in a trap.

"Saranguy!" he exclaimed, as a scowl spread across his lips.

"My name is Tremal-Naik," replied the Indian, his revolver still trained on the sergeant.

"How did you get in here?" he asked.

"That's my secret."

"So I was right after all?"

"It would appear so."

"What do you want?"

"I've come to kill you."

"Ah!" exclaimed the sergeant, gritting his teeth. "You're a murderer."

"Perhaps. Interested in saving your life?"

"What do I have to do?"

"Sit down and answer my questions."

Bhárata slowly returned to his chair. Tremal-Naik picked up the weapons, locked the door, and sat down opposite the sergeant.

"I warn you again, cry out and you're dead. There are six bullets in this gun, and I never miss."

"Get on with your questions," repeated the sergeant, slowly regaining his nerve.

"I have a terrible mission to complete."

"What do you mean?"

"I promised the Thugs I'd kill Captain MacPherson."

Tremal-Naik looked at Bhárata to see what effect those words had had, but the Indian's face remained impassive.

"Did you understand, Bhárata?" he asked.

"Perfectly."

"Well?"

"Continue."

"I have to deliver them Captain MacPherson's head."

The sergeant erupted in laughter.

"Fool! The captain has already left."

Tremal-Naik jumped out of the chair.

"He isn't here?" he exclaimed desperately. "Where's he gone?"

"I'm afraid I can't tell you."

"I've promised the Thugs I'd bring them his head."

"They'll have to manage without it."

"No, Bhárata! I must complete my mission! Where's the captain? I'll comb India if I have to, from the Himalayas to Cape Comorin."

"You won't get any more information out of me."

"So you do know!" exclaimed the hunter.

"Yes."

Tremal-Naik raised the revolver and pointed it at the Indian's forehead.

"Bhárata," he said furiously, "Tell me!"

"I'm a sepoy! Kill me if you must, I won't betray my captain!"

"There's no returning from the grave, Bhárata."

"Kill me if you must."

"Is that your final word?"

"Yes."

Tremal-Naik placed the barrel of his gun against the Indian's forehead. He was about to fire, when a whistle sounded three times from out in the courtyard.

"Nagor!" exclaimed Tremal-Naik, recognizing the Thug's signal.

He stuck the revolver in his sash, grabbed Bhárata, covered the sergeant's mouth with one hand, and threw him to the ground.

"Don't move," he said, "Or I'll kill you."

183

He grabbed a rope, bound the sergeant tightly, gagged him, then ran to a window, raised the blinds and whistled three times.

A shadow stood up from behind a bush and quickly crawled towards the bungalow. It stopped beneath the window and raised its head.

"Nagor!" murmured Tremal-Naik.

"Who goes there?" asked the Thug, after a brief hesitation.

"Tremal-Naik."

"Should I come up?"

The hunter rapidly scanned his surroundings, straining his ears to catch the slightest sound.

"Come up," he said.

The Thug tossed his noose at a window hook, caught it, and quickly climbed up to the windowsill. He was around twenty years old, tall, thin, blessed with extraordinary agility, and judging by his actions, indomitable courage. He was dressed in a simple dhoti and armed with a dagger. His skin glistened with coconut oil; a blue Nagi marked his chest.

"I see you managed to free yourself," he said. "What about the sepoys?"

"Sleeping."

"The captain?"

"He's no longer here."

"Could he have suspected something?" asked the Thug. "We have to find out where he went. Suyodhana wants his head."

"The sergeant refuses to speak."

"We'll force him."

"If only I knew how to make that drink."

"Drink? Some kind of lemonade?" said the Thug with a smile.

"Yes, lemonade. It made me tell them everything."

"I know how to make it, shouldn't be too difficult to prepare some for the sergeant."

He jumped into the room, cast a glance at Bhárata, who was calmly awaiting his fate, grabbed a glass full of water and prepared the same lemonade Captain MacPherson had given Tremal-Naik.

"Drink this," said Nagor, having removed the prisoner's gag.

"Never!" replied Bhárata, recognizing the liquid.

The Thug grabbed the prisoner's nose and squeezed it tightly. Unable to breathe, the sergeant was soon forced to open his mouth; the lemonade was quickly poured down his throat.

"It won't be long now," Nagor told Tremal-Naik.

"Are you afraid of the sepoys?" the hunter asked him.

"Hardly!" laughed the Thug.

"Guard the door, fire at the first man that attempts to climb the stairs."

"You can count on me, Tremal-Naik. No one will interrupt your interrogation."

The Thug picked up a pair of pistols, checked to make sure they were loaded and left the room just as the liquid was beginning to take effect. The sergeant had started to laugh and ramble without pause.

Surprised, Tremal-Naik listened to that torrent of words until he heard the captain's name.

"Excellent, Sergeant," he said, "Where's the captain?"

Bhárata suddenly fell silent. Eyes sparkling, he looked at Tremal-Naik and asked, "Who's that? I thought I heard a Thug... Ha! Ha! Thugs! They won't be around for much longer. The captain promised... and the captain is a man of his word... a great man... not afraid of anything... We'll attack their lair... we'll drown them all... Ha! Ha! Ha!"

"Can I go with you?" asked Tremal-Naik, catching every word.

"Yes, we'll both go! Ha! Ha! It'll be a fantastic sight."

"Do you know where their lair is?"

"Of course we do. Saranguy told us."

"Ah, wretches!" exclaimed Tremal-Naik.

"He drank the lemonade," continued the sergeant, "And told us everything."

"Was the captain present at Saranguy's interrogation?" Tremal-Naik asked nervously.

"Of course; he left as soon as he got the information."

"For Rajmangal?"

"No, no!" Bhárata exclaimed breezily. "The Thugs are powerful; we'll need a lot of men to destroy them."

"He's gone to Calcutta?"

"Yes, to Calcutta, to Fort William! He's going to arm a ship and gather an army… and lots of cannons… Ha! Ha! What a sight!"

The sergeant fell silent. Though he struggled to remain awake, his eyes were growing heavy and he could barely keep them open. The opium was slowly taking effect.

"That's all I needed to know," he murmured. "The captain will never make it to Rajmangal."

Chapter 9
Under Siege

He had not yet finished speaking, when two rifle shots thundered from the lower corridor followed almost immediately by a loud cry. Tremal-Naik rushed out of the room.

"Nagor! Nagor!" he yelled.

Not a sound came in reply. The strangler, who only moments ago had been standing watch by the door, had disappeared. Where had he gone? What had happened?

Alarmed, but determined to save his companion, the hunter headed towards the stairs. A sepoy lay in the middle of the hall, writhing in pain as he took his last gasps of life. A river of blood flowed from his chest into a dark puddle slowly spreading across the floor.

"Nagor!" repeated Tremal-Naik.

Three men suddenly appeared at the far end of the hallway, racing towards a room on the right. Almost at the same instant, he heard Nagor's voice cry out, "Help! They're breaking down the door!"

Tremal-Naik rushed down the stairs and fired two quick shots from his revolver. The three Indians fled.

"Nagor, where are you?" asked the hunter.

"In here," replied the Thug. "They've locked me in!"

Tremal-Naik smashed in the door with a powerful thrust of his shoulder. The strangler, bruised and bleeding, rushed out of his prison.

"What happened?" asked Tremal-Naik.

"We've got to get out of here!" yelled Nagor. "This place is crawling with sepoys."

The two Indians raced up the stairs, ran back into the room and locked the door. Three rifle shots rang out in the hallway.

"Quick! Out the window!" yelled Nagor.

"It's too late," said Tremal-Naik, leaning over the windowsill.

Two sepoys had taken position two hundred metres from the bungalow. At the sight of the two Indians, they aimed their rifles and fired, but the bullets went wide and struck the coconut mats.

"We've been discovered," said Tremal-Naik. "We've got to barricade the door."

Fortunately, the door was thick and the latches were sturdy. Within minutes the two Indians had piled up all the furniture in the room behind it.

"Load your pistols," said Tremal-Naik. "It won't be long before they attack."

"Are you sure?"

"They know there are only two of us. What happened? Why so much noise?"

"I obeyed your instructions," said the strangler. "I spotted two sepoys making their way down the corridor. I fired and sent one crashing to the ground; the other escaped into the room. I followed him, but I tripped. By the time I got back up, the door had been locked. Without your help I'd still be in there."

"You should have held your fire. We may be trapped."

"We can wait it out for awhile."

"And in the meantime Rajmangal will fall."

"What?"

"Rajmangal is in grave danger."

"Who told you that?"

"The sergeant."

"Where is he?"

"Over there, asleep."

"He told you Rajmangal is in danger? It could be a trick."

"No it's the truth. The British have discovered the location of our lair."

"Impossible!"

"Captain MacPherson is heading to Fort William to prepare an expedition as we speak."

"You have to capture the wretch and kill him."

"I know."

"If you do not kill him, the Guardian of the Sacred Temple will never be your bride."

"Do not speak of her," Tremal-Naik said hoarsely.

"So what's your plan?"

"Get out of here and reach Fort William."

"We're under siege."

"I can see that."

"Well then?"

"We're going to escape."

"When?"

"Tonight."

"How?"

"Leave it to me."

"How many men in the bungalow?"

"Sixteen, perhaps eighteen. But…"

He grabbed the Thug by the hand and squeezed it tightly.

"Did you hear that?" he whispered, pointing to the door.

"Yes," said the Thug.

"Someone's coming towards us."

"The sepoys!"

"An attack?"

The floorboards in the corridor creaked, someone was walking towards the room. There was a knock on the door.

"Who goes there?" asked Tremal-Naik.

"A Thug," replied a voice.

"A trick," whispered the hunter.

"Open the door! They're following me!" continued the same voice.

"Who's your leader?" asked Tremal-Naik.

"Kali."

"You're a sepoy. We have a hundred bullets; if you don't get out of here, you're a dead man."

The floorboards creaked again as the man raced off.

"They're afraid," said Tremal-Naik. "They won't try anything for awhile."

"We're still trapped in here," replied Nagor, his uneasiness increasing with each passing minute.

"We're going to escape!"

"Quiet!"

A rifle blast thundered from outside.

"A tiger! A tiger!" cried a soldier.

The hunter rushed to the window.

Two sepoys, who had been hiding behind a bush, had jumped to their feet, carbines in hand, shrieking in fear.

"Darma!" yelled Tremal-Naik.

The tiger sprang forward, threatening to attack the two soldiers, unfazed by their rifles.

"Get out of there, Darma!" commanded the hunter, having spotted other sepoys rushing to aid the men.

Realizing her master was in danger, the intelligent beast hesitated for a moment then raced off with lightning speed.

"Clever beast," said Nagor.

"Yes, brave and loyal," added Tremal-Naik, "And tonight she'll help us escape."

They returned to the barricade and patiently waited for nightfall. During the day, the sepoys approached the door several times and attempted to knock it down, but a blast from a revolver always sufficed to scatter them. The sun set at eight o'clock; night fell quickly after a brief twilight. It would be several hours before the moon appeared over the jungle.

Towards eleven o'clock, Tremal-Naik approached the window and spotted two dim silhouettes, the two sepoys that had been hiding in the bush. He looked for the tiger, but she was nowhere to be seen.

"Are we going to escape?" asked Nagor.

"Yes."

"How?"

"The window. We're only four metres up and the ground is soft."

"What about the sepoys?" asked Nagor. "They'll start firing at us before we hit the ground."

"We'll make them empty their weapons first."

"How?"

"You'll see."

Tremal-Naik grabbed the carpets, gathered all the clothes, pillows and bedding he could find, and constructed a dummy the size of a man.

"Ready?" he asked Nagor.

"Ready. What about the sergeant?"

"Let him sleep, he's no danger to us. Be careful, the sepoys are only fifty paces from the bungalow."

"I know."

"I'll lower the dummy. The sepoys will mistake it for one of us and shoot until their carbines are empty."

"Excellent."

"While they're reloading, we'll jump down and escape. Understand?"

"Brilliant," said Nagor. "It's too bad you're not a Thug!"

"Get ready to jump."

The hunter fastened his noose about the dummy and lowered it out the window, making it sway gently. The two sepoys fired immediately, yelling: "To arms!"

Tremal-Naik and Nagor jumped out of the window, guns drawn. They hit the ground, rolled, shot to their feet and ran off as quickly as they could.

"Follow me!" said Tremal-Naik, doubling his speed.

The sentries sounded the alarm; several rifle blasts filled the air, but none found their mark.

Tremal-Naik raced into the stable. A horse was lying on the ground. He brought it to its feet with a swift kick.

"Hurry!" he yelled to the Thug.

The hunter grabbed onto the horse's mane, the two fugitives jumped onto its back and took off across the heath.

"Where are we going?" asked Nagor.

"To see Kugli," replied Tremal-Naik, whacking the horse's side with the butt of his revolver.

"We'll be captured by the sepoys!"

"Is Kugli under attack as well?"

"After I left him, I spotted several sepoys lurking in the forest."

"We'll be careful. Keep your weapons drawn."

The horse, a beautiful animal with a black mane, quickly covered the ground, jumping over trenches and bushes, despite its double load.

The bungalow had already disappeared in the darkness and the forest was just becoming visible, when a voice yelled out from a thicket of bamboo.

"Halt!"

The two escapees turned and levelled their weapons.

The moon was just rising; ten men lay upon the ground, their carbines trained upon the horse.

"Use your spurs!" yelled Nagor.

A flash of light tore through the darkness as ten rifles thundered simultaneously; the two Indians fired their revolvers in response. The horse jumped forward, neighed softly and fell, dragging the riders to the ground.

The sepoys rushed out of the thicket, but their excitement immediately gave way to terror. A large shadow had jumped out from among a group of bamboo trees, roaring angrily. A swipe of her paws knocked the commander to the ground.

"Darma!" yelled Tremal-Naik, getting up immediately.

"The tiger! The tiger!" yelled the sepoys, flying off in all directions.

The intelligent beast was at her master's side in an instant.

"Excellent, Darma!" he said, stroking her affectionately. "I can always count on you."

The two Indians headed into the forest, smashing through the bushes that barred their path, looking about carefully, fearing a trap. Running at full speed, a half hour later, they arrived at Kugli's hut. Tremal-Naik quickly went in, leaving Nagor behind to look after the tiger. The Thug was lying on the ground, deciphering a letter written in Sanskrit. At the sight of the hunter, he jumped to his feet and rushed towards him.

"Free!" he exclaimed, not hiding his surprise and joy.

"Thanks to your help," said Tremal-Naik.

"And Nagor?"

"He's outside."

"Give me the head."

"What?"

"Captain MacPherson's head, give it to me."

"We've been beaten, Kugli."

The Indian took three steps back.

"Beaten! Beaten! What do you mean?" he asked.

"Captain MacPherson is still alive."

"Still alive!"

"I wasn't able to kill him."

"Tell me everything!"

"He left the bungalow while I was imprisoned in the cellar."

"Where did he go?"

"Calcutta."

"To do what?"

Tremal-Naik did not reply.

"Tell me."

"He's gone to prepare an expedition. He's learned of your lair on Rajmangal."

Kugli looked at him in terror.

"Impossible!" he exclaimed.

"It's the truth."

"Who betrayed us?"

"I did."

"You!"

The strangler drew his dagger and rushed at Tremal-Naik, but the hunter, quick as a flash, grabbed Kugli's hand and twisted his wrist, forcing the weapon to the ground.

"Don't do anything foolish, Kugli," he said, barely containing his anger.

"Tell me everything, you wretch, tell me!" yelled the strangler. "Why did you betray us? A word from me and it's the pyre for your Ada."

"I know," Tremal-Naik said angrily.

"Well?"

"It was against my will. They made me drink yuma."

"Yuma!"

"Yes."

"And you talked?"

"Who can resist yuma?"

"Tell me everything that happened."

Tremal-Naik quickly related all that had transpired in the bungalow.

"You've accomplished quite a bit," said Kugli, "But your mission isn't over yet."

"I know," sighed Tremal-Naik.

"Why are you sighing?"

"Why? Why? I'm not a murderer. The very thought of it makes me cringe. It's horrible, it's monstrous!"

Kugli shrugged.

"You do not know what hatred is," he said.

"You're mistaken, Kugli!" Tremal-Naik exclaimed darkly. "You have no idea how much I hate you!"

"Careful, Tremal-Naik! Your fiancée is still in our hands."

The unhappy hunter lowered his head and stifled a sob.

"Let's turn our thoughts back to the captain," said the strangler.

"What should I do?"

"We have to prevent that wretch from reaching Rajmangal. If he sets foot in our lair, your Ada will die."

"Have you no mercy?" Tremal-Naik said bitterly.

"Mercy has nothing to do with it. If that man sets foot on Rajmangal, we're done for."

"What should I do?"

Kugli did not reply. He rested his head in his hands and began to think.

"I've got it," he said suddenly.

"You have a plan?"

"Yes! The captain will probably requisition a ship and set sail for Rajmangal."

"It's most likely," said Tremal-Naik.

"We have many spies among the military in Calcutta; some are with the garrison at Fort William, others serve aboard British warships. There are even a few officers among them."

"So?"

"You'll go to Fort William and our men will help you get aboard his ship."

"Me?"

"Are you afraid?"

"I do not know fear. Don't you think the captain will recognize me?"

A smile crossed Kugli's lips.

"With a little makeup an Indian can easily transform himself into a Malay or a Burmese."

"Fine. When do I leave?"

"Immediately, there's no time to waste."

"What about the sepoys?"

"They've been chased off, but they could return at any moment."

Kugli put his fingers to his lips and whistled.

A Thug appeared.

"Is the whaleboat still nearby?"

"Yes," replied the Thug.

"Have seven of our bravest men prepare to set sail."

Kugli removed a gold ring from his finger and offered it to Tremal-Naik. It was engraved with a Nagi, the mysterious symbol of the Kali cult.

"Show this to one of our men," he said, "and he'll rally all the Thugs in Calcutta to do your bidding."

"Any further instructions?" the hunter asked as he slid the ring onto one of his fingers.

"Remember, the Guardian is still in our hands."

"Anything else?"

"If you betray us, we'll burn her alive."

Tremal-Naik looked at him darkly.

"Goodbye," he said abruptly.

He left the room and approached Darma who was looking at him uneasily, as if she had already guessed that her master was going to leave her once again.

"I'll see you soon, my dear friend," he said sadly. "Nagor will take good care of you."

He turned about and went off to join the seven Thugs.

"Take me to the boat," he ordered.

The eight men marched off in single file and headed into the forest, their rifles drawn, ready to use them at the first sign of danger.

They reached the river at two the next morning, stopped at a small enclosure, and drew a whaleboat from beneath a pile of bamboo. It was equipped with oars, a mast and a small sail.

"See anyone?" asked Tremal-Naik.

"No one," replied a Thug.

"Time to go then."

The eight men climbed in and rowed off.

Chapter 10
The Frigate

"Give it all you have!" said Tremal-Naik. "We've got to reach the fort before the expedition sets sail. If we're too late, Rajmangal will be destroyed."

"Leave it to us," replied a Thug, an old man who appeared to be in command. "We'll arrive in time."

"How far are we from the fort?"

"Less than ten leagues."

"How much time do we have?"

"The captain will probably wait until high tide. The water will start to rise in about a half hour or so and then we'll fly faster than a steamer."

The Thugs, strong young men accustomed to hard work, began to row with all their might. The whaleboat, a beautiful, well-crafted vessel, was soon flying over the waters.

The night was calm; a slight breeze blew from the mouth of the river. A large full moon loomed above the jungle, casting its silvery light upon the groves of mango and palm trees lining the shore.

Exotic landscapes spread on either side of them. The jungle had been tamed in places, the vast bamboo forests giving way to fields of mustard plants, their yellow flowers shining brightly in the moonlight. Soon the first plantations appeared, sweetening the air with the scent of indigo, saffron, sesame and scialappa. From time to time small villages could be seen among the vegetation, peering from behind high wooden fences or from among the rice paddies that stretched towards the shore. Bungalows became more frequent, bands of black storks and brown ibis dozing peacefully upon their sloping roofs.

They had been advancing for half an hour when a voice thundered from the right bank:

"Halt!"

At the sound of that unexpected challenge, Tremal-Naik stood up.

"Who said that?" he asked, quickly scanning the shore.

"Look down there," said one of the oarsmen. "We're rowing past Captain MacPherson's bungalow."

"They've spotted us?"

"It appears so. The soldiers must have been keeping an eye on the river. Can you see them?"

Tremal-Naik fixed his eyes on the bungalow and spied a group of men on the terrace, their rifle barrels sparkling in the moonlight.

"Halt!" repeated the same voice.

"Keep rowing," said Tremal-Naik. "If they want us, they'll have to come after us."

The whaleboat had just begun to pick up speed when a blast thundered from the terrace.

"Damn!" yelled a voice. "Fire!"

"It's them!" yelled another voice.

"Fire!"

Four rifle blasts tore through the air. Seconds later, the Thugs heard the bullets hiss over their heads.

"Scoundrels!" exclaimed Tremal-Naik, picking up his carbine.

"Careful!" yelled one of the oarsmen. "They're coming after us."

"I'll keep them at bay. Point the vessel towards that grab coming down the river; if she's set sail from Calcutta she may have news of the expedition."

"Look, Tremal-Naik!" yelled the old Thug.

The hunter turned his eyes towards the roadstead by the bungalow and spotted a murpunky manned by five or six sepoys and half-a-dozen oarsmen.

"Row," he ordered, loading his carbine.

Though the whaleboat continued to pick up speed, the murpunky manned by a highly skilled crew, was rapidly gaining ground. Several sepoys sat crouched behind her topsail, carbines levelled and ready to fire.

"Stop!" thundered a voice.

"Keep rowing!" commanded Tremal-Naik.

A sepoy raised his head, exposing it for an instant. Tremal-Naik quickly aimed his weapon and fired. The soldier let out a cry, clutched at the air and fell from sight.

"Next!" yelled Tremal-Naik, taking up another carbine.

A volley of fire came in reply, the bullets strafing the whaleboat's sides.

Another sepoy raised his head, but immediately disappeared, felled by another blast from Tremal-Naik's carbine.

Surprised by the hunter's precision, the sepoys quickly tacked and headed towards the opposite bank.

"Keep your eyes open, Tremal-Naik," said one of the Thugs. "There are several English bungalows along that shore."

"They'll gather reinforcements," added another.

"We won't give them the time," said the Indian, "Point the bow towards the grab."

The ship was only half a mile away. Her bow, of Indian design, was fine and sharp, adorned with exquisite carvings of gods and elephants. Advancing at full sail, her three masts swayed beneath the cool northern breeze.

Within fifteen minutes the whaleboat had drawn up beneath her starboard side. Her captain leaned over the bulwark to address the new arrivals.

"Where are you coming from?" asked Tremal-Naik.

"Calcutta," replied the old man.

"When did you pass Fort William?"

"Five hours ago."

"Did you spot any warships?"

"Yes, a frigate, the *Cornwall*."

"Was she taking on supplies?"

"No, just soldiers."

"That must be MacPherson's ship," said a Thug.

"Do you know where she's headed?" asked Tremal-Naik, gritting his teeth.

"No," replied the captain.

"Where her engines running?"

"Yes."

"Thank you, Captain."

The whaleboat pulled away from the grab.

"Did you hear that?" Tremal-Naik asked angrily.

"Yes," replied the Thugs, taking up their oars.

"We have to get there before the frigate raises anchor or all is lost. Row, row!"

One of the Thugs suddenly let out a cry of triumph.

"Listen!" he exclaimed.

Ears straining to catch the slightest sound, everyone held their breath. A dull roar, like the sound of distant thunder, was slowly growing louder.

"High tide," yelled a Thug.

A large wave had appeared to the south, advancing towards them with the speed of a horse in full gallop.

It thundered past the whaleboat, raising the tiny vessel as it swept towards Calcutta, dragging off thick tangles of grass and branches.

"Pull to starboard!" commanded the chief oarsman. "We'll reach the fort in an hour."

Within minutes the Thugs had manoeuvred into the current and quickly picked up speed.

Dawn broke as they advanced, bathing the sky in a warm pink light. The stars began to fade and silence descended upon the jungle.

As the whaleboat drew nearer Calcutta, the banks of the great river began to change. The great jungle, populated by large packs of tigers, wild buffaloes, jackals and serpents, slowly gave way to farms and plantations. The vast seas of bamboo soon disappeared, replaced by fields teeming with cotton, indigo and cinnamon.

Fruit trees lined the gardens of elegant villas and large villages. Squads of monkeys appeared among the foliage, swinging among the branches; buffalos stood along the shore lazily quenching their thirst. At times a deer would appear, study the tiny vessel then dash off into the bushes.

Perched atop the huts, buzzards and arghilahs slowly awakened from their slumber. Kites and cormorants peered from the mangroves, as coots, ibis, and Brahmin ducks wheeled aloft, filling the air with their cries.

"We're near Calcutta," said an oarsman, after having carefully scanned the shores.

Tremal-Naik, who had barely managed to contain his impatience throughout the journey, shot to his feet and cast his eyes northwards.

"Can you see it?" he asked.

"Not yet, but it won't be long now."

"Row! Row!"

The whaleboat picked up speed. The Thugs, just as eager, rowed with incredible fury, their oars bending beneath each stroke.

At eight o'clock, a cannon blast thundered from upriver.

"What was that?" Tremal-Naik asked anxiously.

"We're not far from Kidderpore, probably some warship raising anchor and saluting."

"Hurry, hurry! We have to arrive in time!"

Ships and boats of various sorts, shapes, and sizes began to appear about them. Bricks, brigantines, schooners and steamers plied the river in large number. Grabs, pariàs from Coromandel, square-sailed pulars from Dacca, flat-roofed budgerows, and elegant flyt-sciarras crisscrossed the waters or rocked at anchor along the shore.

Hand fixed on the rudder, Tremal-Naik skilfully wove through that thickening maze of ships that seemed to stretch across the river.

The Thugs rowed faster, straining their muscles, never pausing for a moment's rest.

By nine, the whaleboat had sailed past Kidderpore, a large village on the river's left bank and come within sight of Calcutta, Queen of Bengal, the capital of British India. Majestic palaces, pagodas, domes, and towers rose against the sky, beyond them, past a wide esplanade, stood Fort

William, the largest fort on the subcontinent, home to a garrison of ten thousand men.

Tremal-Naik's eyes grew wide, stunned by the magnificent sight spreading before him.

"What splendour!" he murmured. "I never dreamed Calcutta would be this grand."

He turned towards the old Thug and asked, "Do you know the city?"

"Yes, Tremal-Naik," the man replied.

"Any idea where the captain could be?"

"No, but we'll find him. We have spies everywhere."

"You don't think he's already set sail?"

"We didn't spot any warships coming down the Hugli," replied the old man. "We can be certain the expedition hasn't left yet."

"Does the captain have a villa in Calcutta?"

"Yes, close to Fort William."

"Are you familiar with it?"

"Perfectly."

"Do you think he's staying there?"

"We'll know soon enough. As I said, we have spies everywhere. See that gunboat anchored near the fort?"

Tremal-Naik turned his head and spotted a small steamship. She had a low hull and weighed about three or four hundred tons, light enough to sail up the narrow branches of the Ganges. A single mast towered over her bow; a large cannon peered menacingly from her stern. A metal plaque beneath her railing bore a name in letters of gold: *Devonshire*.

"There's a Thug aboard that ship?" asked Tremal-Naik.

"Yes, the quartermaster, Hider."

"We have to talk to him."

"We must be cautious, Tremal-Naik."

"No one knows us here."

"Who can say for sure? Let me be your guide, I've been here many times."

"Fine. I place myself in your hands."

The Thug put down his oar for a minute, stood on the thwart, and carefully scanned the gunboat's bridge.

Several sailors bustled about, busily cleaning and organizing the ropes and tools cluttering the deck. They spotted the quartermaster among them, talking to a young cadet.

"That's our man," said the strangler, turning towards Tremal-Naik. "I'll call to him."

He cupped his hands about his mouth and whistled three sharp notes.

The quartermaster turned his eyes towards the river then leaned over the bulwark, just as the whaleboat was passing beneath the gunboat's side. His eyes met the old Thug's then turned away, pretending to study a grab descending the river at full sail.

"He'll meet with us soon," said the old man, turning towards Tremal-Naik. "He understood my signal."

"Where?"

"One of our men runs a tavern not too far from here."

"And he knows we're going to be there?"

"My signal gave him all the information he needed."

"Let's go."

Keeping close to shore the whaleboat resumed its course, advancing towards the centre of the Indian capital.

Ships and boats multiplied before them, spreading across the entire river. Vessels from every nation crowded the jetties as legions of stevedores worked feverishly, hauling cargo between ship and shore.

Crowds of men, women and children lined the ghats, preparing to take their morning bath in the sacred waters of the Ganges.

At dawn, the daily ceremony begins, bathers crowding along the banks until the sun grows warm. Eyes upon the rising sun, they wade into the river until the waters touch their waists. Some dip their heads beneath the waves; others fill a small brass vase and pour water over their heads.

They offer a handful of water to the sun, recite their prayers then wash their clothes. Once dressed, they head for home, taking with them a jar of water to use throughout the day.

The whaleboat, after having weaved through that chaos of ships and bathers and having sailed past an infinite number of beautiful villas, pagodas and gardens, drew to a halt before a large deserted ghat. The old Thug signalled the oarsmen to guard the boat then turned to address Tremal-Naik.

"Follow me," he said.

They ascended the stairs, walked past several betel vendors, crossed the street and headed into the splendid squares along the river.

Though the sun had just risen, the city was alive with activity. Bengalis, Malabars, Brahmins, Morwari, Europeans, Chinese and Burmese streamed through the vast squares as they went about their morning business. Bullock carts piled high with goods advanced through the wide streets, moving alongside gilded palanquins fitted with blue silk curtains.

The old Thug quickly crossed the squares, making his way past splendid palaces into a small district filled with dirty straw huts. He headed down a narrow street and a quarter of an hour later, halted before a squalid old shack.

"This is the place," said the Thug. "Hider should be here soon."

The room was dark and furnished with a few stools and bamboo tables. They sat down in a corner and an Indian, as thin as a fakir, with a face scarred by smallpox, brought them jars of tody and a couple of terracotta bowls full of curry and rice.

The two had almost finished their meal when they spotted the quartermaster entering the room.

He was a tall Indian, about forty years old, strongly built, with sharp eyes and a thick black beard. A small pipe rested between his lips.

At the sight of the old Thug, he drew near, proffering his hand.

"Nice to see you again, Moh."

He fixed his eyes upon the Thug and nodded towards Tremal-Naik.

"Don't worry, Hider," replied the old man. "He's a devoted member, one of our leaders."

"I need proof," said the quartermaster.

"Show him your ring, Tremal-Naik."

The sailor bowed and said, "At your service, envoy of Kali."

"Sit down," said the hunter. "Do you know Captain MacPherson?"

"I know him well," replied the quartermaster.

"Do you know where he is?"

"Has he left his bungalow?" Hider asked.

"Yes."

"When?"

"Three or four days ago."

"I didn't know that; what's he doing here in Calcutta?"

"He's come to prepare an expedition; he's going to attack Rajmangal."

The quartermaster jumped to his feet; his pipe fell from his lips and clattered on the floor.

"Attack Rajmangal! Then my suspicions were correct!"

"What suspicions?"

"The *Cornwall* has been arming for several days now."

"A warship?" asked Tremal-Naik.

"An old frigate discharged to Captain MacPherson."

"Where is she now?"

"At anchor near the arsenal. They've loaded a large amount of food and ammunition and they're fitting the corridors with hammocks. I'd guess they're planning to embark a large number of men."

"Any Thugs among the crew?" asked the old man.

"Two, Palavan and Bindur."

"I know them; we must get in touch with them immediately."

"I talked with them last night, they do not know the *Cornwall*'s destination; it's a closely guarded secret."

"Then there can't be any doubt," said Tremal-Naik, "That's the ship."

"I'm beginning to suspect that as well," replied Hider.

"She must not leave Calcutta!" exclaimed the hunter.

"Who could possibly prevent her from setting sail?"

"Me!"

"How?"

"By killing the captain before she can raise anchor."

"It won't be easy," said Hider. "He'll be on his guard."

"Suyodhana wants his head, I must kill him. They told me he has a small villa here."

"That's true."

"We'll send someone to make sure he's there."

"How?"

"I don't know yet; we'll find a way," said Tremal-Naik.

The old Thug raised his head slowly and said, "We'll know soon enough."

"You have a plan, Moh?" asked Hider.

"We'll send a man."

"Who?"

"Nimpor."

"The fakir?"

"Yes, time to pay him a visit!"

Chapter 11
The Fakir

Having tossed a rupee onto the small table, the three Indians left that dismal tavern and began to make their way through the busy squares. They soon reached the Ganges and headed beneath the trees lining the shore to escape the heat.

Walking upriver, they made their way north past the centre of the city, and towards the Indian quarter. The palaces, wide clean streets and rich palanquins quickly disappeared, replaced by a chaos of shacks, hovels and huts. Narrow muddy lanes teeming with people, twisted every which way; large arghilah roamed among the crowd, sifting through the dirt and refuse as they searched for their next meal.

Having led them through that maze, the old Thug stopped before a large pagoda that towered above the squalor. He looked about then climbed the wide steps and halted before an Indian seated by the entrance.

"This is our fakir," he told Tremal-Naik and Hider.

Despite himself, the hunter shuddered.

The man sitting before him was little more than a skeleton. Red and black tattoos marked his wrinkled face; his brow was plastered with ash and a thick beard fell to his waist. His hair was long and dirty and had probably never felt the touch of a comb or blade. He was naked to the waist, clad in a small loincloth just four fingers wide.

But it was the man's left arm that had made him shudder. The fakir had held it erect so long that the skin and flesh had withered until it looked like coloured bone. His hand had been bound shut with leather straps and the hollow filled with dirt to serve as a pot for a small sacred myrtle. Left untended, his fingernails had pierced through his palm and grew out the back of his hand like dark twisted talons.

There are many kinds of fakirs in India each with their own unique practices of abstinence and austerity. Sannyasis renounce the world and wander the land alone; aghoris live in graveyards and keep company with the dead, dandis always carry a staff even while asleep; akasmuhkis hold their face to the sky until the muscles in their neck become rigid and their heads can no longer move. Nagas shun all clothing, smear their bodies with ash and wander the land with nothing but a sword.

The fakir sitting before them was a paramahansa. They are revered for their holiness, for they are said to be able to live for a thousand years without food or drink, are unaffected by heat or cold and indifferent to pain or pleasure.

"Nimpor," said the old Thug, bowing before the fakir who had not moved, "Kali needs you."

"My life belongs to the goddess," replied the fakir, without raising his eyes, "Who sends you?"

"Suyodhana."

"The Son of the Sacred Waters of the Ganges?"

"Yes."

"How can I help?"

"We need to find a dangerous man. We must kill him; he's planning to attack Rajmangal."

Nimpor's lips twitched almost imperceptibly.

"Who dares attack Rajmangal?"

"Captain MacPherson."

"He's returned to Calcutta?"

"We believe so."

"How soon do you need the information?"

"Tonight."

"He's not in his villa?"

"We're not sure," said Moh.

"We'll find out soon enough."

"When?"

"Tonight, at the villa."

"What?"

"Leave it to me, I'll summon the sampwalla."

"Snake charmers? How can they help?"

"All will be revealed in time, now go. Vishnu summons me to prayer."

Eyes to the ground, the fakir slowly rose to his feet and entered the pagoda, his arm still fixed in the air.

"Where can I find you?" asked Hider, once the fakir had disappeared. "I must return to my ship."

"We're staying with Vindhya while we're in Calcutta," replied the old Thug. "When can we meet again?"

"Tomorrow at noon. There's a lot of work to do aboard ship. We're casting off in a few days."

"Where is the *Devonshire* headed?"

"Ceylon."

"I was hoping you'd help us track down the captain."

"I'm at your disposal until we set sail. Goodbye, my friends, until tomorrow!"

Left alone, Tremal-Naik and the old Thug made their way back towards the British quarter, walked along the Ganges, and soon drew up before the whaleboat.

"Vindhya's place," said the old Thug.

He sat down at the stern, and the small boat set off up the river.

Moh had taken the rudder and the hunter scanned the ghats and palm trees as the whaleboat raced along the shore.

Fires blazed at the base of those stone steps, sending clouds of sparks and smoke wafting over the river.

From time to time a tarè[13] would sound, its sombre notes announcing a cremation had begun. Men could be seen circling a pyre as family and friends chanted prayers to Yama, the god of death.

Once the flames had died, they would gather the ashes and scatter them upon the sacred river, the watery road to heaven.

A couple of times he spotted a dying man, surrounded by his relatives, awaiting death on the shores of the sacred river.

---

[13] Brass trumpet.

When an Indian learns he is about to die, he immediately has himself transported to the Ganges, to be all the better prepared to enter Brahma's kailasson. He finds a patch of grass beneath a tree and calmly awaits his fate. As the time draws near, he's given his last rites. Relatives rub his limbs with mud or sprinkle his face with holy water drawn from the river; the Brahmin crumbles sage leaves upon him as others prepare his funeral pyre.

The whaleboat, after having gone another two miles, sailing past temples, villas and the endless maze of shacks in the Indian quarter, drew up alongside a deserted promontory shaded by latanie and coconut trees.

The old Thug ordered the whaleboat moored and jumped ashore.

"We'll meet you at Vindhya's house," he told his men.

He gestured for Tremal-Naik to follow and set off toward a group of huts built about the remnants of an enormous pagoda. They made their way down several muddy lanes, through a series of overgrown gardens, and halted before a stone hovel thatched with coconut leaves that stood alone by the edge of a swamp.

An old wrinkled Indian sat before it, holding a bunch of dried leaves, his hands and arms smeared with ash, a common practice among ramanandi, fakirs devoted to Rama, the Creator god.

His long grey hair had been matted with red mud and bundled atop his head like a turban. He was clean shaven save for a thin set of whiskers that grew from his chin, so long they almost touched the ground. Three lines marked his arms, chest and forehead, made from a mixture of mud and cow dung. A handkerchief rested on his knees.

The old Thug advanced towards him, bowed and said, "We need your help, Vindhya."

The ramanandi looked up at the Indian.

"Kali's will is my command," he replied.

"We need a place to stay."

"My house is yours."

"And your advice."

"I am at your disposal."

"We're hungry."

"Come."

The ramanandi leaped to his feet, threw away the bunch of leaves and entered the hut.

Moh and Tremal-Naik followed him into a small room. The floor disappeared beneath coconut mats; banana leaves covered the walls, keeping the room cool and fresh. The furnishings were sparse: large terracotta vases that contained the fakir's food, several kaskpanaye, straw boxes used to store roots, and a few mats rolled in a corner that must have served as beds.

The Thug signalled Tremal-Naik to make himself comfortable, then withdrew to a corner with the fakir.

The two whispered for a few minutes, then once they had finished, returned and sat before the hunter.

"This is Suyodhana's envoy," said the old Thug.

"You have my allegiance," replied the ramanandi.

"I've informed Vindhya of our mission," added Moh, addressing Tremal-Naik. "He's a cautious and knowledgeable man; he'll give us precious advice."

"Excellent," said Tremal-Naik, stifling a sigh.

The ramanandi shut the door, drew three cups and a golden bottle from a vase and offered his guests some arak, an exquisite liqueur made from the bark of a yagra tree.

"You may speak freely," he said, addressing the old Thug.

"You know why we're here. Do you think Nimpor will be able to find the captain's hiding place?"

"Yes," said the ramanandi. "Nimpor has friends everywhere; nothing will escape his army of spies."

"Finding him is not enough," said Tremal-Naik. "I have to get close enough to kill him."

"You will."

"How? Captain MacPherson will have taken precautions; it won't be easy to take him by surprise."

"We'll lay a trap for him."

"He's too cautious, it won't work."

A smile crossed the ramanandi's lips.

"We'll see," he said. "He's desperate for information; he'll come if we offer the right bait."

"What do you mean?"

"I have a plan."

"Tell us."

"Let's find out where the captain is first."

"And then you plan to lure him into a trap?"

"Yes."

"He won't be tricked so easily."

"He will," replied the ramanandi firmly. "He may know our lair is on Rajmangal but he does not know how to get into the caverns. He'll do anything to ensure his mission is a success."

"That's true," said Tremal-Naik.

"Without that knowledge, he'll lose the element of surprise," said the old Thug. "He could comb the island for months and never find it."

"Then he'll come here," said Vindhya.

"Here?" exclaimed Tremal-Naik, looking at the fakir in amazement.

"Yes, here."

"Who's going to lead him here?"

"I will."

"How?"

"By promising him information."

"He won't come alone."

"What does it matter?"

"He'll have a large escort."

"He can bring two regiments of sepoys with him if he wishes, it will not matter," said the ramanandi, laughing mysteriously. "There's a secret passage that connects my house to the old pagoda. We'll sneak him off before they can attack." He crossed his arms and added, "Kali is great and she'll smite her enemies! Captain MacPherson thinks he can destroy us, but he'll never set foot on Rajmangal."

"Yes," Tremal-Naik murmured sadly. "One life to free another…"

Chapter 12
Snake Charmers

The sun had already disappeared and darkness was rapidly descending upon the waters of the sacred river when Tremal-Naik and the old Thug left the ramanandi's hut.

The six oarsmen followed a short distance behind, pistols and daggers drawn as a precaution. When they reached the Ganges, the eight Indians jumped into the whaleboat and set off down the river.

It was a beautiful night. Stars filled the sky; the moon peered above the canopy, casting its silvery light upon the bell towers, spires and domes of the Indian quarter's numerous pagodas.

Off in the distance a myriad of lanterns bathed the White City in bright light, further south, rows of bright dots marked the ships and boats anchored along the river.

The oarsmen quickly bent to their task and the whaleboat descended the river with the speed of an arrow, meandering through grabs, pulars, banghs and European ships, then tacked towards the left bank and landed before the remnants of a small ghat that led to an old pagoda.

"Follow me," said Moh.

They moored the whaleboat, disembarked and climbed up the steps.

Tremal-Naik spotted the fakir with the withered arm in front of the pagoda. He was sitting on the top step, wrapped in a large dark dugbah.

"Good evening, Nimpor," said the old Thug. "I knew I'd find you here."

"I was waiting for you," replied the paramahansa, his eyes fixed on the ground.

"Did you learn anything?"

"Nothing definite, however, I have reason to believe the captain is in his villa."

"You didn't see him?"

"No."

"How can we make certain he's there?"

"Listen!"

From off in the distance came the sound of drums, khole and some hulok, the noise steadily growing louder with each passing minute.

"Musicians?" asked the old Thug.

"The sampwalla," the fakir replied, with a smile.

"Part of your plan?"

"You'll know soon enough!"

Moh and Tremal-Naik climbed up onto the top step and spotted a large number of torches meandering along the Ganges, advancing towards the pagoda.

"I think I understand your plan," said the old Thug.

"Wait for us at the villa," said the fakir.

"Come, Tremal-Naik," said Moh.

They went down a set of steps that led behind the pagoda, crossed a small clearing shaded by several coconut and banana trees, and came to a halt before a white stone bungalow with a high sloping roof and a large veranda lined with large blue wooden columns. Tall Palmyra palms sheltered it from the sun.

Though the windows were open the rooms were dark, however, the villa must have been inhabited for an armed sepoy stood guard at the door.

"The captain's bungalow?" asked Tremal-Naik, his voice trembling slightly.

"Yes," replied the old Thug.

"Think he's in there?"

"Could be."

"If I could only get inside!"

"You'd be caught immediately. There's bound to be more than one sepoy standing guard. The captain is a cautious man; he'll have surrounded himself with a large number of soldiers."

"What should we do?" Tremal-Naik asked anxiously.

"Leave it to the fakirs. We'll sit beneath that banana tree and wait for the snake charmers."

The air filled with noise as the procession drew nearer. Soon the temple's steps were bathed in torchlight, its carved pillars gleaming brightly in the glow of the flames.

The throng halted in the clearing, bowed to honour the temple's goddess, then headed off down the steps towards the villa, growing louder as it advanced.

Two hundred people had come to watch the ceremony. Nimpor led the way followed by the sampwalla, snake charmers dressed in simple languti that barely covered their hips, each man carrying a punji, a kind of flute made from a gourd and bamboo reeds.

Next came the bearers, some bore round baskets filled with serpents; others carried large pots of milk, an offering of food for those dangerous beasts.

Twenty musicians followed: drummers pounding kholes, huloks, and tablas, flautists sounding nose flutes and bansuris, and even a few playing sarindas an instrument similar to a violin.

Last of all came six or eight dozen fakirs: sannyassis, dandis, nagas, and akasmuhkis, carrying torches or clay pots filled with offerings.

Having crossed the small clearing, the procession came to a halt before the captain's villa, doubling the noise as it spread into a large circle.

Lanterns and torches bathed the front of the villa in light, anyone appearing at the window or on the veranda would be spotted immediately.

The snake charmers, tall handsome men with long beards and powerful muscles, waited for the musicians to finish, then assembled in the middle of the circle and ordered the baskets containing the serpents to be placed on the ground.

As they made their preparations, Nimpor, always careful to keep his withered arm erect, slipped in among the fakirs, walked past the villa, and halted beneath the banana tree before Moh and Tremal-Naik.

"Keep your eyes on the windows," he said. "If the captain is here, he'll make an appearance."

"We won't take our eyes off them," replied the Thug.

"Neither will I," said the fakir. "I may be old, but my eyesight is excellent. Once the sampwalla have left, go and wait for me at the pagoda."

The snake charmers drew their punjis, formed a small circle among the spectators and began to play, filling the air with sweet melancholy music.

The baskets began to move, the lids rising slowly. Seconds later, a hooded cobra slithered onto the ground. It was more than two metres long with yellow brown scales and dark black rings about its eyes. It hissed menacingly and flashed its fangs; the crowd stepped back, knowing its bite was lethal.

But before it could strike, a sampwalla quickly grabbed it by the stomach and tossed it into the air.

Enraged, it hissed even louder, twisting as it fell. The sampwalla grabbed it by the tail before it touched the ground and squeezed it by the throat, forcing the snake to open its mouth. Ignoring the cobra's angry hisses, he drew a pair of tweezers, pulled out its fangs then tossed it next to the pot of milk.

In the meantime two other serpents peered from the baskets, drawn by the music. One was a boa, a superb snake about four metres long, with blue green skin marked by black rings; the other was a tiny snake just fifteen centimetres long, as thin as a reed with black skin and yellow spots, but far more dangerous, for its bite could kill a man in ninety-six seconds.

They had barely touched the ground when two sampwallas grabbed them by the tail, pulled out their fangs, and tossed them next to the hooded cobra, its anger having vanished as it feasted on the milk.

More serpents slithered out of the baskets, black najas, striped pythons, banded kraits and rough scaled-vipers. Within minutes, the four large jars were surrounded by snakes greedily devouring their evening meal.

The show over, the flutes fell silent and the drums and pipes resumed their play. The fakirs began to dance among the snakes, their wild cries mingling with the thunderous music.

Tremal-Naik and the old Thug had jumped to their feet. The window in the villa had just lit up and a dark shadow had appeared behind the glass.

"Look!" the Thug exclaimed.

"I haven't taken my eyes off the windows!" hissed Tremal-Naik.

The shadow leaned over the windowsill into the glare of the torch-light. A stifled cry escaped Tremal-Naik's lips.

"It's him!"

"The captain!" exclaimed Moh.

"Quick! Get me a rifle!"

"You're mad!"

"He'll escape and I'll lose Ada."

"We'll find him again."

"Yes, we'll find him again," repeated a voice behind them.

Tremal-Naik and the Thug turned about. Nimpor, the fakir with the withered arm, was standing a few paces behind them.

"Did you see him?" he asked.

"Yes," they replied.

"From now on we'll know his every move."

"You have spies?" asked Tremal-Naik.

"Two loyal fakirs."

"When can I kill him?"

Instead of replying, the fakir asked, "Did you see Vindhya?"

"We're his guests," replied the old Thug.

"Do you have a boat?"

"Yes, a whaleboat."

"Take me to him. We'll need to plan our next move. The sampwalla have finished, we may go."

The sampwallas were preparing to leave. They gathered the snakes and returned them to their baskets then formed a column behind the orchestra and set off for the Indian quarter.

As the procession headed off, Tremal-Naik and the Thugs returned to the pagoda. Two dandis stood among the pillars, their staffs visible in the evening light.

The paramahansa drew up before them, pointed to the villa, and said, "Keep your eyes on the captain, follow his every move. Report to me at Vindhya's hut tomorrow before sunset."

"We won't take our eyes off him," replied a dandi.

The small squad descended the steps. Once they reached the Ganges, they jumped into the whaleboat and quickly set off upstream.

The river was deserted, it being past midnight. The odd light shone to the south, lanterns burning aboard the ships and boats anchored along the shore.

Less than an hour later, the whaleboat drew up before the small promontory. Off in the distance, the old pagoda, bathed in moonlight, towered majestically above the coconut trees.

Tremal-Naik and his friends were about to disembark when they spotted a shadow emerge from a mindi bush.

"Vindhya?" asked the old Thug, quickly drawing his pistol.

"It's me," replied the fakir. "Lower your weapon. How was the naga pautciami?"

"Very informative," replied Nimpor, stepping forward.

"You here as well?" Vindhya asked, amazed.

"I have to speak to you."

"Of course."

"Shall we go to your hut?"

"This place is deserted, we can speak freely," replied Vindhya.

"As you wish."

"The captain?"

"We saw him."

"At his villa?"

"Yes."

"Then he's ours."

"You're getting ahead of yourself, Vindhya."

"No, Nimpor."

"You have a plan?"

"An infallible plan."

"Tell me about it," said the paramahansa.

"We have to get him to come here."

"Think it's possible?"

"Definitely, once he's entered my hut, you can rest assured he won't walk out alive."

"You can count on me," added Tremal-Naik.

"We know, Suyodhana is a good judge of men," said Vindhya, "Now listen. I know the captain, he's a brave and determined man; he'll face any danger to obtain information that would facilitate his attack on Rajmangal."

"Continue," commanded the paramahansa.

"I plan to lead him into a trap."

"How?"

"We'll send him one of our men, posing as a traitor. He'll claim to have learned of the expedition against Rajmangal and offer to sell him directions to the entrance of the caverns."

"You think he'll fall for that?" asked Nimpor doubtfully.

"He'll come, I tell you. We'll demand an enormous price and we'll set the appointment for midnight at my hut."

"He won't come alone."

"What does it matter? Tremal-Naik will be hiding somewhere with a carbine. One shot will end his life."

"And the others will attack the hut and kill us," said the paramahansa.

"We'll hide in the tunnels beneath the pagoda," said Vindhya. "They'll never find us."

"How well do you know them?"

"I could find my way blindfolded."

"Then I approve," said the paramahansa, after a few minutes' reflection. "The captain's desire to discover the entrance to the caverns of Rajmangal could lure him into the trap. He won't come alone, I'm sure of that, but a bullet could find its mark, even if he's surrounded by a hundred men. Is Tremal-Naik a good shot?"

"Infallible," declared Moh.

"Excellent, now it's time for me to go."

"One last question," said Tremal-Naik. "Once the captain has been murdered, do you think they'll give up on their expedition?"

"Only the captain is daring enough to lead an attack across the Sundarbans. Once he's dead, Rajmangal will be free of danger! Good night, my friends. Tomorrow one of my most trusted men will contact the captain, come nightfall you'll have his head."

"Shall we have our men take you back in the whaleboat?" asked the old Thug.

"There's no need," replied the paramahansa, "I may not be able to use my arm, but my legs are more than sound."

As if to prove those very words he set off along the winding shore and quickly disappeared into the shadows.

Chapter 13
The Trap Fails

The next evening, Tremal-Naik, Vindhya and Moh left the hut and silently made their way toward the small promontory. They had armed themselves as a precaution; the hunter had grabbed his carbine while the Thugs had tucked their daggers into the rumaals fastened about their waists. Arriving at the old pagoda, they climbed the steps to the landing and sat down among the rubble.

The water sparkled in the moonlight. Silence reigned over the slumbering city, broken only by the soft gurgle of the river as it lapped against the lotus leaves along its banks.

Vindhya climbed up onto the remnants of a column and scanned their surroundings, trying to spot an approaching launch, but not a shadow appeared upon the waters. Tremal-Naik, barely hiding his agitation, had begun to pace among the ruins, circling about a statue of Mohini, one of Vishnu's early incarnations.

"Nothing," said the fakir after a few minutes had passed, climbing down from his observation post. "It must be close to midnight."

"What if he doesn't come?" asked Tremal-Naik, not attempting to conceal his anger.

"He'll come," the fakir replied calmly, "The captain won't pass up such an opportunity."

"The paramahansa is nowhere to be seen, I'm afraid the captain has seen through your plan. Where are our men?"

"Hiding along the river," said the old Thug.

"So they haven't seen anything either?"

"You're mistaken, Tremal-Naik," said the fakir. "There's a man running towards us."

"One of ours?"

Tremal-Naik jumped up onto the column that Vindhya had been using as an observation post and fixed his eyes on the shore. A man was running towards them at full speed. It had to be the dandi, for the runner clutched a staff in one hand.

The Indian ran through several groves of plants, turned past Vindhya's hut and continued on towards the temple.

"A messenger from Nimpor," said the old Thug. "I'm sure it's good news."

The dandi rushed up the stairs and halted before Vindhya.

"He's coming!" he said, panting heavily.

"Who's coming?" they asked in unison.

"The captain."

"Great Shiva!" yelled Tremal-Naik. "He's mine!"

"Is he alone?" asked the fakir.

"No, he's brought six men with him."

"I'd kill him even if he where guarded by a thousand sepoys," the hunter exclaimed excitedly.

"Who are those men?" asked the old Thug.

"Six sepoys."

"Armed?"

"Yes."

"Then he believes we have the information?"

"So it appears."

"We'll wait for him in the hut," said the fakir, "and kill him once he's inside."

"I'll go alone," said Tremal-Naik.

"We should wait until we spot the boat," suggested the old Thug. "The hut is nearby, it won't take us long to prepare the ambush."

"Look, he's coming!" exclaimed the dandi.

Tremal-Naik, the old Thug and Vindhya had rushed towards the ghat, keeping their eyes fixed on the river. A thin black line advanced over the sparkling surface of the Ganges, the waters foaming about it as it drew near.

As it took form, Tremal-Naik spotted six armed men, their rifle barrels shining in the moonlight.

"They're coming," he said darkly. "Brahma, Shiva, Vishnu, give me the strength to commit this last act."

"To the hut," said the old Thug.

"And your men?" asked the fakir.

"They must have turned back by now. They'll be here soon."

The four Indians left the ghat and returned to the fakir's hut.

"Here's the plan," said Vindhya. "I'll pretend to give the captain his precious information."

"And then?" asked Tremal-Naik and the other two.

"You'll hide behind those mats, ready to strike. When you hear me cough, jump out."

At that instant the six oarsmen entered the hut.

"They're about to land," said one of them.

"Excellent," said Vindhya. "Everyone to their places."

While Tremal-Naik, the old Thug and the dandi hid behind the mats, the fakir turned to give the oarsmen their final instructions.

"Go hide among the reeds near the swamp. Do not move until you hear a pistol shot. And now to us, Captain," the fakir murmured, a sinister light flashing in his eyes. "You'll be talented indeed if you manage to escape the noose."

He stood in the doorway and cast his eyes toward the pagoda, waiting for his victim to appear.

Straining his ears, he heard the beating of oars then a dull thud; the launch had docked against the ghat. Minutes later, a figure appeared at the far end of a row of tamarind trees. The captain, to avoid recognition, had dressed in traditional Indian clothing. He was clad in a white dug-bah; a large turban covered most of his face. When he arrived to within ten paces of the hut, he stopped, drew a pistol from his belt, pointed it at Vindhya, and asked menacingly, "Who are you?"

"The man you've come to see, Captain MacPherson."

"Your name."

"Vindhya."

"We'll enter your hut, but I warn you, if it's a trap, I've got two loaded pistols tucked in my belt; and I never miss."

"I'm not a traitor."

"How do I know that?"

"You don't trust me?"

"Perhaps."

"Then turn about and go back to your launch, Captain. I'm a man of my word."

"We shall soon see."

"Did you bring the money?"

"Five thousand rupees, as you requested."

"Enter; you have no need to fear."

The captain took a step forward, cast one last look about, then entered the hut. The fakir had already gone inside and lit the lamp. As soon as the flame lit the room, a cry of anger and amazement escaped his lips.

The man he had believed to be the captain was in fact a well-built Bengali with bold features and a proud face. He had removed his large dugbah and stood before him in the red and white uniform of the Indian sepoys.

"You seem shocked," said the Bengali, a mocking smile spreading upon his lips. "Now why is that?"

"Why?" replied the fakir, barely able to contain his anger. "I thought I was speaking to Captain MacPherson, not one his sergeants."

The Bengali shrugged.

"Do you really believe my captain would have been foolish enough to come here?"

"Perhaps he's too afraid."

"No, just cautious."

"He made a terrible mistake."

"And why is that?"

"I will not tell you anything. I'll only divulge my information to him."

"My name is Bhárata, I'm the captain's most trusted servant, the Thugs' most merciless enemy; he sent me in his place. You have nothing to lose, I'll pay you and no one aside from him will ever learn what you've told me."

The fakir hesitated for a moment then offered the sergeant a seat close to the mats hiding Tremal-Naik and the two Thugs.

"Sit down and listen to me," he said.

He paced about the room, looked out the door one last time, then closed it, bolting it shut with an iron bar.

"What are you doing?" the sergeant asked uneasily.

"Taking my precautions," replied the fakir calmly.

"And I'll take mine," said Bhárata, drawing the two pistols from his belt and resting them upon his knees.

"I'm unarmed."

"Even an unarmed man can be a traitor," replied the sergeant. "Now tell me what you know."

"First, I must ask you a question."

"Ask it."

"Is it true the captain is about to undertake an expedition against Rajmangal?"

"Yes."

"With a ship?"

"They're readying the *Cornwall*, a good frigate stocked with several cannons and large enough to hold two battalions of sepoys."

"But he couldn't possibly know how to get into the caverns. The entrance is well hidden."

"If he knew, I wouldn't have come here with five thousand rupees. He only knows that it's somewhere on the island of Rajmangal."

"I'll guide him," said the fakir, affecting a ferocious smile. "Those wretches have done me great harm, but I'll have my revenge. I would, however, have preferred to have spoken to the captain."

"He's not far from here. If your revelations are important, I'll take you to him."

"Why didn't he come here himself?"

"Like I said, he's a cautious man."

"He'll need a large number of soldiers to attack the Thugs."

225

"That will not be a problem."

The fakir frowned for an instant, but his brow quickly cleared as if he had come to a decision.

"Listen," he began. "I hate the Thugs, especially their leader, the treacherous Suyodhana. Up until a few days ago I was one of them; now I'm determined to avenge the suffering they have caused me."

"What did they do to you?"

"There's no need to discuss that now. I spent several years on Rajmangal; you'll have no better guide to the Sundarbans and the vast labyrinth of caves and tunnels the Thugs use as their lair. I'll tell you what the captain will have to do to surprise them and..."

The fakir had stopped abruptly, suddenly uneasy.

A jackal had cried out from near the swamp. Knowing they always kept their distance from the Indian quarter, he had started at that cry, realizing instantly that it could have been a signal from one of the oarsmen.

They were in danger. The sergeant would have to do.

Bhárata had not flinched, eyes riveted on the strangler.

"Continue," he said, noticing that the fakir had suddenly fallen silent.

"Yes," said Vindhya. "If the captain intends to surprise the Thugs in their lair, he'll have to use the greatest precautions and land on the island without being seen. If he disembarks in the middle of the day, he won't find a single Thug in any of those caverns."

A second cry, longer than the first, sounded from outside. There was no mistaking it; they were in danger. Vindhya pretended not to notice and continued, "It would be best if the captain hid his ship in the Gona-Skuba canal. There's no shortage of islands there, you'll be able to set up camp, and then..."

He stopped for a second time and coughed loudly. As he turned his head he spotted a movement among the mats. The sergeant, his back to that corner of the room, had not noticed, engrossed in the informant's story.

"Then you'll be able to advance on Rajmangal undetected," continued the fakir.

"Like this!" yelled a voice from behind the sergeant.

Bhárata quickly drew his pistols and turned about, but his assailants knocked him to the ground before he could fire. Instantly, three daggers were trained on his chest, ready to run him through.

"Traitors!" he exclaimed, attempting to writhe free of their grasp.

A cry of rage and amazement escaped his lips.

"Tremal-Naik!"

"Yes, Bhárata," replied the hunter.

"Wretch!"

"You didn't think I'd given up, did you?"

"May the devil take you!"

"Quiet! You're in our hands now, there's no need for such insolence."

"Kill me if you must; the captain will avenge me."

"Not as soon as you may think," said Tremal-Naik. "Enough threats, if you value your life, answer our questions."

"This is the second time I've been stupid enough to fall into your hands; kill me if you must."

"You're too valuable a hostage. Just tell me where I can find the captain."

"So you can kill him?" Bhárata asked sarcastically.

"That's none of your concern. Tell me where he is."

"You have but to open the door."

"He's here?" exclaimed Tremal-Naik, the two fakirs and the old Thug.

"Yes, and if I fail to return, he'll order the sepoys to attack the hut."

"Great Shiva!" yelled Tremal-Naik, turning pale.

"Who's worried now?" continued the sergeant, laughing. "You thought he'd be foolish enough to fall into your trap? No, you scoundrels, he outsmarted you, and soon you'll be his prisoners."

"You're lying!" said Vindhya.

"Open that door then!"

Tremal-Naik picked up the prisoner's two pistols and was about to rush towards the door, but Vindhya and the old Thug quickly held him back.

"What are you doing?" asked the fakir.

227

"The captain may be out there!" said Tremal-Naik.

"What about all those men he has with him?"

"Bhárata could have lied."

"Or he could have been telling the truth. Didn't you hear those jackal cries? Our lookouts have signalled we're in danger."

"So, what are we going to do?"

"Nothing, we'll wait for a better opportunity and try again."

"But we're surrounded."

The fakir shrugged.

"It matters not. We'd escape even if there were a thousand of them. Wait."

The Indian was about to go into the adjoining room when a loud knock froze him in his tracks.

"Open up or we'll set fire to the house!" thundered a voice.

"My men!" exclaimed Bhárata.

"No one answer!" whispered the fakir. "Gag the prisoner and follow me. Try not to make any noise."

"Where are we going?" asked Tremal-Naik.

"We're getting out of here."

"What about the captain? I may not get another chance."

"If you value your life, follow me," replied the fakir. "We'll find him again, I assure you, but for the moment, its best we escape."

Bhárata was quickly bound and gagged. At a sign from the fakir, Tremal-Naik picked him up and followed the others into the adjoining room, while the same voice thundered menacingly, "Open up or we'll roast you alive."

The fakir rolled back a coconut mat, pulled up a stone tile then slid back a metal door that opened onto narrow steps.

"Grab the torches," he said, addressing the dandi and the old Thug.

The two Indians picked up two long sticks and quickly lit them.

"Let's go!" commanded Vindhya.

He descended the narrow steps and entered a small cellar; the walls were damp, the swamp being close by. He quickly scanned the room and asked the dandi to climb up onto the remnants of a pillar in the far corner.

"Do you see an iron plate?" he asked.

The dandi tapped the wall and a dull metallic sound echoed throughout the room.

"It's here," he said.

"There's a button in the middle of it, can you see it?"

"Yes, I found it."

"Press it as hard as you can."

The dandi did as instructed, the metal plate slid back and a dark passageway opened before them.

"Do you hear anything?" asked Vindhya.

"No, nothing."

"Everybody up."

"What about you?" asked the old Thug.

"I'll join you in a minute."

Tremal-Naik, Moh and the dandi climbed up into the passageway, taking Bhárata with them. The sergeant put up no resistance, knowing it was impossible to attempt an escape.

Vindhya waited for his companions to disappear, then climbed back up the steps and listened. Outside, the sepoys were yelling, threatening to blow up the hut. Tired of waiting, they began to pound against the door with the butts of their rifles.

"The place is yours," murmured the fakir, as a triumphant smile spread across his lips.

He picked up a third torch, thrust a large heavy knife into his belt, then went back down into the cellar, stopping before the wall opposite the passageway.

He raised his torch and carefully studied it for a few minutes, then drew his knife and struck the wall with all his might. A thick pane of glass, black with age, gave way beneath that blow and a large torrent of water roared into the cellar.

"We'll drain the swamp, but what does it matter?" murmured the fakir. "Now let's get out of here before the water fills the tunnel and drowns us all."

With water storming into the cellar, he scrambled up the pillar and rushed into the tunnel, the sound of the sepoys' pounding on the door thundering above him. He felt along the sides of the opening, found a spring and pushed against it with both hands. The iron door slid shut with a loud clang.

"Now come and get us," laughed the Indian.

And he ran off to join the others.

Chapter 14
Beneath the Pagoda

That damp tortuous passageway was just wide enough for the men to advance in single file. After a few paces it began to slope upwards, curving and twisting as it wound its way beneath the swamp and the old pagoda. Scorpions, spiders and lizards fled in the torchlight, scared off by that unexpected invasion.

The hunter led them forward, tightly gripping Bhárata's arm. But after having gone five hundred paces, Tremal-Naik came to a halt in a small cavern, which at first glance, appeared to be a dead end.

"We can't go any further," he informed the dandi and the old Thug as they drew near. "The tunnel ends here."

"We should wait for Vindhya," Moh replied. "He's the only one that knows his way around here."

"I've heard tell of the caverns beneath the old pagoda," said the dandi. "There's got to be another tunnel hidden nearby."

"If there isn't, we may as well sit down and await our deaths," said Tremal-Naik. "It won't take the sepoys long to find us."

He had just finished uttering those words when they spotted Vindhya running towards them.

"It's done," he said. "Now we can be certain we won't be followed."

"Why is that?" asked Tremal-Naik.

"I flooded the cellar; they won't be able to find the entrance."

"So what are we going to do now?" asked the dandi. "The tunnel is a dead end."

"There's another hidden passageway," replied Vindhya. "I know where it is."

He had just brought his torch to one of the cavern walls, when a frightful discharge thundered off in the distance. The ground shook and a large number of boulders fell from the ceiling, crashing down with a loud roar. Fortunately, the four Indians had heard the explosion in time and rushed into the tunnel, dragging the prisoner along with them.

"What happened?" asked Tremal-Naik. "That sounded like a mine going off."

"I think they blew up my house," Vindhya said uneasily. "I wasn't expecting that."

"Could they have collapsed the tunnel?" asked the dandi.

"I doubt it, however… Listen! Do you hear that?"

Tremal-Naik and his two companions held their breath, straining their ears to catch the slightest sound. From the depths of the dark tunnel they had just crossed, came a dull roar which grew louder with each passing minute.

The four Indians exchanged uneasy looks.

"What's that noise?" asked Tremal-Naik.

"I don't know," said Vindhya.

"It sounds like a river."

"Water!" exclaimed Vindhya, terrified. "They must have blown open the metal door."

"We've got to get out of here," said the old Thug. "Where's that secret passage?"

Vindhya rushed towards a second metal plate in the corner of the cave. He had just spotted the button that would release the spring, when a torrent of water erupted from the tunnel and roared into the cavern.

The impact was so violent it hurled the four Indians and the prisoner against the far wall. Two of the torches went out, but fortunately the old Thug had quickly raised his to keep the darkness at bay.

"Great Shiva!" yelled Tremal-Naik, letting go of Bhárata as the waves knocked them about. "Where's this water coming from?"

"The plate's been blown open and the swamp is draining into the tunnel," said Vindhya.

"Are we going to drown?"

"It's possible," the fakir replied nervously.

"We have to get out of here," said the old Thug.

"Our only way out is underwater."

"You've got to get it open; once the swamp drains, the sepoys will set off after us."

"Yes, better hunted than stuck here to await our deaths," added Tremal-Naik.

"Even if I manage to open the panel we may not be able to get through."

"What do you mean, Vindhya?"

"The water could collect in the caverns beneath the temple and block our path."

"Are they large?"

"Enormous."

"What about the tunnels? Where do they lead?"

"The Ganges."

"Then the water should drain."

"Yes, but a lot of the tunnels will still be underwater."

"If we have to, we'll swim through them. Hurry, Vindhya, find that metal door, we're minutes away from drowning."

"Protect the torch," the fakir told the old Thug, "If it goes out, we're done for."

Though the waves had settled the water was quickly filling the cavern, within minutes it had reached their chests; a minute more and it would be at their chins.

Having studied the cavern walls, the fakir headed towards a corner; took several deep breaths and dove into the water, determined to find the spring that would release the metal panel.

Three times he came up for breath, but his fourth attempt proved successful, he found the button and pressed it with every ounce of his strength. Within seconds a small eddy formed in the corner, followed by a dull roar that quickly grew louder. Grabbing onto a rock protruding from the wall, the fakir quickly pulled himself away to avoid being dragged down by the current.

"We're saved!" he yelled, drawing up beside his friends. "The water's draining into the caverns!"

"And just in time," murmured Tremal-Naik. "The water had reached Bhárata's chin."

The waters were receding, but slowly, they would have to wait for the swamp to drain, before they could risk entering the tunnels.

"We're going to have to wait for a couple of hours," Vindhya informed Tremal-Naik.

"Where do we go from here?" asked the hunter.

"We'll follow the tunnels to the Ganges. It won't be safe to hide in the caverns. Once the swamps have drained the sepoys will set off after us. It won't take them long to pick up our trail."

"Think we can escape?"

"Let's hope."

"What about Bhárata? Are we taking him with us? He's more of a hindrance than an asset now."

"He could still provide insight into the captain's plans," replied Vindhya. "We shouldn't abandon him just yet."

"Besides, he's still a precious hostage," said the old Thug. "If we leave him here, he might lead the sepoys after us."

"We could kill him," said the fakir.

"A needless crime," replied Tremal-Naik. "Bhárata is not the captain."

"Then we'll take him with us," concluded Moh.

As they were discussing their plans, the water continued to drain, finding numerous outlets in the caverns beneath the old pagoda. A half hour later the water level had dropped to the Indians' waists.

The fakir, fearing the sepoys could appear at any moment, decided to scout the path back to his cellar.

He gave the torch to Tremal-Naik, signalled the dandi to follow and headed off into the tunnel.

The rush of water had abated, a sign the small swamp would soon be dry. The two fakirs advanced slowly, grabbing the walls for support. When they had gone three hundred metres, they paused for a moment to catch their breath then headed forward once again, aiding each other to combat the current. They had already gone fifty or sixty metres when they heard several voices echo from the mouth of the tunnel.

"Did you hear that?" asked Vindhya, grabbing the fakir's hand.

"Yes," replied the dandi.

"They've found the tunnel."

"Think so?"

"Quiet, listen!"

A triumphant cry echoed down the passageway.

"A tunnel!"

"We've been discovered," murmured the dandi.

"It won't be long before the sepoys are on our tails," replied Vindhya.

"Let's get out of here."

"Wait. If they'd found the metal plate, we'd see their torches by now."

Careful not to make any noise, they began moving forward once again, reached a bend in the tunnel, and spotted a bright light a hundred and fifty paces from them. Several sepoys were about to enter the passageway.

"Back!" whispered Vindhya. "We've got to head into the caverns. If they haven't drained by now, we're done for."

Driven forward by the current, they rushed through the tunnel and a few minutes later reached the cavern where they had left Tremal-Naik and Moh guarding the prisoner.

"Let's get out of here," said Vindhya.

"What happened?" asked the hunter.

"The sepoys have found the entrance to the tunnel."

"Already?"

"Yes, they'll be here soon."

Tremal-Naik drew his dagger; its blade shone before Bhárata's eyes.

"Walk or I'll kill you," he said.

The tunnel into the old pagoda's cellars was empty, most of the water having drained away. The five Indians headed into it, closed the metal door behind them, to slow the sepoys advance, and set off, keeping the torch held high.

That second passageway was a lot more spacious than the first and wide enough to allow three or four men to walk side by side.

They could hear the water racing on in the distance, following each bend and turn, its dark bellows slowly fading as it disappeared among the caves and tunnels beneath the old pagoda.

Familiar with those dark passages, Vindhya had taken the torch and confidently led the way forward, unfazed by the tunnels' many twists and turns. The ground was almost dry in places, the water having vanished into the porous rock.

For a half hour he guided his friends through that underground maze of endless tunnels, until at last, they came upon a large cavern filled with numerous burial mounds, perhaps the tombs of ancient rajahs.

Carvings and inscriptions covered the walls, honouring Vishnu in his many incarnations. A large shankha had been sculpted into the rock, a black conch shell revered among Hindus for its ability to banish evil spirits.

Vindhya stopped; the far end of the cavern was filled with water.

"We have a problem," he said, a slight tremble in his voice. "The tunnel into the next cavern is underwater."

"Should we turn back?" asked Tremal-Naik.

"That would be foolish; the sepoys are undoubtedly on our trail by now."

"There's no other way out?"

"None," the fakir replied sullenly.

"How long is the tunnel to the next chamber?"

"About seventy paces."

"I'm a good swimmer."

"So are we," said the old Thug and the dandi in unison.

"So?"

"We'll proceed underwater," Tremal-Naik replied determinedly.

"What about the prisoner?"

"He'll follow if he doesn't want to drown." He removed Bhárata's gag and asked, "Do you know how to swim?"

"Yes," replied the sergeant.

"Follow us and stay close."

An explosion thundered off in the distance, echoing throughout the tunnels and the large cavern for several minutes.

"Sounded like a grenade," said Vindhya. "They must have blown up the second metal door."

"Hurry."

They headed towards the far end of the cavern, plunging into the water once again. The incline was steep, the water had gathered there, hiding the path to the second cavern.

"The tunnel is directly in front of us," said Vindhya. "I'll go first."

"Keep an eye on Bhárata," said Tremal-Naik.

The five men took deep breaths and dove in. Four quick strokes brought them to the passageway, they headed into it, swimming quickly, using all their strength.

Twice, Tremal-Naik tried to surface, believing he had reached the second cavern, but both times he bumped his head against the ceiling. At his third attempt, his head finally broke the surface. As soon as his lungs filled with air he yelled, "Vindhya, where are you?"

"Over here," replied the fakir.

"And the others?"

"I'm here," replied the old Thug.

"I'm here," said the dandi.

"Bhárata?"

No one replied.

"Bhárata?" repeated Tremal-Naik.

Once again there was no response.

"Great Shiva!" he yelled. "The scoundrel has disappeared."

"Or he's drowned," replied Vindhya. "There's no time for recriminations; if you wish to live, follow me."

Chapter 15
The Chase

The small squad slowly advanced through the darkness. A large amount of water had accumulated in the cavern, and the four Indians struggled to remain afloat as they searched for a place to rest their feet.

"Where are we going?" asked Tremal-Naik, becoming uneasy. "I'm lost."

"Follow me," said Vindhya. "This cavern connects with the tunnel to the Ganges."

"Can you find it in the dark?"

"I hope so."

"Won't it be underwater as well?"

"No, it's above this cavern."

"What if we can't find it?"

The fakir remained silent.

"Answer me," insisted Tremal-Naik.

"Then we die here," sighed Vindhya.

"The sepoys?"

"I'm not afraid of the captain's men; the tunnels we took are still full of water, they won't be able to track us for awhile. I'm more worried about our strength giving way."

"I'm getting tired," said the dandi, struggling to keep afloat.

"Try to find the tunnel," said Tremal-Naik. "We'll do our best to follow."

The fakir began to swim, found the wall and groped his way forward, attempting to get his bearings.

Following the sounds of splashing water, Tremal-Naik and his companions made their way through the lightless cavern, keeping close to avoid getting lost.

Though they were bold determined men, the profound darkness and the gloomy echo of splashing water began to affect them. Even Tremal-Naik felt a slight terror begin to seep into his bones.

The fakir had already made two unsuccessful rounds of the cavern. He had almost given way to despair, when he unexpectedly struck something hard. He stretched forth his leg and felt a step.

"Found it!" he exclaimed triumphantly.

"The tunnel?" asked the dandi, his voice almost a whisper. "I can barely keep afloat, my strength's giving way."

"A foothold," replied Vindhya.

"Is there room for us?" asked Moh. "I'm exhausted."

"The tunnel's close; I'm standing on a step."

"This way, fakir," said Tremal-Naik.

The fakir reached forward, grabbed a step and yelled: "Come, we're saved!"

Feeling his way forward, he quickly reached the mouth of the tunnel and with one last effort, pulled himself up into the passageway.

"This is it," he said." Come, it isn't far to the Ganges."

"Do you see a light?" asked Tremal-Naik.

"Not yet, we're going to have to make our way through a few more tunnels and caverns."

Following his voice, the three companions soon reached the steps.

Vindhya had already entered the tunnel, advancing blindly, not knowing precisely where he was. The caverns were full of passages he had never explored, he was not sure if the one he had found was indeed the one that led to the river.

"What a disaster if we've come all this way in vain!" he murmured. "I'm not sure we'll find our way in this darkness."

He took two more steps and struck something hard.

"What's this?" he mumbled nervously.

"What's the matter?" asked Tremal-Naik, knocking against him.

"The path is blocked," replied Vindhya.

"Then you made a mistake?"

"Afraid so."

They all fell silent.

"I'm starting to believe we're lost," said Tremal-Naik, attempting as best he could to stifle his anger. "What are we going to do now?"

Vindhya sighed.

"Is that all you have to say," continued Tremal-Naik. "I don't want to die here, understand?"

"I'm at a loss," said the fakir. "Without a torch I haven't the slightest idea where to go."

"What's blocking our path?"

"It's either a rock or a door."

Tremal-Naik drew a gun from his belt, took a few steps forward and began to tap against the obstruction with the butt of his weapon. A metallic sound echoed throughout the dark tunnel.

"It's a metal door," said the hunter. "There may be a way to open it; some kind of button."

He ran his hands along its top, bottom and sides, but to no avail.

"Nothing," he murmured dully.

He gathered his strength and pushed against it, but in vain. The door would not move.

"We'd need a cannon to blast through it," he said.

"Could this passage have been sealed recently?" asked the old Thug.

"No," replied Vindhya. "It may have led to the pagoda at one time."

"Then this isn't the tunnel to the Ganges."

"No."

"We'll have to continue our search."

"How?"

"We'll go back to the cavern."

"If we couldn't find it before, I doubt we'll be able to find it now."

"We'll see," said Tremal-Naik. "Are you sure that tunnel isn't underwater?"

"If it was, there wouldn't be any air in here."

"Let's go find it then," suggested the old Thug.

"What if we waited for the water to drain a bit more?" asked the dandi.

"What about the sepoys?" observed Moh. "Have you forgotten them?"

"They're probably still far off."

As if to refute the dandi's words, a frightening discharge thundered from nearby followed by a brilliant flash that lit every corner of the cavern. The sepoys had set off another mine. The waters, hurled forward by the powerful blast, had smashed against the walls with a deafening roar as a shower of rocks fell from the ceiling.

Tremal-Naik, the dandi, and the old Thug cried out in fear, believing the entire cavern was about to collapse upon them; Vindhya, however, howled triumphantly.

That flash of light had allowed him to spot a second set of steps.

"Over there!" he yelled, recognizing them immediately. "Hurry, into the cavern!"

Without bothering to ensure if his companions were following, he rushed into the water and began to swim with renewed vigour.

"Vindhya!" Tremal-Naik yelled.

"Come," thundered the fakir. "The sepoys are almost here!"

Realizing they were about to be surprised by Captain MacPherson and his men, the Indians dove in after him. Voices could be heard in the tunnel they had swum through. From time to time, flashes of light illuminated the walls and reflected onto the waters. The blast having cleared their path, the sepoys had regrouped and were preparing to storm the cavern.

Just as the fakir reached the steps at the foot of the passageway that led to the river, they heard a voice yell out, "Forward men!"

Tremal-Naik howled with rage.

"That's Bhárata's voice!"

"He tricked us and now he's hunting us down," said the old Thug. "If that rascal ever falls into our hands again, we won't spare him."

At their sergeant's command, twenty sepoys armed with rifles and carrying torches rushed into the tunnel. But when they reached the cavern, they were forced to halt for the water came up to their necks.

"There they are!" yelled a soldier.

Vindhya, Tremal-Naik and the old Thug had already reached the passageway and headed inside, but the dandi, exhausted by the swim, had paused on the last step to catch his breath.

Spotting him, several sepoys rapidly aimed their weapons and fired.

Riddled with bullets, the unlucky fakir tumbled into the water. Hearing the splash, Tremal-Naik turned about.

"The dandi!" he yelled.

"Keep going!" replied Vindhya. "He's dead!"

The three Indians raced into the darkness as the sepoys began to swim towards the steps.

After having gone two hundred metres, Vindhya came to a sudden stop. A large metal door stood before him, but this time, it was open.

"This should hold them off for awhile," he said, once his companions had gone through.

He closed the door behind him with a resounding crash.

"Where are we going?" asked Tremal-Naik.

"Forward, keep going forward," replied the fakir.

"Is it far? I can't see anything."

"No. We're close. We're almost there."

Determined to escape from the captain's sepoys, the three men resumed their wild run, feeling along the walls as they advanced.

It was not long before they spotted a sliver of light at the far end of the passageway. A dull murmur soon reached their ears.

"What's that?" asked Tremal-Naik.

"The Ganges," replied Vindhya.

They soon reached a third larger cavern, lit by a narrow opening barely visible in the high ceiling.

Their sudden appearance was greeted with a deafening shriek from above. Surprised by that noise, Tremal-Naik and the Thug stopped and looked about uneasily.

The walls and ceiling were covered with large black dots. A quiet buzz filled the air as thousands upon thousands of badul, a type of bat with large wings and yellow striped fur, began to stir, annoyed by that unexpected intrusion. They gathered in like a large ball, then scattered in all directions, soaring about the cavern, striking the men with their giant wings.

Tremal-Naik and his companions quickly ran through that chaotic storm and into another tunnel. A rumbling sound soon reached their ears, the river was nearby.

"Come," said Vindhya, "We're safe now!"

They raced forward, the ceiling narrowing with each step, and soon stood before an opening.

"It doesn't look very big," said Tremal-Naik.

"Follow me," replied Vindhya.

With a few steps, the fakir's hips disappeared beneath the water. The tunnel floor sloped downward and led into the river, the Ganges was little more than a metre away.

Advancing cautiously, the fakir was about to plunge into open water, when he stopped suddenly and quickly drew back.

"What's the matter?" asked Tremal-Naik.

"Sepoys!"

Chapter 16
Vindhya's Death

The fakir had not been mistaken. Three launches manned by a dozen sepoys were patrolling the river in the early morning light, attempting to find the mouth of the passageway.

Fortunately, it appeared the soldiers did not know the tunnel's location; otherwise they would have stormed the entrance and trapped the fugitives.

At the sight of them, Tremal-Naik turned pale. He slowly drew back and gave the fakir a menacing look.

"Someone's betrayed us!"

"So it would seem," replied Vindhya.

"Who? You assured me no one knew of these tunnels."

"It is so."

"You lied to us."

"No."

"Then how do you explain those men?"

"Bhárata," said the fakir. "He knew of our plans."

"Bhárata!"

"Yes! He overheard our conversations, he heard me tell you about a tunnel to the Ganges and once he escaped, he ordered his men to keep an eye on the shore."

"It must be so," confirmed the old Thug.

"So, what are we going to do now?" asked Tremal-Naik.

"We'll have to try something desperate," replied Vindhya. "If we remain here, it won't be long before the sepoys find us."

"What about the metal door?"

"They've probably blown it up by now."

244

"You have a plan?"

"We're all good swimmers; we'll dive underwater and try to reach the opposite shore."

"If those soldiers spot us, they'll start shooting."

"I know, but we'll have to risk it. There are always a few corpses float- ing in the river, there's a good chance they won't even spot us. Now get into the water! I can hear the sepoys advancing."

Time was of the essence. In a few minutes the soldiers pursuing them would have stormed their last refuge and taken them prisoner. They took deep breaths and dove into the water.

Tremal-Naik quickly swam three hundred paces then stopped and let the current drag him forward, drawing on all his strength to remain un- derwater. Holding his breath until his ears began to pound, he swam two hundred paces then rolled on his back and gently let his nose and mouth break the surface. Once he had filled his lungs, he submerged again and headed for a patch of thick vegetation lining the far shore.

He had gone a hundred and fifty paces, and was about to come up for another breath when he heard a shot then a cry reverberate through the water.

Someone had been hit.

Though exhausted, he swam on, keeping beneath the waves. When at last he could go no further, a vigorous kick brought him just beneath the surface.

He was about to take a breath, when he struck against something.

Grabbing it with both arms, he slowly poked his head up from the water and opened his eyes.

He barely stifled a cry; Vindhya's body lay floating beside him. The poor fakir had received a bullet in the head; the waters about him were red with blood.

Horrified, Tremal-Naik pushed away the Thug's remains and disap- peared beneath the water. The shore was not far off and fortunately the launch was now more than five hundred metres away.

245

Afraid of sharing the fakir's fate, he swam desperately, coming up for air among the large round ghil leaves floating atop the waters along the shore.

Flocks of brown ibis, Brahmin ducks, and cormorants frightened by that sudden appearance, flew off across the river, cackling loudly.

Fearing that sudden flight would attract the sepoys' attention, Tremal-Naik hid beneath the leaves for several minutes then slowly made his way towards the bushes and reeds. With one last effort he dragged himself out of the water and slithered towards a grove of mango trees. Hidden by the leaves, he pulled himself up onto a large branch and cast his eyes towards the river.

Two of the three launches had drawn up close to the mouth of the tunnel. Several sepoys were coming out of the opening, probably those that had tracked the fugitives through the passageways beneath the old pagoda; the third, however, was making its way down the Ganges.

"They must be looking for the fakir's body," murmured Tremal-Naik. "I wonder what happened to the old Thug."

No sooner had he uttered those words when he spotted something moving among the ghil leaves.

At first he thought it might have been some kind of large fish, but a few minutes later he spotted a head peering out of the foliage.

"The Thug," he murmured.

He put a hand to his lips and howled like a jackal.

Moh raised his head and cast his eyes towards the river. He had understood immediately, a friend was nearby; however, he was hesitant to leave the safety of his hiding place.

"Over here!" yelled Tremal-Naik. "The coast is clear."

The old man rushed ashore, dove in among the grass and crawled to the grove of mango trees.

"I'm glad you're safe!" he said.

"Vindhya has been killed!"

"I know," replied Moh. "I was just ten paces from him when the sepoys shot him."

"What are we going to do now?"

"We'll head south."

"And then?"

"Then we'll try to find the paramahansa."

"What about the captain?"

"We have more pressing concerns at the moment."

"But what if he's already set sail?"

"I doubt it, Tremal-Naik. Quickly now, we've got to get out of here before the sepoys begin to search the area."

"Do you know the way?"

"We'll follow the shore for awhile," replied the Thug.

They were about to leave the grove, when they spotted a Brahmin priest coming out of the nearby rice field. He was a tall handsome man wrapped in a white cloak. His face was framed by a magnificent grey beard and he carried a metal pot in one hand, large enough to contain three of four litres of water.

"Off for his morning bath, no doubt" said Tremal-Naik.

"Our luck may be changing," replied Moh. "He may be able to hide us; the sepoys would never dare violate the home of a Brahmin priest. We'll approach him once he's finished."

Unaware of the two fugitives, the Brahmin walked past the thicket and slowly made his way down to the shore. Keeping his eyes fixed on the sun as it rose above the horizon, he took off his cloak and began to wet his hands and feet. He scooped some water into his right hand, and raised it towards the heavens, letting it run down his wrist. Then, murmuring his morning mantras, he wet his nose, mouth, ears, lips, eyes, stomach and shoulders.

His bath completed, he drew out a green twig and brushed his teeth, then gathered a bit of earth from the riverbed and traced a few marks on his forehead.

Brahmin must complete numerous daily rites designed to test their piety. Once they have bathed, they wash their mantles and take up a small bundle of grass. Facing east, they wade into the river and begin their morning meditation, chanting mantras to ward off evil spirits. They take three sips of water, hold their breath, repeat several mantras, sip more water, cup their hands, stand on one foot, and make three oblations to the sun. After three more sips, they utter ten mantras, then clasp their hands and offer a final prayer to the sun. Lastly they turn to the four corners of the compass, east, south, west and north, repeating a short mantra while facing each direction.

Having finished his morning rites, the Brahmin walked up the shore and sat down by a thicket. He mixed a bit of red ochre with some mud then painted a dot in the middle of his forehead, one on the tip of his nose and a few more upon his arms, making each mark with a different finger. He was about to take a last sip of water from the sacred river, when Moh appeared before him and bid him good morning.

The Brahmin looked at the Indian and was about to throw away the bundle of grass, this being the procedure when one encountered a member of the lowest castes, but the old Indian quickly put up a restraining hand and said, "I'm a sotteri; I serve Kali."

That greeting announced Moh as a warrior, a member of the second of four Indian castes. The first and most noble is that of the Brahmin priests, the third is comprised of farmers, the fourth of servants and artisans.

"What do you want?" asked the Brahmin.

"We would be most obliged if you could hide us until nightfall."

"Do you not have a house?"

"Yes, but it is quite far from here and my friend and I are in great danger."

"Are your lives at risk?"

"Those sepoys crossing the river wish to take us prisoner."

"Have you stolen anything?"

"No."

"Killed someone?"

"No."

"Then follow me," said the Brahmin.

"Will we be safe in your home?"

"A pagoda is sacred."

"The sepoys are coming!" Tremal-Naik said at that moment.

The old Thug cast his eyes towards the water. The two launches that had stopped near the tunnel had picked up Bhárata's sepoys and were quickly advancing across the river.

"Those dogs are still after us!" he exclaimed, attempting to stifle his anger. "They'll be on our heels before long."

"And Bhárata will be leading them," added Tremal-Naik.

"Come," said the Brahmin.

While the sepoys were speeding towards the shore, the Brahmin and the two fugitives rapidly crossed the grove of mangos and headed into a rice field.

They soon spotted the spires of a pagoda just beyond a small forest of coconut trees, peepal, neem and tara palms.

The Brahmin led his guests across the rice field and through the forest and came to a stop before a small pagoda capped by a large dome. A copper statue of Vasuki peered down from its spire, the serpent king that in ancient times had helped the gods churn the great ocean.

The Brahmin rushed up the steps and pushed open a bronze door green with age. Waving the men inside, he quickly drew a heavy latch and barred the door behind them.

"You're in the Temple of Narasimha," he said. "No Indian would dare enter without my permission."

"The sepoys serve the British government," observed Tremal-Naik.

"But they're still Indians," replied the priest.

The temple was bare save for an enormous golden statue that stood in the centre. Narasimha, half man, half lion, was Vishnu's fourth incarnation, the god having taken this form to slay a demon that could not be killed by man or beast.

The Brahmin approached the statue and pushed against a spring hidden in its stomach; a metal panel slid back, opening a hatch large enough for a man to pass through. He helped the two Indians inside and said, "You'll be safe in there; no one will find you."

The statue was large enough to fit six people quite comfortably. The two Indians crawled up to its head and peered through its glass eyes.

The old Thug smiled happily as his gaze swept across the door.

"We'll see anyone that comes in," he said.

"Don't you trust the Brahmin?" asked Tremal-Naik.

"Of course I do," replied the Thug. "Brahmins hate the British as much we do. They despise the sepoys because they're Indians serving a foreign master. He may not know why they're after us, but he's promised to help and he'll keep his word."

"The sepoys could just give up."

"I doubt it. If they've found our tracks, they'll surround the pagoda and demand entry. The search is far from over."

"We're running a great risk then, we're pretty much trapped in here."

"Who could possibly guess we're hiding in here?"

"It's large enough to hide several men. They could grow suspicious and rip it apart."

"Indian soldiers tear apart an incarnation of Vishnu? They'd never commit such sacrilege!"

"That may be, but if they surround the pagoda we'll be trapped in here anyway," said Tremal-Naik.

"They'll grow tired eventually."

"And in the meantime the captain will set sail for Rajmangal."

Moh started at that observation.

"That's true," he murmured. "And if he sets off, it'll mean the end for our brethren."

"And perhaps the death of my beloved," said Tremal-Naik, stifling a sigh. "We cannot allow it, I must kill him!"

"He may put off his departure until Bhárata and the sepoys return."

"Who can assure that?"

"No one, I guess."

"What if he does set sail?"

The old Thug fell silent, at a loss for an answer. At one point, however, he struck his forehead and exclaimed triumphantly, "We've forgotten about the paramahansa!"

"The fakir with the withered arm?"

"Yes."

"What about him?"

"He'll rescue us."

"How?"

"I don't know, but I have great faith in old Nimpor. He's greatly respected. All fakirs and snake charmers obey his every word; he can do anything. Once he learns we're in danger, he'll find a way to help us."

"Who's going to inform him?"

"The Brahmin."

"Ah!"

A shot thundered from outside the pagoda, echoing beneath the great dome.

"The sepoys!" the old Thug exclaimed with a shudder.

"Ssh," said Tremal-Naik.

Chapter 17
The Mattu Pongal

The Brahmin must have been expecting that visit, for at the sound of that shot, he appeared from behind a screen where he had been praying before one of the many incarnations of Vishnu, and headed quickly towards the door.

Peering through the statue's eyes, Tremal-Naik and Moh spied his every movement. The priest drew the large latch and slowly opened the door, then stretched out his arms, blocking access to the pagoda.

Four sepoys with rifles stood before him, led by a sergeant the two fugitives recognized immediately: Bhárata.

"How can I help you?" asked the Brahmin, feigning astonishment.

Unexpectedly finding themselves before a member of such an elevated caste, the five Indians were startled for a moment, but the sergeant quickly recovered and said, "Forgive us, for having disturbed you, Your Holiness, we're looking for two men. We've been searching for them since last night."

"And you think they're in this pagoda?" asked the Brahmin, his amazement increasing.

"We believe so," said Bhárata. "Their tracks disappear nearby."

"No one has entered here."

"Are you certain?"

"I have not seen anyone, search elsewhere."

Having said that he moved to close the temple door, but Bhárata, not entirely convinced, quickly put up a restraining hand.

The Brahmin frowned.

"You dare?" he said.

"I mean no offence," replied the sergeant. "I'm looking for two men; I would appreciate it if you would allow us to search the pagoda."

"No weapons may desecrate Vishnu's temple."

"We'll leave them at the door."

"Very well then," replied the Brahmin, fearing that further resistance would increase the sergeant's suspicions.

"Thank you," replied Bhárata.

He ordered his men to lay down their rifles then turned towards a second group of sepoys that had remained at the base of the steps and said, "Surround the pagoda, if anyone attempts to escape, fire."

He turned about and led four men into the temple, keeping his right hand on the hilt of his sabre, ready to draw it at the first sign of danger.

There was no place to hide in the pagoda, the interior consisting of only one room that the Brahmin used as his residence. Nevertheless, the five sepoys carefully examined each corner, tapping the stones on the floor to make sure they did not conceal any hidden passages. Once they finished inspecting the room, they came to a halt before the giant statue of Narasimha.

Bhárata would have liked to ensure it was empty, but he did not dare commit such sacrilege. Even though he had been in the captain's service for many years, he was still an Indian and he had not renounced his religion.

"Do you swear that no one has sought refuge in this pagoda?" he asked the Brahmin for the second time.

"Yes, Sergeant," the priest replied calmly.

"And yet those two Indians must be hiding around here somewhere."

"Well, go look for them."

"I plan to. Thank you for your assistance. Good day."

The five sepoys cast one last look about the room then slowly made their way out of the temple.

The Brahmin watched them go then closed the door. He paced about the room a few times then sat down by a small hole carved in a block of black stone.

"Ah!" he murmured after several minutes. "They're preparing to surround the pagoda. Well, we can be just as patient. We will not be beaten by a handful of chokadars."[14]

He left the spy hole, headed towards the giant deity and pressed the button. Tremal-Naik and the old Thug immediately popped their heads out of the hatch.

"You have nothing to fear for the moment," said the Brahmin.

"Are they gone?" asked Tremal-Naik.

"No, they've surrounded the pagoda."

"They didn't believe you?"

"I'm afraid not."

"Nothing we can do to change their minds?"

"I doubt it."

"And there's no other way out of here?"

"None."

"No underground passages into the forest?" asked Moh.

"No, I'm afraid not."

"We have to escape," said Tremal-Naik. "It's vital."

"As soon as you set foot outside, those traitors will capture you," replied the Brahmin.

"I have an idea," said the old Thug, "Is there someone you can trust?"

"Yes, a boy that brings me food."

"When will he arrive?"

"Shortly."

"Does he know Calcutta?"

"He was born there."

"Have him relay a message to a paramahansa named Nimpor. He's our friend; he'll help us escape."

"Where can the boy find him?"

"In Krishna's pagoda. He's known as the fakir of the flower, there's a seedling growing from his left hand."

"Very well," said the Brahmin. "What's the message?"

"That his friends, Tremal-Naik and Moh, are surrounded by sepoys in this pagoda."

---

[14] Lackeys

"Anything else?"

"Tell him the sepoys are led by Captain MacPherson's sergeant."

"You'll have word from the paramahansa before nightfall," said the Brahmin.

He brought them a bowl overflowing with rice and fish, a bottle of tody and several small bananas. He then closed the hatch, inviting the Indians to eat well and relax, reassuring them that they had nothing to fear.

Not having eaten since the previous night, Tremal-Naik and the old Thug quickly devoured the food. Once they had finished the meal, they stretched out as best they could, lay their daggers beside them and quietly fell asleep.

They had been sleeping for several hours when they were awakened by the sound of the hatch sliding open. Fearing the sepoys had returned, they grabbed their daggers and sprang to their feet.

Darkness had invaded the interior of that giant god; however, the open hatch provided enough light to allow them to make out the face of the Brahmin priest.

"The boy has just returned," he said.

"Did he find the paramahansa?" the two prisoners asked in unison.

"Yes," replied the priest.

"Is there a message?" asked Tremal-Naik.

"You'll escape tonight."

"How?"

"I do not know yet, however, I've been instructed to light the temple and prepare for the Mattu Pongal. Yesterday every home in the Indian quarter celebrated the Sarkarai Pongal."

"He's coming here?"

"Yes, and I think I know what the paramahansa plans to do," said the priest. "They'll carry the statue of Narasimha to the Ganges and bathe it in its sacred waters. At the right moment, you'll slip out and escape."

"Does Nimpor know we're hiding inside it?"

"I instructed the boy to tell him."

"It must be late," said the old Thug. "The sun is about to set."

"What about the sepoys?" asked Tremal-Naik.

"They're still standing guard outside," replied the priest. "Rest assured, we'll outsmart them."

"Won't they object to the festival?"

"They would not dare. No one, not even the British authorities, can prevent us from celebrating our festivals. I'm going up to the roof to keep an eye out for the arrival of the paramahansa and his men."

He closed the hatch and went off to spy on the sepoys. They had set up camp a short distance from the pagoda, placing sentries in several places to thwart any attempt at escape. The priest made his way to a ladder that spiralled up the dome, climbed to the top and slowly took in his surroundings.

His eyes scanned the rice fields and small farms then rested upon the City of Palaces, its dimming skyline still visible in the distance. The sun was setting, its last rays reddening the waters of the sacred river and the countless spires towering among the dark green vegetation.

The sky was clear, save for a cloud of marabou, cackling loudly as they searched for their next meal.

Ships and boats of all sizes gracefully plied the waters, boatmen filling the air with song as they sailed their crafts downstream.

Having scanned the riverbanks, the Brahmin fixed his eyes upon a group of huts surrounded by thick bushes and shaded by groves of palm trees. A long dark mass was slowly approaching, meandering through the rice fields, a handful of torchbearers lighting their way.

"It's them," he murmured.

He watched the mass transform into a jubilant crowd. Soon tom-toms, trumpets, huloks and tambourines mixed with cries of celebration.

"It won't be long now," said the Brahmin.

He bent over the iron railing and looked at the sepoys. Having also heard those sounds, Captain MacPherson's soldiers had drawn their rifles in fear of a sudden attack.

"Let's prepare the Pongal then," said the Brahmin.

He climbed up one of the four spires, picked up a wooden club, and began to sound a giant metal gong. Sharp brassy notes filled the air, shattering the silence about the pagoda and echoing into the nearby groves and rice fields.

The Brahmin continued that deafening music for two minutes, then, spotting several Indians from a nearby village running towards the temple, he went down into the pagoda and opened the door.

Bhárata and two sepoys were standing on the steps.

"What's the meaning of all this noise?" asked the sergeant.

"We're preparing to celebrate the Mattu Pongal," the priest replied.

"Are you planning to let that crowd into the pagoda?"

"Certainly."

"I cannot permit that."

The Brahmin frowned, crossed his arms, and calmly asked, "When were the sepoys given the power to interfere with Hindu celebrations?"

"There are two men hiding in your pagoda," replied Bhárata. "They could easily escape among all those people."

"Search for them before Vishnu's faithful arrive."

"I don't know where they're hiding."

"Neither do I."

Then, without further thought to the sergeant, he turned to address the ten or twelve farmers that had rushed to the call of the tom-tom.

"Light the fire for the Pongal," he instructed.

"I will not allow that procession to enter the pagoda," said Bhárata.

"You are free to do as you wish," replied the Brahmin.

He turned his back to the soldiers and re-entered the temple.

The farmers quickly built a large bonfire at the base of the steps then set off for their houses to collect pots, rice and milk for the Mattu Pongal.

The harvest festival is one of the most popular among Hindus. It lasts for two days. The first day, the Sarkarai Pongal, is a family celebration that's held in the home. They purify the stove with cow dung, fill a new pot with rice and milk then gather round the fire at noon to watch it boil. If it boils rapidly, the coming year will be filled with prosperity, a slow boil indicates new hardships. Once the rice is cooked, a bowl is offered to Lord Indra, ruler of the clouds. They give thanks, ask for a good harvest then serve the remaining rice to all those that have come to attend the ceremony.

The second day, the Mattu Pongal, is for offering thanks to cattle, animals the Hindus hold sacred. Bulls and cows are bathed, their horns are painted and garlands of flowers are placed around their necks. They are taken to the village centre then paraded through the countryside, accompanied by musicians, fakirs, snake charmers, dancers, and priests, stopping at each pagoda for pongal, rice boiled in milk. The celebrations last for hours and the nights are filled with revelry.

The large pots had just begun to boil, when the procession, led by the paramahansa, arrived before the pagoda.

Five hundred people had gathered for the Pongol, howling happily as they drove their cattle forward. Drummers beat their hauks and tom-toms as musicians played their bansi, filling the air with their high pitched notes.

When they reached the steps they fanned out into a large semicircle, Bhárata's men quickly retreating, as the celebrants filled the clearing.

At a sign from the paramahansa, two rows of devadasis came forward. The music grew louder and they began their dance, silk scarves twirling gracefully, their gold and silver bangles flashing in the firelight.

Once their performance ended, the music began to fade and the cows were led to the large pots of rice and milk. Nimpor climbed the temple steps and drew up before the Brahmin priest, who was standing in front of the door.

"Your Holiness," he said, bowing, "This humble paramahansa asks your permission to honour Narasimha. The fakirs wish to bless him in the sacred waters of the Ganges."

"The fakirs are blessed men," said the Brahmin. "If that is their wish, they may enter the pagoda and take the statue to the river."

"No," said a nearby voice. "No one but the Brahmin may enter the pagoda."

The paramahansa turned and found Bhárata standing before him.

"Who are you?" he asked.

"A sergeant of the sepoys."

"Ah! A chokadar," Nimpor said sarcastically.

"Careful, paramahansa! Your tongue is a little sharp."

Nimpor turned about, pointed to the large crowd gathered before the pagoda and said menacingly, "Look at all those fakirs! Not one of them fears death! If you try to prevent them from entering the temple, they'll start a riot. No one has the right to interfere with our religious ceremonies, not even the British. We will not tolerate any kind of interference from you or your sepoys. We have over five hundred devotees here; you have but a dozen men."

Bhárata believed it best not to reply. He knew the fakirs would not have retreated before a dozen rifles; his men had no hope against such large numbers. He gestured in annoyance and withdrew, retreating to the far side of the steps.

The paramahansa raised his good arm and twenty fakirs immediately rushed up the steps and into the temple.

Each man carried an iron rod, a deadly weapon in angry hands. Had they met with resistance, they could have easily massacred the sergeant's sepoys.

The statue of Narasimha was raised and taken outside. The fakirs in the square greeted its appearance with deafening cries; the music grew louder and the devadasis quickly resumed their dance.

"Forward!" thundered the paramahansa.

Supporting the enormous statue with their iron rods, the twenty fakirs descended the steps and began to walk towards the Ganges, preceded by the dancers and musicians, and followed by the snake charmers, the cows and the rest of the devotees.

Bhárata and the sepoys, unaware the two fugitives were concealed inside the god, had remained stationed about the pagoda, still convinced that the Brahmin had hidden the Thugs in some underground chamber.

The paramahansa, pleased that all was going according to plan, led the noisy throng to a place along the river thick with vegetation.

He stopped fifty paces from the shore, put up a hand and gestured for all to halt. Born by twenty loyal men, the statue advanced through the crowd and into the reeds as it was carried to the river.

They gently lowered it onto a sandbank then took two steps back, encircling the statue to better hide the escape. Assured the path was clear the fakir quickly ran his hand along the metal.

Instantly, the hatch sprung open.

"Now!" said Nimpor.

Tremal-Naik and the old Thug quickly slipped out and disappeared among the reeds and lotus leaves.

"Narasimha has been blessed," the paramahansa announced loudly. "We shall return him to his home."

The twenty men grabbed their iron rods, picked up the giant statue and headed back towards the musicians and devadasis. The large procession immediately regrouped and noisily made its way back to the pagoda.

Chapter 18
Too Late

The paramahansa had remained behind, crouched on the sandbank, pretending to bathe. Once the procession was a good distance away, he stood up and said, "Come, hurry!"

Tremal-Naik and the old Thug followed him into the bushes.

"Thanks for coming," said Tremal-Naik. "Without your help, we'd still be trapped in the pagoda."

"No need to thank me, there's still much to do," replied Nimpor.

"Any news of the captain?" asked Moh.

"Yes, things look bad for Suyodhana."

"Tell us everything," said Tremal-Naik.

"They're going to set sail for the Sundarbans tomorrow at dawn."

"Great Shiva!" exclaimed Tremal-Naik, turning pale. "So soon!"

"The *Cornwall* tested her engines today."

"Who told you that?"

"Hider."

"Then all is lost!"

"Perhaps not. We'll hurry back to Calcutta and find out his exact plans."

"Where's the ship anchored?"

"Near Fort William."

"We'll go there immediately."

"It's quite far," observed the old Thug.

"Your whaleboat's waiting for us not too far from here," said the paramahansa.

"Our men managed to escape?"

"Yes."

"Let's go," said Tremal-Naik. "If the *Cornwall* has already raised anchor, we're done for; Rajmangal will be destroyed."

The three men raced down the shore, the drums and trumpets of the procession echoing faintly in the distance. It was not long before they reached the six Thugs; the whaleboat was only a few feet away, hidden among the reeds.

"Have any soldiers been buzzing about here?" asked the old Thug.

"No," one of the oarsmen replied.

"Can we reach Fort William before dawn?" asked Tremal-Naik.

"It'll be difficult but not impossible," said one of the Indians.

"Fifty rupees if you succeed," said the paramahansa.

"All we need is your blessing," replied the Thugs.

The whaleboat quickly set off, descending the river with the speed of a steamer. Moh had taken the rudder; Nimpor and Tremal-Naik at his side.

The Thugs rowed with all their might, the helmsman skilfully guiding the little boat around the sandbanks dotting the river. The Hugli was deserted at that late hour and the tiny vessel could fly over the waters without fear of being spotted.

"When did you see Hider?" the hunter asked, turning his gaze from the shore.

"This morning," replied Nimpor, "before I received the Brahmin's message."

"He's certain the captain plans to leave at dawn?"

"Yes. Two companies of Bengali infantry embarked yesterday. They've fitted the ship with two heavy pieces of artillery and taken on a large quantity of supplies and ammunition. The stokers fired up the engines this morning shortly before noon."

"Was the captain aboard?"

"He did not know."

"Are your men still aboard?"

"Yes, both of them."

"Excellent. I'll need their assistance," said Tremal-Naik.

"You have an idea?"

262

"Yes, I'm going to board the frigate."

"You're going to kill him aboard his own ship?"

"There's no other option."

"It won't be easy," said the paramahansa.

"I will not fail," Tremal-Naik replied determinedly.

"The British do not take murder lightly, especially when it's committed by an Indian."

"I know."

"Do you think the captain's death will put a halt to the expedition?"

"He's the driving force; he's the only one that knows their final destination."

"But what if the ship has already set sail?"

"Shiva will protect me."

"What do you mean?"

"I'll go to Rajmangal and wait for the captain there."

"It would be best if the captain never reached the island."

"I don't see any other option."

"I may have a better idea. Hider's ship is departing for Ceylon tomorrow night. If the *Cornwall* has already set sail, you could have the *Devonshire* take you to the mouth of the river. That gunboat is a lot faster than the frigate."

"How can I get aboard?"

"Hider will arrange everything."

While they were talking, the launch continued to advance along the Ganges with ever-increasing speed.

Dawn had started to break as they reached the outskirts of the City of Palaces. Crews began to stir aboard the numerous ships lining the shore. Men appeared among the confusion of masts and sails, stretching their arms, as several songs echoed through the calm morning air.

Tremal-Naik stood up, his eyes fixed on Fort William, its massive walls towering before him in the morning light.

"Where's the frigate?" he asked savagely.

The paramahansa had also gotten up and was anxiously scanning the shore with his dark menacing eyes.

"Look, over there, in front of that floodgate," he yelled at one point.

Tremal-Naik turned his gaze and spotted a frigate several metres from the fort's moat. Though built for speed, she must have carried a great amount of cargo, for she lay low in the water.

Thick smoke swirled out of her stack. Numerous soldiers and sailors bustled about her deck, hauling cables, stowing boxes and barrels, while others stood at the bow, awaiting the order to raise anchor. It would not be long before the ship set sail.

"He's escaping! Hurry, hurry, or all is lost!" howled Tremal-Naik.

The paramahansa cried out in anger, then slumped back down on a thwart and murmured, "Too late! Suyodhana's days are numbered!"

Gathering what remained of their strength, the six Thugs doubled their efforts. Water splashed over the launch's bow, her sides shaking as she flew over the waves.

"Hurry! Hurry!" repeated the hunter, his howls growing louder as his anxiety increased.

"It's no use," the old Thug said at last, abandoning the rudder.

The frigate had left the dock and was descending majestically down the river, spewing torrents of smoke into the air. The oarsmen, exhausted by that long run, had abandoned their oars, eyeing the vessel ferociously as it sailed past them.

Tremal-Naik picked up a rifle leaning against a thwart and aimed it at the ship.

A man had appeared on the bridge; the hunter had recognized him immediately.

"The captain!" he gasped.

The paramahansa tore the rifle from him before he could fire.

"Do you want to get us all killed?" he said.

Tremal-Naik turned towards him, fists raised, eyes burning with rage. "Didn't you see him?"

"Yes," Nimpor replied calmly.

"I could have killed him."

"What if you missed?" asked the paramahansa. "We'd be done for."

"You're right," murmured Tremal-Naik.

"Don't worry; success can still be ours. There's still a chance to save your Ada," continued the old fakir. "Have you forgotten Hider? He's waiting for us near the *Devonshire*."

Tremal-Naik remained silent, turning his eyes towards the disappearing frigate.

"Head for the shore!" commanded the paramahansa.

The whaleboat tacked and slowly made her way upstream, heading towards the Strand. She was about to dock, when a sailor rushed out from behind an enormous mound of cases and barrels, and ran towards them, yelling, "Quick, come ashore!"

It was Hider, the *Devonshire*'s quartermaster.

At the sound of that voice, Tremal-Naik shot to his feet, and with a leap worthy of a tiger rushed up the steps toward the shore.

"He's gone!" he yelled, approaching the quartermaster.

"I know," replied Hider.

"When does your ship set sail?"

"Tonight at midnight."

"Then there's still time."

"What do you mean?" asked the quartermaster.

"We can still reach the *Cornwall*."

"How?"

"With the *Devonshire*," Tremal-Naik replied determinedly.

Hider looked at him but remained silent, believing perhaps that the hunter had gone mad.

"Understand?" Tremal-Naik asked excitedly.

"No."

"Your gunboat is faster than the frigate."

"Yes, that's true."

"Then we'll overtake the captain's ship and sink her."

"Sink the frigate! How?"

"Don't you think it's possible?"

"It'd be difficult; I'm not in command of the *Devonshire*. If I attempted to sink a British ship, the captain would clap me in irons in an instant."

"He won't get the chance; I have a plan. Are there any Thugs aboard the gunboat?"

"Six in all."

"How big is the crew?"

"Thirty-two men," replied Hider.

"We've got to get another ten men aboard."

"Impossible!"

"Anything is possible if you have the determination," said the paramahansa who had been following their conversation. "Tremal-Naik is Suyodhana's envoy; you will do as he wishes."

"If he can devise a way to get those men aboard, I'll see to it," said the quartermaster. "I'll do anything to protect Suyodhana and our men."

"What's the *Devonshire* loading now?" asked Tremal-Naik.

Chapter 19
Stranglers and Englishmen

The clocks in the City of Palaces had truck midnight, when the *Devonshire* pulled away from the dock and began to make her way down the Hugli.

The night was dark, thick black clouds stretched across the sky, shrouding the moon and stars. Kidderpore lay before them, a few lights blazing from the huts and ships that lined the shore. Behind them, Calcutta slowly faded into the night.

Standing on the gangway, the captain shouted final orders, his metallic voice thundering above the rumbling engine and churning wheels. Several crewmen worked in the dim lantern light, stowing the last barrels and cases that encumbered the deck.

Kidderpore had just disappeared from sight, when Hider left the wheel and silently made his way across the bridge. He walked past an Indian sealing the main hatch and nudged him with his elbow.

"Come," he whispered, as he walked by.

A few minutes later the two men made their way down the steps to the common room, quickly looking around to ensure they were alone.

"Well?" asked Hider.

"No one suspects anything."

"Did you count the marked barrels?"

"Yes, ten of them as promised."

"Where did you put them?"

"Beneath the stern."

"Close together?"

"Side by side," said the Thug.

"Did you warn the others?"

"Everyone is ready. They'll attack at our signal."

"We must be cautious. The crew could set fire to the powder and blow up friends and foes alike."

"When are we going to strike?"

"Tonight, once I've taken care of the captain."

"What shall we do in the meantime?"

"Send two men to secure the armoury, then find the two stokers and take command of the engine."

"It won't be the first time I work in the boiler room."

"Excellent. I'll start to put the plan in effect."

Hider climbed back up to the deck and cast a look at the gangway.

The captain was pacing back and forth, his arms crossed, smoking a cigarette.

"Poor captain!" murmured the strangler. "You don't deserve this."

He headed towards the stern, went down to the lower deck, and once assured no one was about, stopped before the captain's cabin. The door was ajar; he opened it and found himself in a small, elegantly furnished room. He quickly advanced towards a table on which sat a crystal bottle full of lemonade.

A sly smile spread across his lips.

"Every morning the bottle returns empty," he murmured, "The captain, always has a drink before he goes to sleep."

He inserted a hand beneath his shirt and pulled out a tiny vial filled with red liquid. He sniffed its contents several times then poured three drops into the bottle.

The lemonade bubbled, reddened then turned back to its original shade.

"He'll sleep for two days," mumbled the Thug. "Now let's go find my friends."

He left the cabin and opened the door that led into the hold. A faint sound emanated from beneath the stern, followed by a snap, as if a firearm had just been loaded.

"Tremal-Naik!" the Thug called out.

"Is that you, Hider?" whispered a voice. "Let us out, we can barely breathe."

The Thug picked up a lantern he had hidden in a corner earlier that day, lit it, and walked towards the row of barrels.

He quickly removed the lids and the ten stranglers climbed out, rubbing and stretching their limbs. Tremal-Naik rushed towards Hider.

"The *Cornwall?*" he asked.

"She's heading towards the open sea."

"Can we catch her?"

"Yes, if the *Devonshire* picks up her pace."

"We have to board her; Ada's life depends on it."

"First we have to take possession of the gunboat."

"I know. Do you have a plan?"

"Yes."

"Quick tell me everything. It'll be a tragedy if we don't reach the *Cornwall* in time."

"Relax, Tremal-Naik. There's still hope."

"Tell me your plan."

"First, we'll take possession of the engines."

"Any Thugs in the boiler room?"

"Three stokers. The four of us won't have any problem tying up the engineer."

"And then?"

"Then I'll go and see if the captain has drunk the sleeping potion I slipped into his lemonade. You'll be waiting in the transom and jump onto the bridge at my signal. Caught by surprise, the British will surrender."

"Are they armed?"

"Only with knives."

"Excellent, we've got to hurry."

"I'm ready. I'm going to tie up the engineer."

He put out the lantern and made his way back up to the bridge, arriving just as the captain was leaving the gangway and heading towards the stern.

269

"So far, so good," murmured the Thug.

He filled his pipe and headed into the engine room. The three Thugs were at their stations, by the boilers, whispering among themselves.

The engineer was smoking, seated on a chair, reading a book.

With a glance, he signalled his men to be ready then moved towards the lantern that hung from the ceiling, above the engineer's head.

"Mind if I light my pipe, Mister Kuthingon?" said the quartermaster. "The wind keeps blowing out my matches."

"By all means," replied the engineer.

He stood up to give Hider some room. With one quick move the strangler grabbed him by the throat and slammed him onto the table.

"Mercy!" the poor man stammered, turning purple beneath the quartermaster's iron fist.

"Keep quiet and you'll be fine," replied Hider.

At a sign from their leader, the Thugs bound and gagged the engineer then dragged him behind a large pile of coal.

"Make sure nothing happens to him," said Hider. "I'm going to check on the captain."

"What about us?" asked one of the Thugs.

"Do not leave your post, no matter what happens."

"Very well."

Hider calmly lit his pipe and went up the stairs.

The gunboat was sailing past groves of trees, her ram slicing through swatches of floating vegetation.

The crew was on deck, smoking and talking amongst themselves as they gazed upon the river. The Officer of the Watch was walking along the lunette, chatting with the master gunner.

Hider, extremely satisfied, rubbed his hands happily, returned astern, and went below without making a sound.

When he arrived at the captain's cabin, he placed an ear against the door. Loud snores filled the air. He drew his dagger as a precaution, turned the knob and entered.

The captain had drunk most of the lemonade and was fast asleep.

"A cannon blast would fail to wake him," smiled the Indian.

He left the cabin and headed into the hold. Tremal-Naik and his companions were waiting for him, their revolvers drawn and ready.

"Well?" asked the hunter, jumping to his feet.

"The engine room is ours and the captain is fast asleep," replied Hider.

"And the crew?"

"They're on deck, unarmed."

"Let's go up."

"We must be cautious, my friends. We'll have to trap the crew in a crossfire before they can take refuge in the forecastle. Otherwise we could be in for a long siege. Tremal-Naik, you'll below with five men, I'll take the others to the common room. When you hear the first gunshot, rush up to the bridge."

"Fine."

Hider picked up an axe, drew his revolver then led five men across the hold, into the common room and up the stairs.

"Now!" commanded Hider.

The six men sprang onto the bridge, filling the air with savage cries.

Surprised by that unexpected noise, the crew rushed to the bow to see what had happened.

A revolver blast knocked down the master gunner.

"Kali! Kali!" shouted the Thugs.

A terrible rain of bullets followed the stranglers' war cry.

Several men fell to the deck. The others, surprised by that sudden, unexpected attack, rushed to the stern, yelling in terror.

Cries of "Kali! Kali!" filled the air.

Tremal-Naik and his men had swarmed upon the quarterdeck, daggers and revolvers drawn.

A series of discharges filled the air.

Confusion spread throughout the gunboat. The ship, now without a helmsman, began to drift with the current.

Caught in a crossfire, the British began to panic. Fortunately the Officer of the Watch was quick to take command. He drew his sabre and jumped down from the lunette.

"To arms!" he shouted.

The crew immediately gathered round him and rushed to the stern, drawing their knives.

The clash was terrible; Tremal-Naik's Thugs were quickly routed by that avalanche of men.

The officer seized a cannon but the victory was short-lived. Hider had rallied his men and attacked from the rear, weapons levelled, ready to fire.

"Lieutenant!" he yelled, pointing his revolver at him.

"What do you want, you wretch!" yelled the officer.

"Surrender and I promise no harm will come to you."

"No!"

"We have fifty bullets each. It's foolish to resist."

"What are you going to do with us?"

"We'll put you in a lifeboat, where you go after that is up to you."

"And the gunboat?"

"That's none of your concern. Now surrender or I'll order my men to fire."

"Let's surrender, Lieutenant!" shouted the sailors, realizing they were at Hider's mercy.

After a brief hesitation, the lieutenant broke his sword and threw it into the river.

The stranglers rushed at the sailors, disarmed them and escorted them into the whalers. The engineer and the unconscious captain were quickly brought up to join the crew.

"Good luck!" shouted the quartermaster.

"If I ever catch you, I'll hang the lot of you!" the lieutenant replied, shaking his fist.

"As you wish."

As the two launches headed towards then shore, the gunboat resumed her course.

Chapter 20
Aboard The Cornwall

So far the plan had worked. The frigate had a fifteen hour lead, but the gunboat, faster and lighter, could still reach her on the open water if she held her speed.

Once they had cleared the deck of the dead and tended to the wounded, Tremal-Naik and Hider made their way to the lunette, while a topman armed with a powerful spyglass took position on the crosslet.

Udaipur had taken command of the engine room and the hunter quickly summoned him to the bridge.

"We need more power," said Tremal-Naik.

"We're sailing at maximum pressure, Captain."

"It's not enough. We have to overtake the *Cornwall.*"

"Increase pressure to five atmospheres," said Hider.

"We could blow up the ship."

"We'll take the risk."

The engineer left the bridge and rushed down into the engine room.

The gunboat flew like a bird. Torrents of black smoke spewed from the stack; steam roared through the turbines; the wheel churned furiously shaking the ship from bow to stern.

"Heave the log!" ordered Hider.

"Fifteen knots and five tenths," a sailor yelled out a few minutes later.

"We're really racing now," said the quartermaster.

"Do you think we can catch the frigate?" asked Tremal-Naik.

"I hope so."

"On the river?"

"On the open sea. It's only a hundred and twenty-five kilometres from Calcutta to the Bay of Bengal."

"How fast can she go?"

"Six knots an hour and that's under ideal conditions. She's too old to go any faster."

"She must not reach Rajmangal."

"If she does, what's the plan?"

"We ram her and attack her crew."

"You're a determined man, Tremal-Naik," the quartermaster said with a smile.

"I have no choice. I need the captain's head."

"You're running a great risk!"

"I know, Hider."

"The captain could recognize you."

"I'll kill him before he gets the chance."

"And if you fail?"

"I will not fail," Tremal-Naik said adamantly.

"He's a tough man."

"I'm tougher. I have reason to succeed."

"The Guardian of the Temple of the East?"

"If I were to lose her, I'd kill myself."

"I pity you, my friend," said Hider, moved.

Tremal-Naik looked at him uneasily.

"What do you mean?" he murmured.

"Nothing."

"Do you know something I don't?"

"No," said the Thug, a trace of sadness in his voice.

Tremal-Naik fell silent. Hider took one last look at the hunter, let out a deep sigh, then left the lunette and headed for the bow.

Jungles, swamps, and villages flew by as the gunboat continued to devour ground, slashing through the water with ever-increasing speed.

At four o'clock, the gunboat sailed past Diamond Harbour, a small port near the mouth of the Hugli. A white cottage shaded by six coconut trees stood near the shore, the British flag fluttering atop the new semaphore tower that had recently been erected before it.

The river soon grew wider and the island of Sangor appeared in the

274

distance, marking the entrance to the sea.

"Sandheads off the bow!" yelled a sailor from atop the crosslet.

The cry tearing him from his thoughts, Tremal-Naik rushed to the bow, as the sailors scrambled up the shrouds and ratlines. All eyes turned toward the vast sandbanks that stretch from the Ganges into the Bay of Bengal.

The waters were deserted, not a lantern or ship appeared on the horizon.

A cry of rage erupted from Tremal-Naik's lips.

"Topman!" he yelled to an Indian scanning the waters with a spyglass from atop the crosslet.

"Yes, Captain!"

"See anything?"

"Not yet."

"Udaipur! Increase pressure!"

"We're already at maximum pressure," observed the engineer.

"To six atmospheres!" yelled Hider, gritting his teeth. "Four more men to the engine room."

"We'll blow up the ship," grumbled Udaipur.

Four Indians went down into the engine room and filled the boilers with coal. Thick black smoke spewed from the stack as the gunboat began to bounce over the waves.

"Set a course for Raimatla!" Hider ordered the helmsman.

Engines pounding feverishly, steam hissing and roaring through the pipes, the distance separating them from the island was quickly disappearing.

Silence reigned over the bridge. All eyes were scanning the horizon, hoping to spot their prey.

"Ship off the bow!" the topman yelled at one point.

Tremal-Naik started.

"Where?"

"To the south."

"Can you make her out?"

The topman did not reply. He stood up on the crosslet and put the spyglass to his eye.

"It's a steamship!" he yelled.

"The frigate! The frigate!" yelled the Indians.

"Quiet!" thundered the quartermaster. "Topman, where's she headed?"

"East, she's hugging the coast of Raimatla."

"Can you make out her bow?"

"Yes."

"Describe it."

"Straight as an arrow and she's got a ram."

The quartermaster rushed towards Tremal-Naik.

"It's the *Cornwall*," he said. "There's no other ship in Calcutta that could match that description."

Tremal-Naik howled triumphantly.

"Are you sure she's heading east?" he asked again.

"Yes, sir. She's taking the long way around the island; the captain probably fears the canal isn't deep enough."

"Then we can ambush her?"

"On the other side of the island if we cut through the canal. But…" said Hider.

"Quiet, I'm in command here."

Flying at three times the frigate's speed, the gunboat quickly rounded the island. At ten she left the canal bounded by Raimatla and the nearby shores and hid behind a small deserted island opposite Jamera. Hider quickly scanned the waters for the enemy ship, she was still far off.

"Tremal-Naik!" he yelled.

The hunter appeared on the bridge completely transformed. His brown skin had been dyed olive green, white markings made his eyes appear larger, his teeth, white as ivory just a short time ago, had been blackened with betel. So disguised, with a rattan hat on his head, a cha-wat[15] of red calico about his hips, and two long poisoned krises tucked into his sash, he was almost unrecognizable.

---

[15] Loincloth.

"How do I look?" he asked the quartermaster, who was studying him with admiration.

"If I didn't know better, I'd swear you were a Malay."

"Do you think the captain will recognize me?"

"I doubt it."

"What are the names of the two Thugs aboard the *Cornwall*?"

"Palavan and Bindur."

"Excellent! Have the men prepare a launch."

At a sign from the quartermaster a yole was lowered into the water.

"What's your plan?" he asked.

"To get myself rescued by the frigate."

"What about us?"

"Hide the ship in the canal near Rajmangal. When you hear an explosion, raise anchor and come look for me."

He grabbed onto a rope and lowered himself down into the yole, which was rolling gently among the waves.

A resounding whistle filled the air and the gunboat rapidly sailed off. An hour later she was no more than a black dot barely visible on the horizon.

Almost simultaneously, another dot appeared to the south, a thin black plume of smoke stretching over it.

Tremal-Naik fixed his eyes upon it.

"The *Cornwall*!" he exclaimed.

With thoughts of Ada in his heart, he grabbed the oars and began to row furiously.

The ship was advancing, forcing her engines, growing larger with each passing minute. Tremal-Naik continued to row, trying to cut across her path.

At noon, only five hundred paces separated the yole from the frigate. It was the moment the hunter had been waiting for. He waited for a wave to knock against his tiny vessel then hurled himself to one side, tipped it over, and grabbed onto the keel.

"Help! Help!" he thundered.

Several sailors rushed to the frigate's bow. Within seconds, a launch manned by four men was lowered into the water and set off to rescue the castaway.

"Help!" repeated Tremal-Naik.

The launch flew over the waters. Five minutes later, the tiny vessel drew up alongside the yole.

The hunter grabbed a sailor's outstretched hand and climbed aboard.

"Thank you!" he panted.

The sailors took up their oars once again and returned to the *Cornwall*, which had reduced speed to await their arrival. A ladder was lowered, and the Malay, streaming with water, was taken to meet the Officer of the Watch.

"Name?" the officer asked.

"Paranga, from Singapore," replied Tremal-Naik, looking about curiously. "I served aboard the *Hannati*, a merchant ship bound for Bombay. She sank four days ago, a hundred miles from the coast."

"In calm waters?"

"Yes, she sprung a leak beneath the stern."

"And the crew?"

"Drowned. The life boats had been damaged and sank moments after they'd pulled away from the ship."

"Are you hungry?"

"I ate my last biscuit more than twelve hours ago."

"Master Brown! Take this poor devil to the galley."

The quartermaster, an old sea wolf with a grey beard, pulled a cigar stub from his mouth, gently placed it in his hat and led the Malay below. A pot of steaming soup was placed before Tremal-Naik, and the hunter attacked it greedily.

"You have a good appetite, young man," smiled the quartermaster.

"I have an empty stomach. What ship is this?"

"The *Cornwall*."

Tremal-Naik looked at the old man in surprise.

"The *Cornwall*!" he exclaimed.

"The name bother you?"

"On the contrary. I have two friends aboard a ship with a similar name. Two Indians."

"Well, there's a coincidence! What are their names?"

"Palavan and Bindur."

"They both serve aboard this ship, young man."

"And they're sailing with us now?"

"Yes!"

"I'd like to see them if possible, sir. What luck!"

"I'll send them to you immediately."

The quartermaster went up the stairs. Minutes later, two Indians appeared before Tremal-Naik. One was tall, thin, and gifted with monkey-like agility; the other was of average height, strong limbed and looked more Malay than Indian.

Tremal-Naik looked about to ensure they were alone, then stretched out his right hand and showed them his ring. The two Indians fell to their feet.

"Who are you?" they whispered.

"An envoy from Suyodhana, the Son of the Sacred Waters of the Ganges," whispered Tremal-Naik.

"Speak; our lives are in your hands."

"Can anyone overhear us?"

"Everyone is on deck," said Palavan.

"Where's Captain MacPherson?"

"In his cabin; still asleep."

"Do you know where the frigate is heading?"

"No. Captain MacPherson said he'd tell us when we reached our destination."

"So even the officers have been kept in the dark?"

"Yes."

"Then, if I kill the captain, the secret will die with him."

"Undoubtedly, we fear the frigate is heading for Rajmangal."

"You're correct, but the frigate will never reach her destination."

"What do you mean?"

"We're going to blow her up before she reaches the island."

279

"Give the order and we'll set fire to the powder."

"How long before we reach Rajmangal at our current speed?"

"We should be there by midnight."

"How many men aboard?"

"About a hundred."

"Excellent. I'll kill the captain at eleven then we'll blow up the ship. There's just one last thing."

"Speak."

"For my plan to succeed, the captain must be deeply asleep."

"I'll slip a sleeping potion into his water," said Palavan.

"Can I get to his cabin unseen?"

"The cabin communicates with the battery. I'll make sure the door is open."

"Excellent. That's all. Meet me here at eleven."

Tremal-Naik began to eat once again. He devoured a steak large enough to feed three men and drained several glasses of gin. Not wanting to return to the bridge lest he be recognized by the captain, he stretched out on the hammock and tried to sleep.

A thousand thoughts swirled through his head: Kammamuri, the Thugs, Suyodhana and his blood-filled pact. Ada's face appeared before him and he smiled, knowing that soon she would finally be his bride. But whenever his thoughts turned to the captain, he grew uneasy, almost horrified by what he had to do.

The hours passed slowly. No one came down to the cabin, not so much as a word or a signal from the two Thugs.

The hunter began to worry; perhaps Palavan and Bindur had been discovered.

At eight o'clock the sun began its descent and night fell quickly upon the blue waters of the Bay of Bengal. Tremal-Naik, gripped by a thousand anxieties, climbed the stairs and made his way towards the bridge.

Soldiers and sailors were everywhere; many had gathered at the bow, their eyes fixed on the east; others clung to the ratlines, crow's nest, crosslets and yardarms. Several men moved about the stern, stocking the launches with provisions.

His eyes turned to the lunette. Four officers were strolling about, smoking and chatting animatedly. Captain MacPherson was nowhere to be seen.

He returned to his hammock and waited.

The ship's clock struck nine, then ten, then eleven. The last chimes had not yet faded when two shadows silently descended the stairs.

"Hurry," whispered a voice, "We don't have a moment to lose. We're within sight of Rajmangal."

Tremal-Naik immediately recognized the two Thugs.

"And the captain?" he murmured.

"Sleeping," replied Bindur. "He drank the potion."

"Let's go."

Tremal-Naik's voice trembled slightly as he uttered those words. Palavan opened the door and entered the battery, coming to a stop before a second door that led into the transom.

"We cannot fail," said Tremal-Naik.

"Our lives are in Kali's hands."

"Are you afraid?"

"We do not know fear."

"Listen closely."

The two Thugs drew nearer, their eyes blazing darkly.

"I'm going to kill the captain," he said sadly. "Bindur, go down into the powder magazine and light a fire."

"What about me?" asked Palavan.

"Get three life preserves then go join him. Now go, and may the goddess protect you."

Tremal-Naik grabbed an axe, silently opened the door and entered the cabin. A talc lantern filled the room with a dim light.

The hunter caught his reflection in a mirror and was frightened by what he saw.

His face was horribly twisted; large drops of sweat beaded along his brow, his eyes gleamed like daggers.

He quickly looked away and his gaze fell upon the bed, it was covered with a thick mosquito net. Several soft breaths reached his ears. He took three steps forward and raised the veil with a trembling hand.

Captain MacPherson lay before him, smiling, perhaps dreaming of better times.

"Suyodhana's will be done," murmured the Indian.

He raised his axe, but lowered it immediately, almost as if his strength had suddenly given way. He wiped his brow and checked his hand, it was damp with perspiration.

"What's happening to me?" he asked, surprised by that sudden wavering. "How can I have lost my nerve? Who is this man? Why can't I kill him?"

He raised the axe a second time, but lowered it just as quickly. An inner voice had stayed his hand; he could not spill this man's blood.

"Ada! Ada!" he exclaimed almost in rage.

He turned pale and took a few steps back. The captain had sat up.

"Ada!" exclaimed MacPherson excitedly.

Tremal-Naik, shocked and frightened, did not move.

"Ada!" repeated the captain. "Who speaks of my daughter?"

Then he noticed the Malay.

"What are you doing in my cabin?" he asked.

Tremal-Naik's mind raced, filling with a terrible suspicion.

"Who are you?" he asked, his voice barely a whisper. "Which Ada do you mean? My Ada?"

"Your Ada?" exclaimed the captain, stunned. "I'm talking about my daughter!"

"Where is she?"

"She was kidnapped by the Thugs!"

"Powerful Brahma! Can it be true? A word, Captain, I beg you! What's your daughter's name?"

"Ada Corishant."

Tremal-Naik buried his face in his hands and let out a cry of horror.

"My fiancée! I was about to murder her father!" He dropped to the foot of the bed and exclaimed, "Forgive me, forgive me!"

The captain, stunned, looked at Tremal-Naik, wondering for a moment if this were a bizarre dream.

"Explain yourself!" he exclaimed.

Tremal-Naik, his voice broken by sobs, quickly informed him of Suyodhana's infernal plot.

"And you know where my daughter is?" asked the captain, jumping to his feet, pale with emotion.

"Yes, I'll take you there," said Tremal-Naik.

"Return her to me and I promise that if she loves you, she'll be your bride."

"Thank you, Captain! My life is yours."

"There's no time to waste; we must fly to Rajmangal. I'm planning to attack the Thugs' lair."

"A moment, I have two accomplices aboard awaiting my order to set fire to the powder."

"We'll hang them."

They ran out of the room and rushed up to the bridge.

"Quick! Send four men to the powder magazine! Two traitors are about to blow up the ship!"

At those orders twenty men rushed into the munitions room. Minutes later, they heard two cries followed by several gunshots.

"They jumped overboard," said an officer, rushing onto the bridge.

"Let them drown!" said the captain. "Is the powder secure?"

"The traitors didn't have time to smash open the barrels."

"God is with us! Full steam towards the Mangal!

Chapter 21
Freedom

The *Cornwall,* having miraculously escaped destruction, was flying at full speed towards the Sundarbans. Tremal-Naik had explained everything, and Captain Corishant wanted to reach Hider's gunboat before the crew realized what had happened and went off to warn the formidable Suyodhana of the thwarted attack and subsequent betrayal.

The sailors and infantrymen had drawn their weapons in anticipation of attack, while the gunners had taken position behind the six cannons, determined to sink the *Devonshire* if she attempted to escape.

Standing on the forecastle and armed with a strong pair of binoculars, the captain eagerly scanned the darkness, guiding the helmsman past the numerous shoals. At his side, Tremal-Naik anxiously studied the jungle, trying to spot the mouth of the Mangal.

"Soon, soon!" he repeated. "If the Thugs notice our advance, our Ada is lost!"

"Now that I know where she is and that you can lead us into their lair, I'm certain we'll succeed, my good friend," replied the captain. "After three long years, I'll finally be able to see her again! What joy! Revenge will finally be mine."

"And to think I was about to kill you. Your head was to have been her wedding present! Great Shiva! What terrible vengeance!"

"You were determined to murder me?"

"It was the only way I could have obtained my beloved's freedom. But something held me back at the last minute. A voice. A feeling. It was more powerful than anything I'd ever experienced. If that potion had been more potent, and you hadn't heard your daughter's name…"

"What potion?" the captain asked, surprised.

"The one Palavan slipped into your water."

"When?"

"Last night."

"I didn't drink it. Ah!"

"What's the matter?"

"The water tasted bitter, so I poured it out."

"The Mangal!" yelled the Officer of the Watch.

"Where?" asked the captain.

"Straight ahead, sir."

"Are you sure?"

"Yes, sir. See those two lanterns burning down there?"

The officer had not been mistaken. Two bright dots, one red, one green, shone in the darkness less than half a kilometre from the *Cornwall*.

"The *Devonshire*!" exclaimed Tremal-Naik.

"Reverse engines!" commanded the captain.

Carried forward by her momentum, the ship advanced another fifty or sixty metres, then came to a complete stop.

"Lower three launches into the water. Have forty men and three firelocks readied for the mission," ordered the captain. He turned to Tremal-Naik and added, "My daughter's fate is in your hands, succeed and she'll be your bride."

"At your orders, Captain," replied the Indian.

"Take the gunboat's crew prisoner."

"Yes, sir."

"Make sure no one escapes."

"No one will."

"And hold your fire if you can, we don't want to warn the Thugs."

"We won't fire a single shot. Hider is waiting for me; I'll catch him by surprise."

"Well then, good luck, my brave friend."

Once the launches had been readied, Tremal-Naik boarded the largest one and gave the order to set sail.

The captain had remained aboard the frigate, leaning against the bow parapet, clutching the railing as he tried to steady his nerves. He watched the launches row off and disappear into the night.

Several minutes passed as he waited in anxious silence.

Then suddenly, he heard a shot, then a crash, then all fell silent once again.

The captain turned to the officers standing next to him.

"See anything?" he asked, his voice barely a whisper.

"Yes!" yelled one. "The lanterns are tacking about!"

"The gunboat's coming towards us!" yelled the others.

A hurrah erupted off in the distance, a cry of victory.

The captain let out a deep sigh of relief.

"God is with us," he murmured. "It won't be long now, Ada!"

A short while later the *Devonshire* dropped anchor just off the frigate's bow. Tremal-Naik came aboard.

"Hider and his men have been taken prisoner," he reported.

"Thank you, my brave friend," said the captain, tightly shaking the Indian's hand. "Were they surprised?"

"Yes, Captain. They were waiting for me, expecting I'd be delivering your head and let me approach unchallenged. By the time they discovered our true intentions, they were surrounded and dropped their weapons without any resistance."

"On to Rajmangal then."

"The frigate is too large to sail up the Mangal."

"Then we'll take the gunboat. Another twenty determined men with me."

They abandoned the frigate, boarded the *Devonshire*, and were soon sailing up the Mangal. Tremal-Naik had taken command and made her fly over the muddy waters.

Her speed grew rapidly as tons of coal disappeared into the boilers. Steam raced through the valves, whistling sharply as the ship trembled from bow to stern.

The pressure gauge soon marked six and a half atmospheres! But Tremal-Naik and the captain, gripped by a burning impatience that verged on delirium, were not yet satisfied. Their voices thundered continually, demanding more power from the stokers and engineers roasting about the boilers.

Three hours crept by like three centuries for the hunter who desired nothing more than to see his beloved Ada.

The canal began to narrow and small islands appeared before them, but the *Devonshire* maintained her speed, slicing through thick masses of rotting vegetation as she rushed towards the Thugs' lair.

Suddenly a cry shot out from atop the mainmast.

"The banyan tree!"

The giant tree's three hundred trunks had appeared to the north of them. Tremal-Naik's heart raced, pounding violently.

"Ada!" he exclaimed. "At long last!"

He jumped down from the lunette and rushed towards the stern.

The shore was deserted save for a few marabous perched on the branches of the banyan tree, cawing mournfully. The hunter shivered at the sight of them.

"Halt engines!" he yelled.

The wheels stopped but the gunboat, driven forward by her momentum, rammed her bow into the shore.

The captain drew up beside Tremal-Naik, who was clutching the bulwark frantically.

"No one?"

"No one."

"Then we'll surprise them in their lair. Is the entrance nearby?"

"Yes, Captain."

"Excellent, we'll move on them immediately!"

"Wait, there may be guards posted. I'll go in alone. They know me; they'll let me pass. I'll whistle when it's safe."

He ran off towards the tree like a madman, climbed up it, reached the trunk and let himself fall through the opening. A torch shone at the foot of the stairway, beside it, a Thug armed with a carbine, stood guard.

"Who goes there," he said.

"Tremal-Naik. I've completed my mission," said the hunter. "Where's my Ada?"

"She's in the pagoda, waiting for her wedding present."

The Thug approached an enormous drum that hung from the ceiling and struck it three times. A moment later another drum sounded in reply from deep inside the cavern.

"They're expecting you," he said, handing the hunter the torch.

Quick as a flash, Tremal-Naik drew his dagger and lunged at the Thug. Grabbing him by the throat and plunging the blade into his chest took only an instant. The strangler fell without a sound.

Tremal-Naik pushed the body aside and whistled. Gathered about the base of the tree, the captain and his men quickly made their way down.

"The way is clear," said the Indian.

"And my daughter?" whispered the captain.

"She's waiting for us in the great cavern."

"Forward men! Load your rifles!"

"No, let me go first. It'll be easier to take them by surprise."

"Go, we won't be far behind."

Tremal-Naik set off, walking quickly. Now that the supreme moment was finally at hand, he was tormented by doubt and worry. On the verge of happiness, he could not shake a feeling of imminent danger. He began to run, making his way through that maze of tunnels in less than ten minutes.

The large drums were thundering when he reached the pagoda that housed the large statue of Kali, the beloved goddess of the Indian Thugs.

Lamps blazed beneath the vaulted ceiling, filling the room with pale blue light. Suyodhana, cloaked in a large yellow silk dugbah, sat before the statue upon a cushion of crimson silk. A tiny fish swam in a marble basin set before him. A hundred Thugs stood on either side of him, as still as statues, naked to the waist, skin glistening with coconut oil, each chest marked by a Nagi, the goddess' mysterious symbol.

Panting, amazed, Tremal-Naik had come to a stop in the middle of the pagoda, every eye fixed upon him.

"Welcome," said Suyodhana, smiling strangely.

"Where's my Ada?" Tremal-Naik asked anxiously.

A dull murmur ran through the circle of Thugs.

"Be patient," said the leader of the sect. "Where's the captain's head?"

"Hider is making his way through the tunnel; you'll have it in a few minutes."

"You killed him?"

"Yes."

"Brothers, our enemy is dead!" yelled Suyodhana.

He sprang up like a tiger, his eyes fixed on Tremal-Naik.

"Listen," he said. "Do you see that woman of bronze standing across from us?"

"I see her," replied Tremal-Naik. "But she's not the one I seek."

"I know, but she is powerful, more powerful than Brahma, Vishnu, Shiva and all the others. She lives in the land of darkness, she speaks to us through that fish you see swimming in that basin, she is just and demanding; she despises incense and prayers, but revels in human sacrifice. She is the symbol of Indian freedom and the destruction of our white-skinned oppressors."

Suyodhana paused to gage the effect those words were having on Tremal-Naik, but the hunter remained cold, unmoved by the leader's enthusiasm. His mind was filled with thoughts of Ada, his goddess, his life.

"Tremal-Naik," continued Suyodhana, "You are strong, clever, relentless; you are, like us, an Indian who languishes beneath the yoke of our oppressors. You have proven yourself worthy, and I offer you a place among us. Will you join our cause?"

"Me!" exclaimed Tremal-Naik. "Me! A Thug!"

"Do we horrify you? Because we strangle our enemies? The British kill us with guns and cannons; we fight back with our nooses, the weapons of our mighty goddess."

"What about my Ada?"

"She'll stay with us on Rajmangal, as will Kammamuri, who has become a Thug."

"And she'll be my bride?"

"Never! She belongs to our goddess."

"Ada Corishant is my goddess, I shall never serve another!"

For the second time a dull murmur ran through the circle of Thugs. Tremal-Naik looked about angrily.

"Suyodhana!" he exclaimed. "Do you break your word? Do you deny me that woman now, after I've fulfilled our pact, a pact that you proposed? Are you a liar?"

The leader paused for a moment, all eyes upon him.

"She's yours," he said coldly.

An Indian struck the tom-tom twelve times.

A deadly silence descended upon the pagoda. The Thugs appeared to be holding their breath.

A door opened and Ada entered the cavern, dressed in white silk, her golden breastplate glimmering in the lantern light.

Two cries broke the silence.

"Ada!"

"Tremal-Naik!"

The hunter and the young woman rushed into each other's arms. Almost immediately they heard a voice thunder, "Fire!"

The Thugs, frightened and amazed, rushed into the tunnels, leaving twenty men on the ground behind them. Suyodhana, leaping like a tiger, had bolted down a narrow passageway, closing a heavy door of teak wood behind him.

The captain rushed towards his daughter yelling, "Ada! Finally!"

"Father!" the young woman yelled, and fainted in his arms.

At a sign from Tremal-Naik, the soldiers turned back towards the pagoda, afraid of getting lost in the dark tunnels.

"Let's get out of here!" said the captain. "Come, brave Tremal-Naik, my Ada will be your bride! You've earned her hand."

They headed off towards the tunnel, but before they left the immense cavern, they heard Suyodhana's terrible voice thunder menacingly, "We'll meet again in the jungle!"

Titles in the Series

The Tigers of Mompracem
The Tigers of Mompracem are a band of rebel pirates fighting for the defense of tiny native kingdoms against the colonial powers of the Dutch and British empires. They are led by Sandokan, the indomitable "Tiger of Malaysia", and his faithful friend Yanez De Gomera, a Portuguese wanderer and adventurer. Orphaned when the British murdered his family and stole his throne, Sandokan has been mercilessly leading his men in vengeance. But when the pirate learns of the extraordinary "Pearl of Labuan" his fortunes begin to change... perhaps forever...

The Pirates of Malaysia
Fortune has not smiled on Tremal-Naik. Wrongfully imprisoned, the great hunter has been banished from India and sentenced to life in a penal colony. Knowing his master is innocent, Kammamuri dashes off to the rescue, planning to free him at the first opportunity. When the ever-loyal servant is captured by the Tigers of Mompracem, he manages to enlist their help. But to succeed, Sandokan and Yanez must lead their men against the forces of James Brooke, "The Exterminator," the dreaded White Rajah of Sarawak.

The Two Tigers
Just when Tremal-Naik's life was getting back to normal, the Thugs of the Kali cult return to exact their revenge by kidnapping his daughter Darma. Summoned by Kammamuri, Sandokan and Yanez immediately set sail for India to help their loyal friend. But the evil sect knows of their arrival and thwarts them at every turn. Have our heroes finally met their match? It's the Tiger of Malaysia versus the Tiger of India in a fight to the death!

The King of the Sea
A mysterious figure has armed the Dyaks and led them into battle against Tremal-Naik. Yanez races to the rescue but soon learns that Sandokan and his Tigers are also under threat. Despite eleven years of peace, the new Rajah of Sarawak, Brooke's nephew, has ordered the pirates to evacuate their island home or face all out war. Is this the end for the Tigers of Mompracem?

To read sample chapters visit us at www.rohpress.com

LaVergne, TN USA
07 April 2011
223239LV00002B/94/P